Marginal Mormons

What happens when a High Priest becomes addicted to crack cocaine? Should an unemployed bank teller take in a homeless protester from the Occupy Movement? Who is Salt Lake City's newest superhero, a masked man wearing temple clothes who mysteriously shows up at crime scenes?

Is there a way to splice the empathy gene into the genome of every human? Can a schizophrenic woman on anti-delusional drugs keep her belief in an intangible God? Will a childless biochemist find fulfillment by taking part in a mission to Mars?

Not every Latter-day Saint has a mainstream story to tell, but these soul-searching folks are still more than the marginal Mormons headquarters would like us to believe.

Praise for Johnny Townsend

In *Zombies for Jesus*, "Townsend isn't writing satire, but deeply emotional and revealing portraits of people who are, with a few exceptions, quite lovable."

Kel Munger, *Sacramento News and Review*

In *Sex among the Saints,* "Townsend writes with a deadpan wit and a supple, realistic prose that's full of psychological empathy....he takes his protagonists' moral struggles seriously and invests them with real emotional resonance."

Kirkus Reviews

Inferno in the French Quarter: The UpStairs Lounge Fire is "a gripping account of all the horrors that transpired that night, as well as a respectful remembrance of the victims."

Terry Firma, Patheos

"Johnny Townsend's 'Partying with St. Roch' [in the anthology *Latter-Gay Saints*] tells a beautiful, haunting tale."

Kent Brintnall, Out in Print: Queer Book Reviews

Selling the City of Enoch is "sharply intelligent...pleasingly complex...The stories are full of...doubters, but there's no vindictiveness in these pages; the characters continuously poke holes in Mormonism's more extravagant absurdities, but they take very little pleasure in doing so....Many of Townsend's stories...have a provocative edge to them, but this [book] displays a great deal of insight as well...a playful, biting and surprisingly warm collection."

Kirkus Reviews

Gayrabian Nights is "an allegorical tour de force...a hard-core emotional punch."

Gay. Guy. Reading and Friends

The Washing of Brains has "A lovely writing style, and each story [is] full of unique, engaging characters....immensely entertaining."

Rainbow Awards

In *Dead Mankind Walking*, "Townsend writes in an energetic prose that balances crankiness and humor....A rambunctious volume of short, well-crafted essays..."

Kirkus Reviews

Marginal Mormons

Johnny Townsend

Print ISBN: 978-1-961525-05-4
Ebook ISBN: 978-1-961525-06-1

This book is a work of fiction. Names, characters, events, and dialogue are the product of the author's imagination or are used fictitiously. Any resemblance to actual persons, living or dead, is entirely coincidental.

Printed on acid-free paper.

2023

Second Edition

Cover design by Nemanja Vranjkovic

Contents

Edith Goes to Mars

"I want to go to Mars," Edith said suddenly, putting a forkful of carrots back on her plate.

Her husband, Carter, shrugged and kept eating. "So go."

"There's this study being conducted by the University of Hawaii," Edith went on. "They're trying to decide what kinds of prepackaged and stored foods would be best for astronauts on an extended Mars mission."

"Uh-huh."

"So they're taking applications for a team of six volunteers. They'd live on a hardened lava flow on the big island of Hawaii for four months, to simulate the Mars landscape. They'd live in some kind of compound, and if they leave the compound, they'd have to wear spacesuits."

Carter scooped a spoonful of broccoli onto his plate.

"The study participants would have to do tests on each other to monitor taste, and I think they'd have to do some other kinds of experiments to take up their time and be useful during the four months. They're looking for people with a science degree. I want to go."

"So go."

Edith bit her lip. "I've already sent in my application." She paused. "I spent three hours on it this morning."

"Studying poison dart frogs in the jungles of Central America isn't enough excitement for you?" Carter laughed.

Edith had long been interested in poison dart frogs, initially for their lovely coloring, but later because their poison, epibatidine, offered insight into developing the most potent of pain killers, without any addictive side effects. She'd been raising the frogs for years now. Carter no longer complained about the wingless fruit flies she also had to raise in containers in the living room. The biggest obstacle was that poison dart frogs didn't create poison when raised in captivity.

"Well, that'll be a problem. The Mars study takes place a year and a half from now, during the summer when I usually go to Costa Rica. Plus, since the study takes four months, it means I won't be able to teach for the summer semester and probably not the fall semester, either."

"Can you get out of teaching?" Carter asked doubtfully. "You've only been at the university five years. No tenure yet. Surely, you're not eligible for a sabbatical?"

"No." Edith could feel her bobbed hair bobbing as she shook her head. "That'll be a problem. Plus, this is a volunteer study. I'd get a $5000 bonus at the end of it, but that won't make up for four months of not working."

"Well, we certainly don't have to worry about that." Carter shrugged. "Unless I lose my job."

"So it's okay?"

Carter laughed again. "Honey, when have I ever said no to you?"

Edith smiled and ate another carrot. It was true Carter had always been cooperative with her feelings. He did half the housecleaning and half the cooking. He let her make the decision of where to go on vacation. He let her handle the bills and other finances, saying he got enough of that at work. And he didn't make a fuss about her toenail fungus.

The biggest issue in their marriage had been the fact that she didn't want any children. She knew that women who'd never borne children were more likely to develop breast cancer, and both her mother and grandmother had died of the disease, so it wasn't a very smart decision on that score. She also heard lots of people lament the fact that she wouldn't have anyone to take care of her in her old age. And naturally, she wondered if she was simply being selfish not to have children.

Perhaps she was. Edith had always worried about her weight, and even now kept it at a steady 135 pounds, not bad for someone who was almost 5' 6". She'd always been afraid that carrying children would cause irreversible weight gain. Yet it wasn't just that.

The real reason Edith didn't want kids was simply because she was afraid to be ordinary. Almost every other woman had children or at least tried to have them. Edith wanted to be able to explore the jungles. She wanted to take off for Paris for two weeks. She wanted to…to…to go to Mars if the opportunity ever came up.

"You said *no* that time I asked if we could build a batbox behind the house." Edith tried to focus on her husband again.

Carter's eyes twinkled. "Only because I was afraid they'd eat your flies."

"The flies are inside the house."

"Okay, okay. So I don't like bats."

Edith smiled. She liked being told no *sometimes.* She didn't feel it was any better for the wife to be a tyrant than the husband.

After dinner, Carter went to check his email and Edith did the dishes, remembering how she'd always helped her mother with them. The memory made her think again about the daughters she never had, and that made her think again about the Church.

While it was one thing to get Carter to agree to her desire to remain childless, it was quite impossible to ignore the Church's insistence on the importance of motherhood. Mormons were many things, but while their greatest claim to fame may have been a living prophet, their second was a strong emphasis on family.

Edith and Carter had spent most of the past twenty years lying to their fellow ward members about their fertility. Now that Edith was forty-six, that wasn't such an issue any longer, but all the secrets and lies over the years made Edith worry she was only destined for the lowly Telestial Kingdom, where liars went along with the fornicators.

Of course, even if she'd been honest about her decision all this time, the Telestial Kingdom might still be the highest degree where people who refused to procreate could go. She'd probably go to Spirit Prison rather than Paradise when she died, waiting there until Judgment Day. She might not even come forth in the first resurrection but need to wait till after the Millennium to get her body back.

It was a price she was willing to pay to have the life she wanted.

Edith had worked at a Hancock fabric shop in her early married years, enjoying the craft of sewing, of creating beautiful things, pointing out to the other women in Relief Society she was still a "real woman," even if she "couldn't bear children." But at the age of thirty, she read an article about poison dart frogs and became absolutely captivated.

She'd decided to take a few Biology courses at the local university, just for fun, and before she knew it, she'd earned a degree, with a 3.8 average to boot. She wanted to continue her studies and applied for a Master's program in Biology, dismayed when the university turned her down for not being qualified.

So be it, she thought. She'd get a doctorate in Chemistry instead. It wasn't as if she hadn't had to take tons of chemistry and organic chemistry courses, anyway, to study the frogs. Biochemistry was half chemistry as well as half biology, wasn't it?

At the age of forty-one, she graduated with her PhD. With only that and her employment background of cutting fabric, she applied for a teaching position in North Carolina and got it. Carter had quit his job as an accountant and moved with her, also finding work in Raleigh. The man was supposed to be the head of the house, Edith knew, but she and Carter had always made decisions together. And it wasn't just a formality. He thoroughly considered her viewpoint, and as often as not, the "family" decision was to do what Edith wanted.

Edith wondered if that was how Heavenly Father and Heavenly Mother interacted. Was it *her* idea to have humans inhabit this planet on the edge of the galaxy? Had *she* decided it would be the third planet out and have a moon? Did *she* have any input on which plan of salvation her husband accepted from their two competing sons?

Or did she just sit at home, spitting out spirit babies as fast as she could produce them? Was that all women were good for, not only in mortal life but for all eternity, too?

When Edith had finished the dishes, she called Carter and they sat down to watch an episode of *How I Met Your Mother*. It was a stupid show, slightly charming on occasion, but tonight it left Edith feeling empty. She'd never have any children to tell the story of how she and Carter met. It had been one evening when Edith had grown irritated with a neighbor who never picked up after her dog.

Carter, who'd lived a few blocks away and was taking a casual evening stroll, had caught sight of Edith in the woman's front yard, hammering a sign: "There's no such thing as a Poop Fairy." Carter had talked her out of leaving the sign, instead suggesting that they keep an eye out the next time the woman took her dog for a walk and ask if they could join her to get better acquainted. Through mild social pressure, they were able to help the woman accept that she needed to clean up after her dog.

It wasn't the most romantic story in the world, but Edith felt it illustrated who they were.

Yet did it even matter who they were, if there was no one to pass that on to?

Teaching college chemistry courses helped a little. Edith was still passing on vital information to future generations, but it wasn't really the same thing. And yes, she did get to teach Primary and Sunday School classes at church. For the longest time, that had felt like enough. It wasn't so important that she taught her own children as long as she was teaching *somebody's* children.

But the possibility of going to Mars hit Edith hard. What did space exploration mean? Humans couldn't even take care of their own planet, and now they wanted to start exploring and exploiting others?

It somehow struck her as being like the politicians who clamored to send troops to Afghanistan and Iraq and Iran, but who wouldn't be sending their own children to fight, sending somebody else's instead.

Would Edith ever truly understand the importance of life, if she didn't help create it herself? If her own offspring weren't at risk of environmental collapse, or terrorism, or political oppression, if she didn't have to worry about the tax burden and national deficit stretching decades into the future, could she fully engage in the debate over how to solve those problems?

Edith wanted to help advance the possibility of a future Mars mission by participating in this study, yet somehow, her desire to go to the campsite in Hawaii just to make sure she had an interesting life, that she had some fascinating adventures while she could, seemed to taint what she'd originally thought a noble goal. She'd volunteered in the Pre-Existence to come to Earth, but now she wondered if she wasn't cheating somehow on the required testing.

"How about a walk around the block?" Carter asked when the show was over. "You seem pensive."

Edith smiled. "No, just thinking." It was one of her favorite movie lines, from *Yentl*. She liked that Carter always made the comment whenever he could sense she was worried, to get that very reaction. They went out the front.

"Thinking about what?" Carter asked, locking the door behind them.

Edith's smile faded. "About whether my life has any meaning."

"Whoa."

She put her hand on Carter's arm. "You make good money, and I make decent money. We don't have any kids to support. Do you think we should take a couple of years off and go on a mission?"

Carter didn't say anything.

"We might end up somewhere like Bosnia, making microfiche of old records so we can do temple work for people who never had a chance to hear the gospel. Or we might be sent to South Africa to preach. Or maybe Japan."

Carter nodded. "Are you so addicted to adventure that the jungle is no longer enough?"

The comment irritated Edith. "What if I am?" she said. "What's wrong with wanting an interesting life?"

"Well, a mission would be awkward right now."

"I wouldn't want to do it until after the Mars study anyway. I'm just thinking ahead."

"Doesn't planning your life take away some of the excitement?"

Yes, thought Edith, it did, but she needed something intriguing to happen *right now*. If she couldn't have that, she at least needed to prepare for such an event. "We've never gone skiing. Maybe we can take off next weekend…"

"Honey, what's the matter?"

Edith hadn't finished menopause. Her grandmother had her last child at forty-six. If Edith could manage to get pregnant soon, she could have the baby and still be ready in time for the study in Hawaii. Maybe it wasn't too late to keep herself from making a permanent mistake.

They kept walking in silence, Carter holding Edith's hand tightly. When they turned the corner, Edith saw a woman in her early thirties walking a dog, with her young daughter, maybe eight, walking along beside her. The age of accountability. Edith gripped Carter's hand more tightly and heard him grunt from the pressure.

Edith watched as the woman let the dog squat on the sidewalk and make a deposit. She started to smile, remembering her first encounter with Carter, but then she stopped in her tracks. The woman walked on without picking up the feces. Edith suddenly felt an uncontrollable rage.

"What the hell do you think you're doing?"

The woman turned and looked at Edith in surprise.

Edith broke away from Carter and ran up to the woman. "You've got an impressionable young girl here, your *daughter*, and this is the example you set? You pick up that dog shit right now."

The woman looked embarrassed, which almost made Edith gloat, but she was too mad for that. The woman looked down at her daughter, looked back at Edith, and turned around stiffly and started walking off.

"Listen, you!"

Then she did it. Without warning, with no thought to accompany it, Edith reached down with her bare hands and grabbed the warm dog turds. She took a deep breath and threw them at the woman.

"Edith!" Carter shouted.

The woman screamed, and the little girl took off running. The dog broke free of the mother and followed the girl. The woman calmed herself down, pulled out her cell phone, and called 9-1-1.

Edith's first thought was disqualification. The Mars study application specifically asked that the volunteers be able to get along well with others.

"Let's get out of here." Carter took Edith's elbow and started leading her away.

"I know where you live," the woman said coolly, lowering her phone. "I've seen you out walking before."

They hurried home anyway, Edith hoping the threat was a bluff. She washed her hands, with Carter at the bathroom door, looking at her worriedly. "*What* is going on?"

But how could she explain herself? How could she say that motherhood was wasted on the unenlightened? How could she tell him that she could be standing at her own daughter's wedding right now if she'd had a child when she was supposed to?

How could she explain the degree to which she felt she'd wasted her life, when all she'd done was improve herself at every step? Could she make anyone understand how even now, she wanted more than anything to win a Nobel Prize for finally developing an epibatidine variant that wasn't lethal?

There was a sharp knock at the door. Carter closed his eyes in resignation. "Edith…"

"I'll get it."

She walked to the front door and opened it to two police officers. Boy, that was quick, she thought. If it had been a real emergency, these guys would be nowhere to be found. Edith wasn't sure why seeing men in uniform irritated her so much, but she immediately thought of all the men running the Church even today without any input from women.

She thought of all the male politicians in their nice suits debating to make birth control illegal, with no women allowed on the debate floor. She thought of a military run exclusively by male generals as they sent children off to die.

These police officers would never understand what she was going through. Authority, war, control. That was all men cared about.

She glanced back at Carter, feeling a stab of guilt. "That's her," said the dog woman from further back on the pathway.

Edith was arrested for assault and brought down to the police station. As it turned out, the bail was more than Carter could withdraw from an ATM, so Edith was stuck there for the night. She shared a large cell with a very drunk, frizzy-haired white woman and a surprisingly flat-chested Latina prostitute. Edith hoped she wouldn't be fired when news of the arrest reached the university.

Edith sat on a bench and looked at her two cellmates. More evidence of bad parenting, she thought. Maybe that was why it was so important for Mormons to have lots of children. Not only to provide physical bodies for their spirit brothers and sisters, but to instill righteous teachings in the minds of the young.

Edith laughed, generating a nervous look from the sex worker and an angry shout from the drunk woman. Righteous teachings, she thought, like how to assault a neighbor. She'd thought she was long past regret over her choice of not bearing children, but perhaps she should think about getting some therapy.

The question, of course, was whether she should see an LDS therapist or a secular one. A male therapist or a female one.

Around 11:00, as Edith tried to calm herself down to get some sleep, the guard came by. "You have a visitor," she said gruffly.

At this hour? Maybe Carter was coming back. He must have bribed someone or talked awfully nicely to get permission so late. What in the world was he going to say to her now? Was he finally going to put his foot down and demand…demand… what?

The dog woman came up to the cell door. The guard stood aside watchfully. "You the woman who put the 'Pick up after your dog' sign in my yard last week?"

Edith shook her head.

"I can't bend down to pick up the poop," the woman said. "I have severe back pain. And I can't take any medications because I'm a recovering addict." She looked coldly at Edith. "We had to adopt the dog last week when my sister OD'ed. I make my daughter come with me when I walk the dog so I can get her used to the responsibility herself. I can only do so much at one time. Carrie would never come if I made her pick up the poop, too. One lesson at a time."

Edith wondered why the woman was even bothering to explain. It was none of Edith's business. Edith wasn't supposed to be judging others in the first place, whether she knew their particular situation or not. Wasn't that something *her* mother had taught her?

"You must not have kids," the woman continued.

Then it was true. Edith *didn't* understand even basic things that all those average parents out there knew instinctively. She sighed deeply, rubbing her forehead with the heel of her hand. "I'm sorry," she said.

The woman looked at her for a long moment. The guard shifted her feet. "They let me in," the woman finally went on, "because I said I'd drop the charges."

Edith raised her eyebrows.

"Under one condition."

"Yes?"

"That you come over twice a day and walk the dog with Carrie. And *you* teach her about picking up the poop." She paused. "But you need to be the one to pick it up for the first few weeks. Don't scare her off from doing the right thing."

The right thing. Edith almost laughed again. She wondered about her violent response. Weren't men the ones who were usually so aggressive? *Men are from Mars* and all that sort of thing. Perhaps she was only now demonstrating true equality by being a jackass herself. "That's very generous of you." She nodded slowly. "I accept your offer."

"Okay. I'll drop the charges." Edith watched as the woman motioned for the guard to take her back to the office where she could do that.

"Oh, not yet," said Edith.

"Huh?"

"I don't want you to drop the charges till morning."

"You feel the need for more punishment?" the woman asked with the slightest smile. "Believe me, after a few weeks with Carrie at 6:00 in the morning…"

"No." Edith laughed. "It's just that I've never been in jail before. I want something I can write about in my journal." Even if she had no one to leave a journal to.

"You're an odd woman." She chuckled. Edith wondered if the dog woman thought *she* was on drugs. "But I like odd women. I'm Nancy."

Edith nodded. She kind of liked Nancy, too. All this time she'd thought "family" meant children, but it could mean friends and neighbors as well, couldn't it? She certainly needed to think more about extending her family beyond Carter, as great as he was. Maybe she could see about getting Nancy into a drug trial for non-addictive pain treatments once they were further developed. There was the human family to think about, too.

"See you in the morning," Edith said.

"Goodnight." Nancy looked at the other two cellmates and shook her head as she left.

Edith turned to her companions, both of whom were looking at her suspiciously. Think of this as a space capsule, she told herself. She was on a months-long mission, trapped in a small space with people who had fractured nerves, and she had to get along.

Humans, it turned out, *did* develop poison while in captivity. But maybe she could put this on her resumé if she ever got as far as an interview with the University of Hawaii. Should she teach these women a Primary song?

Edith moved over to sit next to the Latina woman, realizing only at that moment that the girl was young enough to be her daughter. Edith wondered if the woman was already irreversibly damaged, or if there was yet some way to help her live a good life.

Had she been forced by circumstances to do sex work or had she chosen it for "the experience," as Edith was choosing her own non-standard evening tonight?

Perhaps the woman already had a great relationship with her own mother.

But Edith could still be an aunt.

Could be…could just be herself.

"Tell me about your life," Edith said in fluent Spanish. All those summers in Central America were paying off.

The woman smiled uncertainly and then began talking. Edith took her hand and listened.

Drug of Choice

Oh, my god, he thought. Yes, *my god*. The situation was worthy of an expletive. Dwayne could not believe what was happening. After forty years of marriage, he was finally falling in love. God had certainly tried him sorely many other times in the past, but this…this was simply *cruel*.

"Dwayne, Brother Thompson is pulling up out front," Samantha said. "You shouldn't keep him waiting."

"Okay, Sam." Dwayne gave her a peck. "You have a good day."

Dwayne headed outside into the brisk December weather. At least there was no snow on the ground. It was about two hours from Springfield to Nauvoo, and Dwayne didn't want to waste any more of his day than he had to. He hated these temple cleaning assignments.

It was challenging enough to live the gospel every day without also being pressured to fiscally support the maintenance of the Church and its programs. Twice a week, local members had to go to the temple to perform routine cleaning chores that the Church was too stingy to pay for itself.

"Hi, Clark," said Dwayne, opening the back door of the car and slipping into the seat. "Hi, Jim." These were two of Dwayne's good friends from the High Priests Group, both sitting up front. There was a fourth guy in the back, too, however, a guy Dwayne didn't know very well, from the Elders Quorum. "Hey," Dwayne said.

"This is Stephen," offered Clark.

Dwayne and Stephen shook hands across Clark's lap. Dwayne had to force himself to smile. He'd hoped for a pleasant drive at the very least, with his two buddies. He didn't feel up to being on guard the whole trip.

And why did Stephen have to be so good looking? It just pushed Dwayne's newfound misery right back in his face. Why, *why*, did Randy have to be such a great guy?

Dwayne had been attending the Gay Men's Recovery Group for just over four years. His dean at the college said it was either that or be fired for missing so many of his teaching assignments. The meetings had turned out to be a godsend. Not only did they give him the strength to finally give up crack, but they also provided a wonderful outlet to be with other men.

Samantha had long ago resigned herself to marriage with a gay man, and she only requested that Dwayne not do anything in Springfield that would "embarrass her." So for the past fifteen years after giving up sex with one another, Dwayne confined himself to trysts only when he was out of town, usually in Chicago.

Who knew that Dwayne would find the man of his dreams in the recovery group? Right here in town. Dwayne home taught a member couple who'd been in AA for twenty years and ran the LDS Recovery Program in Springfield, but how could Dwayne possibly ever participate in a Mormon group? Years ago, he'd learned a very important truth: gays go to hell, but drug users just go to rehab. Mormons were far more likely to accept his drug addiction than his homosexuality.

"Clark tells me you used to work on the *Journey with Joseph* pageant," Stephen said.

Dwayne almost didn't hear the remark, he was so caught up in his own thoughts. But he tried to smile and pretend he was in a good mood. "Oh, yes, I was prop master for eight years. My wife Samantha was the costume designer."

"That must have been a very spiritual experience," Stephen noted, "telling the world about Joseph Smith."

"Oh, definitely, definitely." Dwayne thought about the times he'd caught various cast members giving each other blow jobs in the dressing rooms. And there was that one evening when Oliver Cowdery—

"What was your best experience?" Stephen pressed.

Well, it certainly wasn't the time he'd confided to a visiting General Authority that he was gay and very happy to be able to serve the Church in a typically gay theatre capacity. Dwayne had been released from his position almost immediately.

Of course, he'd never actually been excommunicated, despite going to the authorities on at least four occasions to confess his homosexuality. God must want him in the Church. Dwayne did still believe, after all. He had, in fact, contributed greatly to the Church over the years, financially, certainly, and obviously with the pageant, but also by sending his two sons on missions, and having served a mission himself, back in Holland all those many years ago.

"Oh, we'd frequently receive letters from people who'd seen the production and then asked the missionaries to come by and were eventually baptized. Happened all the time."

"That's wonderful. Sure a lot better than that damned *Book of Mormon* musical on Broadway. We should be able to sue them for slander."

Dwayne tried to keep his face blank. Going to New York to review the play for a Springfield newspaper had been satisfying on more than one account. The trip to New York led to two nights with attractive young men, and the play itself had been eye-opening. Many Mormons were offended by the language and some of the scenes, but Dwayne found the play both charming and faith-promoting.

These young missionaries in Uganda found a way to make the gospel relevant to people who were suffering in a way that most Americans could not even begin to comprehend. It proved to Dwayne all over again that the Church was true. He wished other Mormons were not so short-sighted, that they could recognize truth and beauty even when it came in non-traditional forms.

"There was one time," Dwayne continued, "when we needed a large number of costumes to re-stage a Book of Mormon sequence in the pageant. Samantha asked for a priesthood blessing because she just couldn't see a way to get the job done."

"Yes?" said Stephen.

"So we went up to Chicago, and Samantha found this shop with almost fifty Armenian traditional dresses that could be easily modified to hint at the Middle Eastern background of the Nephites and Lamanites. For her, it was a miraculous answer to prayer. The dresses were just perfect, right down to the color choices. And they ended up saving her a couple of thousand dollars."

"The color choices?" asked Stephen. "You're sounding a little prissy there."

Dwayne could feel Clark stiffen beside him. Clark knew all about his homosexuality. "You should know I support gay rights," Dwayne said coldly, "both in and out of the Church."

"What?" Stephen's eyes widened. "How can you say that? Gays are destroying our society. They're—"

"Did you hear what Bishop Andrews said last week about the new Bishop's Storehouse schedule?" It was Jim from the front seat.

"What did he say?" Clark asked, apparently as eager to change the subject as Jim. Dwayne relaxed just a little and let the others talk. He wasn't prepared for a debate today. Normally, he could quote scripture and the various General Authorities, but today, he needed to be in the right frame of mind to meditate on his problem when they arrived at the temple.

Dwayne brooded in silence for the next fifteen minutes. He thought about how he'd known even from the age of six he was gay, though he didn't have a word for it way back then. One Christmas, he'd even asked his parents for a boy doll along with a tea set.

He'd never been interested in sports. He loved movies and the theatre. He'd learned from a very early age that people didn't like gays, and so he learned to lie. People always believed him. He'd become so good at lying that once he'd even passed a polygraph test.

Of course, that was years later, after all the troubles started.

Dwayne had met Samantha at Brigham Young University after returning from Holland. In those days, the Church encouraged gay men to marry because that would "cure" them. Dwayne had believed the leaders, and Samantha was truly a wonderful woman, so they'd married. Seven years passed before he came out to her, but by then, she already knew. By this time, too, they'd discovered they couldn't have children.

Dwayne had briefly wondered if his sterility was a sign he shouldn't have married, that maybe he was unfit to be a father, but the Church also said that raising a family was the most important thing a person could do in their lifetime. So after a few more years, he and Samantha adopted a baby boy through the Church. Four years after Kevin entered their lives, Keith did as well.

Things got so complicated then. Dwayne and Samantha went to marriage counseling, which only seemed to make things worse, and despite some uncomfortably negative feelings toward each other, they ultimately decided they were still best friends and wanted to stay together. They had a Celestial marriage, after all, and they were going to make it work.

By this time, they were also working on the *Journey with Joseph* pageant and had become Mormon celebrities of a sort. That came with relatively high Church recognition, mostly because of Samantha's position. Once, they were even invited to dinner with the Prophet. Dwayne knew then that God had to approve of him, that somehow his being gay was acceptable, whatever the Church might say publicly on the subject.

Perhaps the leaders were just misinformed and never bothered to ask God what He thought. Maybe Dwayne would be a catalyst and help the Church see the light. Once, he even told an Apostle about his homosexuality, and the man said basically, "Go your way and sin no more." Anyone else would have been excommunicated on the spot. God *had* to have a moral purpose for keeping him in the Church.

The talk in the car shifted to sports, and Dwayne tried to tune it all out. He heard Stephen say something about some guy named Drew Brees and then make the comment, "What would Breesus do?" Dwayne thought the remark distasteful.

After a while, the discussion switched to politics, which was just as uncomfortable. "Mitt Romney's coming back up in the polls," Jim said. "I don't think he's great, but the other candidates are even worse, and at least a good Mormon is more likely to do the right thing once he's in office. That's what we do, after all—we do the right thing."

Dwayne was not a Republican, nor was he a Democrat. He voted for the individual, the person he thought would make the best political leader. He was obviously for gay rights, but that wasn't the only issue he voted on. Sometimes, Republicans were the best choice, regardless of their stand on homosexuality. But he often felt he didn't fit in with his LDS friends, despite his generally conservative views, and he didn't fit in with his mostly liberal gay friends in the recovery group, either. He couldn't help but lonely most of the time.

That's what had made meeting Randy so wonderful, and so awful.

Like him, Randy had also used crack, so there was an immediate bond on that score. He'd fallen into drug use just as innocently as Dwayne had. Dwayne had been cruising for sex and picked up a guy who offered him a hit. Dwayne had never seen the odd glass tube with some kind of filter in it, but he was feeling radical that night. He watched while the guy put in a rock and held the stem so Dwayne could draw in some smoke.

It was as if a train had struck him. Fifteen minutes passed before he was even able to speak again. Over the next few months, gay-cruising morphed into drug-cruising. It was almost exactly the same activity, just looking for a different target. The truly miraculous thing was that for Dwayne, cocaine removed all desire for sex. When he smoked, he wasn't gay. So maybe this was God's solution for his awkward situation.

Randy was Catholic and felt extreme guilt over being gay, and he used crack as an escape from his feelings. Randy was a good man and understood about religion. So many other gays simply dismissed it outright. Randy even listened while Dwayne told him about the Church. It was almost like being back in Holland.

And now, this Sunday, Randy was going to be baptized.

Dwayne really needed some time at the temple to think. They pulled up to the building outside of Nauvoo a few minutes later, and once inside, Dwayne showed the man at the front desk his temple recommend. His had been revoked four and a half years earlier when he'd been caught driving under the influence.

It was being barred from the temple which made him finally realize he needed treatment. Not Samantha questioning him ever more fiercely about why the money was disappearing, not the police finding him with three dime bags of cocaine while they were monitoring a drug dealer, not waking up one morning to discover he'd spent the entire night at a crack house.

After the stake president had taken away his recommend, Dwayne had gone first to High Plains for two weeks of In-Patient treatment and then to Pine Ridge for four months of After Treatment. There'd been one lapse after that, during which he'd given his car keys to a drug friend, who never came back, and when Dwayne was forced to report the car stolen, he'd been charged with Loitering in the First Degree and ended up in Westcreek. But that had been the end of it.

After a year of being clean, Dwayne had been able to get his temple recommend back, and though he was still occasionally tempted, he'd stayed clean ever since.

"We need help today with cleaning both the men's dressing rooms and the male temple workers' dressing rooms," said the man at the front desk.

"Let's get to it," Clark said.

Dwayne worked mostly with Clark for the next hour and a half. The cleaning was routine and not overly difficult, and the two men chatted about the wards they were called to monitor. As a professor, Dwayne enjoyed giving talks at his assigned ward, and he knew he did a decent job. Even in his own ward, he'd once given a great talk on the subject of keeping a journal.

He'd caught Samantha reading his personal entries one day, which really burned him up, so he'd included a quote in his talk from some literary figure: "People who read another person's journal get what they deserve." Samantha had been madder than a hornet over that, but as far as he knew, she'd never looked at his journals again.

Despite his years of lying, Dwayne was honest these days. The recovery program had taught him that. Odd that he hadn't learned such a thing at church. But if Samantha asked him about sex, he told her. If she asked him about any sensitive subject at all, he answered truthfully.

She usually didn't ask.

Now it was time to be honest with himself.

What was he going to do about Randy? Randy believed in the gospel, so he wasn't asking Dwayne to leave his wife. Still, to have a real, ongoing, legitimate relationship with Randy while still married seemed more like adultery than the random hook-ups he'd had before. Was it time to leave the Church altogether, just as he was bringing another soul to Christ?

Something Randy had said the other day was still banging about in Dwayne's head. As they discussed the strict requirements of living the gospel, Dwayne had commented that people would do all sorts of things because of it that didn't come naturally, such as home teaching or forcing oneself to become a leader. Sometimes, he reflected, people would do things which even seemed to hurt them, like paying tithing or postponing college to go on a mission.

Randy had simply said, "Sometimes, I think religion is an addiction. We get hooked when we're young, and we're slaves to it the rest of our lives."

"But—but not the *true* church," Dwayne had spluttered.

Randy had shrugged. "Sometimes, even that still feels like methadone."

"But don't you *want* to get baptized? I thought you believed."

"I do believe," Randy had said sadly. "Just like you. But that means I can never be with you again. Not in the way I want to be, anyway."

"You mean we can never have sex again?"

"I believe in the Church."

"Well, so do I!"

Randy put his arm on Dwayne's and said softly. "You're already sixty-five. It won't be so bad for you. But I'm only thirty-six. That's a long time to be celibate."

"But…but…"

"100% abstinence is the only way not to stay a slave to addiction."

That's when Dwayne had his revelation. Didn't 100% abstinence instead actually mean *being* a slave to addiction? He went to church every Sunday, and often more than that, what with one meeting or another. It was like a hit. He *needed* the Church. Just like he needed to read the scriptures every morning, for at least five minutes a day. Just like he needed prayer every morning and again every evening.

Just like he needed to believe. *Not* believing, even for a moment here and there, was like going through withdrawal. It was simply too awful to bear. He'd never understood before what Karl Marx had meant.

Of course, you could really only push the comparison so far. The fact was that drug use ruined people's lives. The Church was saving his.

Now that the cleaning was done, Dwayne wanted to spend a few minutes alone in the Celestial Room, only he knew he wasn't dressed appropriately to enter. Instead, he went into the bathroom by himself and sat down. He was alone in the temple, and it was time to meditate.

Could he live the rest of his life in a sexless marriage with Samantha, no longer enjoying sex with men, either? Was his reluctance to accept that homosexuality was wrong just like his former reluctance to face his drug abuse? He wondered if one could really believe the Church was true without believing the General Authorities when they stated so emphatically that homosexuality was a sin.

Dwayne had been able to live a double life before, but maybe now it was time to make a real decision. He'd given up alcohol. He'd given up crack. Perhaps now it was finally the moment to give up men as well.

Some Church leaders had always insisted that homosexual sex was by definition an addiction. Dwayne had never believed the claim and wasn't sure he did even now. Giving up processed flour for whole meal flour or pasteurized milk for organic didn't mean you were overcoming an addiction. It just meant you had decided to live on a higher level.

But if he was going to use the food analogy, wasn't there some evidence that people could become physically addicted to sugar? Or that there was a subgroup of people who were addicted to eating in general? Perhaps people could turn any normal behavior into an addictive one.

Dwayne had seen "drama queens" addicted to creating unnecessary disasters in their lives because they thrived on crisis. And he'd certainly seen some people who only enjoyed the infatuation stage of a romance, inevitably short-lived, so they'd go from one partner to another to another in short order, always seeking the high of infatuation.

Was love the same thing? Dwayne had known Randy for over eight months now. His feelings for the man only seemed to grow deeper with time. But perhaps love was a drug, too, and the only viable form was the love one felt for Heavenly Father. Anything else was a synthetic substitute.

Dwayne cleaned himself up and joined the other men in the lobby. They all clapped each other on the shoulders for a job well done and then climbed back into the car for the return journey to Springfield. They talked about sports again, and about politics some more, and about other members of the ward. Even Dwayne talked amicably. He was sure none of the others could even tell what he was really thinking.

When he got out of the car, he pulled out his cell phone before going up to the house. He punched in some numbers.

"Hello?"

"It's me."

"Will you do it?" Randy asked.

"Yes, I'll baptize you."

There was silence on the line for a long moment. "I'm so glad, Dwayne."

Dwayne nodded, even though he knew Randy couldn't see him. The request had been that Dwayne only agree to baptize Randy if Dwayne could also agree to complete repentance and absolute chastity for the rest of his life. Only then could Dwayne put on his white clothing with Randy and get into the warm water with him and hold him there during the sacred ritual. One moment of ecstatic, wonderful intimacy that would have to last the rest of his life.

He loved Randy. He'd do it.

"I'll see you in the morning, Dwayne."

"See you."

Dwayne sighed and hung up, and he walked slowly to his front door and unlocked it. Samantha was in the kitchen preparing some early holiday cookies. "Did you have a good time, dear?" she asked, looking up briefly from her dough.

“Yes, thank you.” Dwayne took off his shoes and breathed in the smell of cinnamon from the kitchen. He slowly walked over to join Samantha. “Can I help you?” he asked softly.

Samantha gave him a funny look but nodded. Dwayne washed his hands and then picked up a wooden spoon and took over the stirring.

Losing God

What a year it had been. Miranda was fifty now. Fifty! Her hair was gray, and she could no longer afford to color it. SSI was demanding she repay the last year of benefits she'd received, all because she earned over a thousand dollars a month at the hospital. No one had told her there was a limit. She'd just been trying to be dedicated and hardworking, an industrious Mormon girl to the end.

NAMI was going to take away her free cell phone, too, but Miranda hardly talked to anyone anyway. There just wasn't much to say these days. Certainly, no one called *her*, but sometimes her old friends answered, more often now that she wasn't crazy anymore.

Well, she'd always be crazy, but at least now it was under control. So why didn't people like her more these days? It would be nice to get at least *one* call once in a while. The loss of the phone would still be a big blow regardless. Miranda was just happy that the other nurse's aides had been reprimanded for being on their cell phones too long at work. Miranda never called anyone from work.

It never ceased to amaze her how the other girls always tried to get out of their duties. They dilly-dallied all through their shift and then tried to rush through everything at the last moment. Miranda, on the other hand, did all her work as quickly as possible, so she'd have time left over if any emergencies came up. The problem, of course, was that because all her work was done by the middle of her shift, she looked like she was being lazy during the last few hours when she wasn't actively doing anything and everyone else was scrambling.

But she always got her work done, and the other girls didn't. So why did everyone complain about *her*?

Miranda entered the Harvey Tunnel and took a deep breath. She knew she'd be murdered on her way to or from work one of these days. Imagine, a fifty-year-old white woman in New Orleans walking through a dark tunnel at night. People would sure be sorry they'd talked bad about her then.

Miranda kicked at a piece of crumpled paper on the ground. She knew people weren't really talking about her like they used to. Nobody even noticed her at all, to be honest. She was poor, all alone in the world, a nothing. Back when she'd believed everyone was plotting against her and railed at the injustice of it all, at least she'd felt important.

How much longer until the end of the tunnel? Miranda missed her car. She'd managed to keep it even during her brief weeks of homelessness last year. But it hadn't run in over nine months now, and she'd finally sold it for scrap.

If she hadn't tried to kill herself in despair and gotten locked up in the hospital, she would never have been diagnosed. It was embarrassing to be labeled a paranoid schizophrenic, to have that in her *file*, but she had to admit she wasn't hearing voices as much now that she was on medication.

She smiled, remembering the time she'd told her doctor the police were tapping her phone. The doctor had increased her meds, but that didn't change a thing. Miranda knew the police were still listening to her. That just proved it wasn't a delusion, if increased meds didn't change her perception.

Yet the anti-delusional drugs did change one thing. Miranda no longer believed in God.

It had come as a shock at first, until she realized what was happening. Now that she was on anti-psychotics, naturally she saw reality more clearly.

Maybe more people should be on the drugs.

Miranda breathed a sigh of relief as she exited the tunnel. It was another two miles to her apartment, but this next stretch was easy. She thought for a moment and then took out her cell phone and called Ed. She might as well use her minutes while she still had them.

She'd never liked Ed that much, ever since he'd stood her up once on a date over twenty-five years ago. He was a black guy from the old Single Adult group at church way back when. Miranda had looked up his number on the computer at work earlier in the afternoon, when she'd looked up all her old friends' numbers. She and Ed talked every few years, but it had easily been three years since their last conversation.

"Hello?"

"Hi, Ed, it's me, Miranda."

"Miranda?"

"From church."

There was a long pause. "Oh, hi, Miranda."

"Guess what I'm doing right now."

There was no answer.

"I'm walking home from work."

"Okay."

Eventually, Miranda caught him up on the past few years and asked him how he was doing. He was still only in the Elders Quorum, still unmarried, and working in real estate.

"Must be hard in this economy," Miranda said.

"It's okay. The only thing that really matters is getting married in the temple. But you know that."

"Why won't anyone marry you?" she asked. He was a man, after all. It was completely within his control.

"Not many women at church want to marry an African American."

"Why don't you move to…to…" She thought of all the times people had told her to move to Salt Lake.

Ed laughed. "It doesn't matter anyway. God will reinstate polygamy in the Millennium, and I'll have plenty of wives then."

Just like a man to say something so repulsive, Miranda thought. "I have a book about Warren Jeffs I could lend you."

"Oh, I never read any books that aren't published by the Church."

Talk about delusional, thought Miranda.

She said goodbye and kept walking past a grungy, dilapidated apartment complex. She dialed Jerry's number next. He'd also been part of the Singles group before moving to Dallas twenty years ago. If the benefits people were going to take her phone at any moment, she wanted one last evening of contact with the world. Oh, God, what if she became homeless a second time? She'd have to try to kill herself and get evaluated all over again so she could requalify.

What a bother.

She didn't know why she hadn't looked up Jerry's phone number sooner. It would have helped to talk on these long walks home. Something to do besides dodge aluminum cans and fast food wrappers. "Hi, Jerry," Miranda cooed into the phone. She knew she still had a sexy voice.

"Who is this?"

"Miranda, from New Orleans."

"Miranda! Where've you been? I called you several times last year, but your phone was always disconnected."

"I was homeless."

"What?!"

She again told her story, smiling. It was fun to hear people's reactions. Of course, several people had told her for a very long time that she needed psychiatric help, but she'd simply thought they were all part of the plot against her. She supposed some of them were thinking, "I told you so," but really, it was a little exciting to be crazy. It made her special.

Still, telling the story was a one-time thing. No one wanted to hear it a second time. And what else did she have to talk about, now that all the nurses and doctors weren't truly out to get her?

"I broke up with my fiancée," Jerry said.

"Really?" Maybe Miranda wasn't the only cursed Mormon out there, the only loser. Maybe it would be okay to go back to church. Perhaps the Relief Society president and the bishop's wife weren't really spreading lies about her masturbating on the pews.

What might life have been like if all those years she could have felt comfort at church instead of believing she was the center of hateful gossip? She wondered if it was too late to go back.

But what would be the point, if there really was no God? Then the Church couldn't possibly be true. It didn't seem fair to dangle the Church in front of her for just a brief moment and then snatch it away.

Yet if there were no God, who was doing the snatching?

Miranda and Jerry commiserated with each other for a few more minutes over their unmarried status, and then Jerry said he had to meet some buddies from work. "I love you, Miranda."

Miranda felt a thrill run through her body, even though she understood he meant it solely as a friend. But it was more than she got anywhere else, so it felt good anyway.

Miranda passed a desolate block filled with weeds. The streetlight here was broken, too. There was an abandoned car, its tires missing, one window broken.

Sometimes, Miranda wished she could die and end this terrible ordeal. What was she going to do if SSI cut her off? She was only working PRN and never knew how many hours she was going to have. She just couldn't face living on the street again.

This time, she wouldn't even have a car to sleep in. The threat of homelessness *sounded* exciting, but actual homelessness was boring. So much of life was boring now that she saw things as they were. A doctor's smile only meant he was nice, not that he was in love with her.

A nurse's scowl only meant she was having a bad day, not that she'd hired a private detective to take nude pictures of Miranda to put on the internet. The cashier at the grocery wasn't really telling jokes about her behind her back. He didn't even notice she existed.

Miranda sighed, but when she did, she thought she heard a noise. She looked over her shoulder as a precaution, and then gasped and started walking faster. There was a black guy behind her, about twenty years old, skulking along. He was following her.

It was almost a relief, really. Just because you were officially paranoid didn't mean *some* people weren't after you. Better to be noticed by a mugger than by no one at all.

This guy probably needed money for drugs. Ha! As if he'd get anything from Miranda. All she had on her was a five dollar bill.

Would he kill her if she didn't hand him more than that?

Miranda smiled. It was comforting to be the center of attention again. It felt good.

She dialed another number. "Tammy?" she said a moment later.

"Miranda?"

"There's a black guy following me home from work. I just wanted to let you know in case you don't hear from me again."

Miranda heard a sigh. "Are you taking your meds?" Tammy sighed an awful lot. Miranda was sure the woman had no idea how condescending it was.

"Yes! There really *is* a guy!" Miranda squealed into the phone. It felt almost like old times.

"Miranda—"

"He's coming!"

"Ma'am? Ma'am?" the teenager said, coming right up on her.

"Yes?" Miranda answered bravely.

"This is a rough part of town. Do you mind if I walk with you?"

Miranda was floored. He was being *chivalrous*? "You want to *protect* me?" she asked disbelievingly.

"No, I just figured gangbangers wouldn't come after me if I was with a white lady."

He'd called her "lady."

"I gotta go," Miranda said into the phone and hung up. Miranda looked at the boy. He was attractive but way too young for her. Even fantasizing that something would come of it wouldn't be particularly fun anymore if she couldn't make herself believe for even a few minutes.

All Miranda did was walk to work, empty bed pans, walk home from work, and watch TV at home in her tiny apartment. There was no excitement to life any longer. She wondered if she *should* stop taking her meds.

"Sure, we can walk together." Miranda shrugged. "I have another mile to go."

The boy nodded and they continued walking. Miranda didn't know what to say to someone so young, and the boy didn't seem to feel a need to talk, so they walked along in silence.

Half a mile more. You'd think with all this exercise, she'd have lost some weight, but she was still a size fourteen. That alone proved there was no God.

They came to another desolate block filled with abandoned houses and weeds, and Miranda felt glad the boy was with her. Maybe she should—

The boy grabbed her arm. "Give it up!"

"Huh?"

"Give me your money!"

"I don't have any money."

He took out a knife. Miranda almost felt scared, but suddenly, she realized she just didn't care. She handed the boy her five dollars. He glared at the single bill, grabbed the phone from her hand, and then pushed her down and ran up the street.

Miranda groaned and slowly pulled herself to her feet, brushing herself off. She didn't feel any particular animosity or anger. This was just the way things were. Maybe she'd tell Katrice about it at work tomorrow. Katrice sometimes seemed nice.

In the old days, there'd been a crisis every day. Each one had made her feel alive. But now she had a normal, average, run-of-the-mill life, and somehow, for some unexplainable reason, it just wasn't enough.

She missed the exquisite torture of all those years.

"Please, God, help me," she prayed. She looked up into the dark sky, her eyes darting from one star to another and then to another.

She stooped to rub her sore knee and continued walking home.

Mock Judgment Day

I'd been out of work for almost a month and becoming more desperate each day. I was either overqualified or underqualified for almost everything. The only jobs that might take me sight unseen were ones that barely paid above minimum wage and certainly wouldn't help me make the mortgage payments. I began wondering if God were punishing me.

I'd always paid my tithing, had put my daughters Deeann and Gloria through college and sent Gloria on a mission as well, and now that I was in my mid-fifties, I'd been hoping to coast until retirement, when I planned to go with my wife, Eileen, on a mission as a couple.

Then came the layoff.

Was this because I hadn't given as much as the bishop asked in addition to my regular tithe? Was it because I'd passed up the last four ward temple sessions? Because I sometimes read anti-Mormon blogs? I wasn't *trying* to be rebellious. I just wanted to know about the things my two daughters kept bringing up, so I'd be better prepared to answer their questions.

Why did my one-year-old grandson have epilepsy? Why did my two-year-old granddaughter have a club foot? I tried to find loving answers for my daughters, even if that meant going temporarily over to the dark side. I hoped Heavenly

Father would understand. Though he couldn't have been happy I'd even glanced at the home page for either Resign from Mormonism or CES Letter. And it seemed God could get angry at just about anything, so I very well might have tested his patience.

I remembered when I was growing up, my father would always smile grimly when something bad happened to me. "It's for your own good," he'd say.

When I sprained my ankle falling off my bike, it was for my own good. When I broke my arm falling out of a tree, that was for my own good, too. When I split my nose playing basketball, when I came in last place in the Church regional speech contest, when I was too sick to go to my high school prom, it was all for my own good.

"Heavenly Father afflicts those he loves," my father assured me, smiling.

"So I guess he really loved Job," I'd replied sarcastically one day, upset over my first car being stolen.

"That's right, son."

"Maybe it's better not to be loved by God too much," I returned.

My father slapped me hard across the face.

Then he hugged me tightly and said, "It's because I love you. I don't want you to fall away. That's why Heavenly Father tests you, too. It helps keep us in line. It's like whipping a toddler who keeps getting too close to the fire. We can't understand reasoning on God's level. All we can understand is the whipping."

I went to the bishop the following Sunday and repented of my dissent, trying from that time on to be a better and more faithful Latter-day Saint. I'd certainly been tested many times in the years since, and I always had a love/hate relationship with God's love/hate relationship with me.

Just yesterday, though, when my younger daughter Gloria asked me why Heavenly Father wouldn't let her become pregnant a second time, I'd said automatically, "Perhaps it's for your own good."

The look of hurt in her eyes made me turn away. I hadn't been able to sleep all night. I tried so hard to be better than my own father, but sometimes, after a lifetime of training, it was difficult not to follow in his footsteps. I needed to call and apologize, but my worry over my joblessness kept pulling my focus elsewhere.

I applied for my required three jobs a week, all in downtown Seattle, to be eligible for unemployment benefits, and last week, I'd applied for eight, even though I knew I wasn't right for most of them.

I was growing more willing to take just about anything, even something temporary, so I applied for a one-day job as a juror on a mock jury. I'd never served on a real jury and thought it might be interesting, and the pay, even though it would be deducted from my unemployment check, would still help me feel like a real person. I hoped.

What I felt, though, was the same humiliation as the day I'd failed a science test in high school, and as punishment, my father forced me to scrub the bathroom with a toothbrush. "That'll teach you a lesson," he said.

Just like the time in grammar school when I'd lost the school spelling bee and Dad forced me to pick up trash along the highway. Like the time in junior high when I lost my solo in Band because I'd missed a key rehearsal due to illness and had then been made to weed our neighbor's yard. Dad always felt that "consequences" for my actions would make me a better person. Punishment, punishment, punishment. Sometimes, the whole purpose of life seemed to be punishment.

"Brock, do you want to have sex tomorrow after you get back from jury duty?" Eileen asked around 9:00 Monday evening. I'd mentioned in the morning I wanted to have sex sometime that day.

"No. I want to have sex now."

"But it's so late for you." I usually preferred sex while I was still alert, not right at bedtime. At 11:00 pm, sex felt like a chore. At 7:00 pm, it felt like sex.

"The defense deserves for me to be in a good mood."

Eileen smiled. "Okay, I'll see what I can do."

Our sex life wasn't very dynamic, with our encounters occurring maybe once a week and often scheduled. I found I had to give Eileen a few hours of warning to let her work herself into being in the mood. She acted sometimes as if sex were not only a chore at any hour but even something to dread.

I wondered how we'd manage throughout eternity if we ever made it to godhood. She didn't seem up to all the sex required to bear billions of spirit offspring. Perhaps that was why there was polygamy in heaven, to make eternal sex easier on the women. I wondered if sexually reluctant goddesses ever made Heavenly Father irritable.

I remembered one ex-Mormon blog that suggested God had committed incest when he got his own daughter Mary pregnant with Jesus. Since that wasn't a very sexy thought, I focused instead on Eileen. I tried hard not to make her feel she was forced to undergo some type of trial when she was with me physically. It was difficult not to feel a bit like an abuser when I knew she wasn't having a good time, but what options did I have?

Was she "being taught a lesson"?

Was I?

The following morning, I woke up early and caught the light rail downtown, getting off at the Pioneer Square station. While filled with dozens of homeless folks and various other grungy people, this part of town was still lovely because all the old buildings were made with such craftsmanship and attention to detail.

I walked down to First Avenue South to the address listed in my email and entered a five-story building made of brown stone. I was supposed to go up to Suite 500, and rather than take the cage elevator, I chose to climb the stairs to admire the walls covered with intricate wood paneling.

Puffing a bit on the top floor, I saw a sign that said, "Mock Jury in Basement." I frowned. Would it have hurt to put that sign in the lobby?

Then I heard my father's voice in my head. I walked back down the stairs and, once on the basement level, saw signs leading to a large back room. I was the first person to arrive, though there was the typical forbidden tea and coffee on a table along with some pastries cut in half.

In the center of the room was a small meeting table, which somehow had permanent stains on its surface. The eight chairs around the table didn't match, half of them covered in white fabric with some kind of abstract pattern and half simple wooden chairs. One of the white chairs was also stained, I noticed. Along the wall were a few other chairs of yet a third type, some kind of faux brown leather. A plastic ficus tree was in one corner. I sat at the table, looking up at the fluorescent lights in the ceiling. Some of the white acoustical tiles that made up the ceiling were stained as well.

Pay attention, I told myself. Learn something today.

Ten minutes later, a tremendously obese white man in his mid-twenties walked into the room. He must have weighed 400 pounds or more. A minute later, a goofy-looking white man came in, with a severe overbite, and after him, two well-dressed white women, an attractive African American man around thirty-five, and an African American woman a decade younger. In all, thirteen of us showed up, all white except for the two Blacks who'd come in. No other ethnicities.

"Have you done this before?" asked a woman whose nametag said Janine. "It's my first time, but it has to be better than delivering phone books. I did that last month. God, how awful."

A couple of the others commiserated over the phone books, and two people, including the Black man, whose name was Emory, said they'd been part of other mock juries. "Easy money," he said, "and we're doing something useful."

Just before 9:00, a middle-aged African American woman came into the room and took attendance. One person was missing, but that didn't seem to concern her. She handed out confidentiality paperwork, which we all signed, and after another ten minutes, two other women came into the room, an Asian woman and a white woman. I got the impression they were the attorneys.

"Everyone, pick up your chairs and put them along the wall in two rows," said the Asian woman, who introduced herself as Linda Wong. We did so, and I ended up as Juror number eight. I smiled. The age of accountability. It was a sign I was doing the right thing in assessing guilt in this case.

"We're going to give you the facts," said the other woman, who introduced herself as Sandra Thompson, "and then we'll let you deliberate." She sat down and started taking notes, which confused me, until I saw that she was writing down our reactions to the information Ms. Wong was giving us.

"The facts are these," said Ms. Wong. "Deressa Davenport is a mother of five. Three of her adult children were out of the house at the time of the incident. One child, Lydia, was thirteen, and the youngest child, Harmony, was seven. One of Harmony's friends, Brianna, was playing at the house and overheard Mrs. Davenport say the F word. It was not directed at the children, but Brianna went home to her own mother and reported that Harmony's mother had a 'potty mouth.' Brianna's mother, Helen Nagle, was upset and called DCPSA, the Department of Child Protective Services Agency."

We'd all been given legal pads and pens, and I was writing down what seemed important. We'd been told we wouldn't be allowed to ask questions but had to go on what we and the other jurors remembered about the case. I wasn't sure where this was going. Mrs. Davenport had clearly been at fault, but it also didn't seem like the biggest crime in the world. Perhaps she needed to be taught a lesson, but I would be lenient, I decided.

"DCPSA assigned Brenda Rathke to investigate the case. Brenda had been with the agency two years. She interviewed Deressa Davenport but did not interview any of the three children who had been present in the house at the time of the alleged incident. She interviewed one neighbor, who said she had never heard Deressa cursing even once. But Brenda's report claims that three neighbors confirmed Deressa's cursing in front of her children. There is nothing in the report to substantiate this claim. Brenda's report also claims that she interviewed two psychologists who insisted that such cursing would be detrimental to the children's welfare, but again, there is nothing in the file to substantiate this. The conclusions are listed in the report, but no documentary material is there to support them."

I still wasn't sure where this was going. There seemed to be no sexual or physical abuse going on, and the verbal problem didn't seem to really qualify as abuse. You didn't need to curse to verbally abuse someone in any event. My father never cursed.

"A week after the report was filed, DCPSA officers came and physically removed the two children from the Davenport household. The children were placed in foster care, where the older girl was molested by another foster child two months later. Deressa, who was a single mother at the time of these incidents, spent all her money fighting DCPSA. She eventually lost her home and had to move in with one of her grown daughters."

Everyone was scribbling away, a few gasps escaping some of the jurors. I was still confused. The state could actually take away someone's children, just over use of the F word? It seemed mind-boggling. I could hardly make it through a single movie these days, there was so much vulgarity spewing out of everyone's mouth. I'd taken to reading children's books because adult books were so abrasive to my spirit.

Did society really think cursing was an actionable offense? I wasn't sure if that proved there was still hope for the nation or not. Children did deserve a beautiful, innocent childhood, so perhaps the action was justified. Wasn't the mother ultimately responsible for what happened to her daughters in foster care, since her poor parenting was what put them in foster care to begin with?

"The case was appealed, and all five of Deressa's children testified that their mother was loving and wonderful. But we have an email from Brenda Rathke's supervisor and another from the supervisor's supervisor, both saying basically, 'DCPSA is above reproach. No one can tell us what to do. We make the rules.' Brenda was promoted because of her work on this case."

The attorney went on and on for another fifteen minutes, stating injustice after injustice. I wanted to believe a government agency would do the right thing. Could it be that someone in such authority over children might act inappropriately? I kept wondering what might have happened if I could have been raised by someone other than my own father. Perhaps I should be grateful my upbringing wasn't any worse than it was. Maybe Heavenly Father putting me under the care of my father was in fact "for my own good."

As I continued to listen to the attorney, I was horrified to learn that the original incident had occurred seven years ago. Lydia was now twenty and living on her own, and Harmony, fourteen, was still in foster care. DCPSA simply refused to back down, and they even refused to allow one of Deressa's older daughters to act as a foster parent for Harmony.

Ms. Wong finished speaking, and Ms. Thompson held up a sheet of paper. "You'll need to choose a foreman," she said. "He or she will ask the jurors to answer these questions. We'll give you forty-five minutes to deliberate, and then we'll be back."

Everyone looked around at each other for a moment, and then I said, "Emory has done this before and seems to know what's going on. How about we pick him to lead us?"

There was no debate. Most people seemed relieved to have it decided that quickly. Emory got up and moved to the front of the room, where he picked up the piece of paper. "Do you feel that Deressa Davenport was wronged in this case?" He looked up at us. "Okay, I'll go down the rows and everyone answer one at a time. Juror number one?"

"Yes."

"Juror number two?"

"Yes."

And so it went. It seemed impossible for anyone to vote against the poor woman, and no one did. "Of course, we've just heard one side of it," Janine pointed out. She was Juror number nine and sat right next to me.

"True," I said, "but we can only go on what we know, not what might be said later. They may come in after we're done and give us new information and make us vote again."

I thought for some reason about all the times at church when the bishop or stake president asked us to sustain someone for a position, and the only thing we knew was that the bishop or stake president was in favor of it. Then we had to say "Aye" in front of everyone and raise our hands, or dissent publicly and give a reason.

In all my years at church sustaining people, only once had I ever seen someone dissent, and it was my father. Everyone in Priesthood meeting had gasped. Then my father simply said, "I've never even met this man. How can I say I believe he'll do a good job?"

"You're only saying you'll *help* him do a good job," he was told. "That's what 'sustain' means."

But I understood about making decisions based on inadequate information, and the peer pressure involved in making those decisions. That was one of the few times I was actually proud of my father, despite being mortified at the same time. In the car on the way home, he said calmly, "I hope you learned a lesson."

Emory read the next question. "Do you believe the state should be held responsible for taking Deressa Davenport's children away without just cause?"

Two jurors were opposed to this point. One man, a white guy in his mid-forties with gray hair and an acne-scarred face, said, "You can't hold the state responsible for what one or two employees did. Fire the employees."

A young woman sitting on my left, Juror number seven, said, "If we hold the state responsible, where does that lead? Do we sue the state because our mail was late?"

"It's systemic," said the morbidly obese young man, who was sitting in the front row. "I was raised in foster care. The whole organization is corrupt."

"We can't punish the system just because you don't like it," said the acne-scarred man.

"All the poor mother did was use the F word," Janine reminded us. "Give the goddamn bitch a break."

Everyone laughed, and we continued deliberating. I wasn't sure we needed to come up with a unanimous vote or not and was just about to suggest we move on to the next question when a final vote pulled the two dissenters over to the side of the majority.

Emory picked up the piece of paper. "One question left," he said. "How much money do you think the woman is entitled to in compensatory damages?" He looked at the paper a moment longer. "There's a note. In the State of

Washington," he went on, "there are apparently no punitive damages, no repayment for lost income or anything like that. It's all lumped together under 'Compensatory Damages.' Whatever we say she gets is what she gets, and it has to cover everything."

"I don't think she deserves anything," said the acne-scarred man. "She gets her kids back. Her name is cleared. That's it."

"But her children were taken away," said Janine.

"So what price do you put on children?" the man asked. "Twenty thousand dollars? Five million? Children are priceless. It's demeaning to put a dollar figure on it."

"And you don't think it's demeaning to say they're worth absolutely nothing at all?" said Janine.

"So she wins the lottery because someone was mean to her? Boo hoo, you hurt my feelings."

"You're being disingenuous," I said. "It's clearly much more than hurt feelings." I felt a small surge of adrenalin flowing through my veins, even over such a minor comment. I usually avoided confrontations whenever possible.

We went around the room then, juror by juror, and each said the amount we thought the woman was entitled to. Two people said zero, a couple of people said $500,000, and then there were a few suggestions of $750,000 and $1,000,000 and even $1,500,000. But then Emory concluded with, "I think she should get $5,000,000."

Everyone gasped. The acne-scarred man started complaining loudly, his diaphragm in good shape, and people argued for the next several moments over the responsibility of a parent and the responsibility of a higher authority. But when I heard the words "higher authority," I was suddenly drawn back to one of those anti-Mormon blogs I'd read recently, one that claimed that the God Mormons worshipped, and that most Christians worshipped, wasn't a very nice being.

He allowed his children to suffer from painful and disfiguring diseases. He allowed them to be beaten and raped by their Earthly parents. He allowed them to starve to death. He allowed them to be raised by fathers who made them feel like dirt their whole lives.

If this woman was guilty of abuse for using bad language, it struck me that Heavenly Father was guilty of neglect at the very least.

If that was a sin for *us*, why wasn't it a sin for *him*, too? Was he like the DCPSA? Was he above the law?

I felt a little dizzy and looked at my knees to steady myself. My mind was reeling like the time I'd seen one of those optical illusions, and what at first appeared to be a lamp suddenly turned into two faces looking at each other.

What about the Flood, I asked myself. I'd quickly glossed over that blog the other day, feeling too uncomfortable to read it carefully, but now I couldn't seem to stop from dwelling on the questions it had raised. Heavenly Father hadn't just "allowed" Nature or Free Will to take its natural course when he created a worldwide flood. He'd deliberately murdered untold numbers of his children.

What would happen to a human parent who killed his own children? Josh Powell, that repulsive man, had very likely murdered his wife, but we *knew* he'd attacked his two sons with a hatchet before burning them to death. How I'd hated having to deal with the comments at work about "Mormon family values." Why did that jerk have to be a Mormon? It looked like the DCPSA had made another terrible mistake in that case, even worse than this one.

But it was one thing for humans to be imperfect and make poor judgment calls on complicated cases. It was another thing for Heavenly Father, all-knowing, to behave this way. Was it possible he *wasn't* a very nice guy?

I looked around the room nervously. I was in a building constructed in 1902, according to the plaque out front. Another powerful earthquake like the one Seattle had had a decade ago could bring this building down right on my head.

I almost laughed. I was wondering if Heavenly Father was nice, and I believed he might strike me dead just for considering the possibility he wasn't?

Perhaps it was understandable why there were doubters out there. But I also believed Heavenly Father loved me. The Church told me so all the time. At least, he loved me while I was obeying his commandments. But if a human father was nice to his kids only when they obeyed every order he gave them, and then made them sick or killed them if they disobeyed, wouldn't we be calling the police?

Something didn't seem right.

After more debate, we finally agreed to average everyone's dollar amount. Even the two zero amounts had been raised to $100,000 by this point, and the overall average turned out to be $2.25 million.

The attorneys weren't back yet, so a few of the jurors took off for a smoke break. I wondered if lung cancer were a punishment from God or just the natural consequence of the action. God always said he didn't create universal laws and principles himself. Even he had to obey them.

Okay, so maybe cancer wasn't God's doing. Carcinogens existed, with or without his input. But the Flood? I couldn't get past that one. If we were to believe the Bible at all, he was fully responsible for that massacre.

And now I started wondering about consequences *for him.* Was there an eternal DCPSA that would take Heavenly Father's children away from *him*? Did he get custody no matter what awful things he did? Who would sit on God's jury?

There were millions of other gods, after all. Would he be judged by a jury of *his* peers? I knew Judgment Day was coming for me, for everyone in my family, and for all my friends. But was there going to be a Judgment Day for Heavenly Father, too?

And if there was, would I testify?

And if I did, what would I say?

I took a quick pee break in a unisex bathroom out in the hallway and then hurried back, not wanting to walk in on the attorneys if they returned. They ended up coming back five minutes later, and Ms. Wong asked us only one question. "What dollar amount did you come up with?"

It seemed awfully crass.

"Okay," she said, sounding disappointed at Emory's answer. "I want everyone to stand up in a row, according to the dollar amounts you personally decided upon, lowest amount over here and highest amount over there."

We all complied. It felt good not to be sitting any longer.

"Okay. I'm going to give you a few more facts," Ms. Wong continued. "And if they change your mind to go either up or down on your amount, I want you to move to the right or left accordingly." She paused and then said, "Would it make a difference if you knew that the younger girl, Harmony, was also molested while in foster care?"

Everyone looked at each other in confusion. Did we put a dollar figure on that, too?

"Would it make a difference if you knew we had an email from a senior person at DCPSA saying they'd lose face if they backed down now?"

A couple of people moved toward the higher end of the dollar range. I thought these last two facts were pretty damning, but I still hadn't moved yet.

"Would it make a difference if we told you there's a letter from the DCPSA dated two years after the girls were taken stating that they'd return custody of the older girl only, as long as the mother refused to file charges?"

There was some shuffling of feet.

"Would it make a difference if we told you Deressa Davenport had won Mother of the Year in the State of Washington four years before this incident occurred?"

More shifting, but no one moved.

"Would it make a difference if we told you that Deressa was a Mormon, and that she was excommunicated from her Church as a result of being publicly 'proven' to be a bad and abusive mother?"

My mouth fell open. Did we actually excommunicate for things like that? I remembered Sonia Johnson had been ex'ed for fighting to support women's rights. Some intellectuals had been ex'ed for, well, for thinking too much.

"Are you serious?" I said.

Ms. Thompson wrote something down on a piece of paper.

Ms. Wong smiled. "Would it make a difference if I told you that when Lydia was molested, she was infected with HPV, the virus that can cause cervical cancer years later?"

A couple more people moved over to the higher amount side of the room. I still hadn't moved, mostly because I was too shocked to think clearly.

"Would it make a difference if I told you we have an email from someone at DCPSA stating that the two daughters were being deliberately placed in homes where the most difficult boys lived?"

"Oh, my god," said Janine. "You can't be serious. Do you really have all this evidence?"

"We've only told you a fifth of all the egregious things the state has done."

"But it wasn't the state," the acne-scarred man insisted. "It was just a handful of employees."

"I think I'm afraid of the government now," said Janine. "Anyone with that much power…"

"What you have to decide," Ms. Wong said, "is whether or not you think Deressa Davenport deserves any compensatory damages for what she and her family went through, and what dollar amount you want to put on that."

I thought about that "handful of employees" claim. Was Heavenly Father responsible for things one of his children did against another one? Could he help it if his son Satan was mean to us and led us astray? Could he help it if the North Koreans hated the South Koreans? Perhaps he couldn't help it if my father wasn't perfect, since no one at all was perfect.

So did that mean Heavenly Father was absolved of everything his children did to each other? What would have happened to *me* if I'd let my oldest daughter kill my youngest daughter? Well, it would probably have been Deeann who went to jail, not me.

But if I'd *known* she was plotting against Gloria and I'd done nothing about it? Heavenly Father was all-knowing. He *let* his children run amok and kill each other. He let them be cruel to each other in millions of different ways. Didn't that make him complicit? An accessory?

And he still got custody?

I moved to the far end of the room. "I don't know what dollar amount you want us to go for," I said. "And I don't know if you can give direction. But I'm willing to go pretty high. I don't know what kind of ballpark figure we're talking about. I just want to make sure this woman gets *something*."

Ms. Thompson wrote another note down on her paper.

Was Heavenly Father "letting" me be unemployed, or was he responsible? Was he accountable for all the homeless people I'd walked past to get to the attorney's office this morning? Was "heaven" supposed to be our compensatory damages?

An eternity with the man who'd wronged us?

I decided I was going to write a comment on one of those blogs I'd been visiting recently. Maybe I'd tell the story of how as a teenager I'd called an attorney to see how much it would cost to be emancipated from my "eternal family." Perhaps I'd put a dollar figure on hearing the bishop praise my father in Sacrament meeting for his parenting skills.

To hell with whether anyone in the ward found out. It looked like the Church could abandon its own as easily as any drug-addled mother could. I thought of my wonderful cousin who'd been excommunicated years ago for being gay and who ended up committing suicide the following day.

If churches could toss aside the needs of their own without any consequences, if states could do it, if even God could do it, what hope was there for any justice in the universe?

Ms. Thompson had us all sit down again. She handed us each a sheet of paper asking us to write our main reasons for voting as we did, and to put our final individual figure down for the award. I still didn't know if I was guessing right or not but put down $25 million. Even if Ms. Davenport won the case, the state was sure to appeal. Who could ever really force the state to pay?

Did my personal verdict against God count any more than the verdict of this mock jury against DCPSA?

I turned in my paper, and Ms. Thompson handed me an envelope with my check. $50. I looked at it, feeling suddenly very cheap, as if I'd been begging at an intersection. Then I grew angry again at Heavenly Father for reducing his children to beggars.

Walking back to the light rail station, I passed a Bank of America and went inside to cash my check. Then I climbed down into the tunnel and waited for the train. I ended up sitting next to a group of five mentally disabled teenagers who seemed to find everything funny and laughed loudly the following twenty minutes until I stepped off at my station. I caught an 8 back to my neighborhood and walked the last few blocks to my house.

"Hi, Eileen." I closed the door behind me and kissed her as she came up to greet me.

"How'd it go?"

"Let's call Deeann and Gloria and have them over for dinner Sunday."

"Both families?" Eileen said in surprise. We usually alternated Sundays.

I nodded and took off my coat. "I'm going to take a nap."

"You okay?"

"I'll help prepare the girls' favorite meal."

"All right."

"And we'll play some fun games or something afterward." Maybe just ask everyone how they were really doing.

I went to the bedroom and took off my shoes, feeling very tired, though it was still not quite 1:00. Maybe later in the afternoon I'd call my father. He'd left several messages over the past few months, saying things like, "I haven't heard from you in a while. Don't you love your old dad anymore?" and then chuckling nervously. I never called him back.

Perhaps I was the one being cruel now. I knelt briefly beside the bed and clasped my hands. I wanted to pray but couldn't quite bring myself to do it. I stripped down to my Mormon undergarments instead and slipped under the covers. I pulled the comforter up to my chin and tried to pray again.

But it was time for emancipation.

I climbed back out of bed and logged onto the computer.

Partying with St. Roch

I could see that Dennis had a drinking problem. It wasn't as bad as Glenn's had been, of course. I'd dated Glenn for almost a year before he died of cirrhosis, holed up in his apartment with empty beer cans around his bed. He'd frequently point to my flat stomach after we had sex and say, "You may have a six-pack, but *I've* got a whole keg," and then he'd pat his extended abdomen.

I'd thought it was just a beer belly, but some of that enlargement was due to his damaged liver. After that experience, I vowed I'd never date another drinker.

Then I met Dennis at the Unitarian church in Uptown New Orleans on Nashville. We were both excommunicated Mormons, and we hit it off singing about a God who loved all people equally. We dated for five months and then moved in together, about one month before Dennis's T-cells dropped to 50 and he was diagnosed with full-blown AIDS.

It was late 1989, and we were looking forward to New Year's, hoping for a repeat of the Gay Nineties, at least in name, working together for gay rights with several organizations, not the least of which was ACT UP, carrying signs and shouting slogans in front of City Hall as we demanded more access to medicines. Shortly after we moved to St. Roch in the Marigny, Dennis developed an addiction to Coke.

That's Coke with a capital C.

He began having me purchase every three-liter bottle of the off brand the local Schwegmann's grocery stocked when I went to do our weekly shopping. I'd pile twelve of the monstrous bottles into my cart and plod my way to the checkout. Every single week, people would smile and ask, "Having a party?"

"Nothing but fun at my house," I'd reply, smiling back.

"Kirk, you only bought eight bottles today," Dennis complained this afternoon. "I'll never make it through the week."

"I'll stop at the store again tomorrow."

"I need this. I get so little pleasure out of life."

"I'll stop at the store again tomorrow."

The sodas were not diet. I was afraid that at any moment, Dennis would have diabetes to add to his problems, but something about the HIV or his particular metabolism seemed to defy the sugar overload. He remained thin as a rail despite a full daily allotment of calories just from the cola alone.

His other favorite treat was chocolate, which was a debatable violation of the Word of Wisdom. And perhaps because the caffeine kept him from fully hydrating despite the vast amounts of liquid he consumed, he also drank a great deal of black tea.

"Do you think I'm a hedonist, Kirk?" Dennis asked. "Do you think I should be obeying all the commandments now that I'm about to die?"

"Shut up and fuck me," I said, forcing a smile.

I was still negative, and Dennis always used a condom when we had sex. The irony was that he was basically a top. He'd only bottomed maybe three or four times ever, but he'd done it just once without a condom, and now he was paying the price. Every day, priests and pastors across the country were still proclaiming that AIDS was God's punishment for our abominable sins, thereby infecting everyone with their hatred. It was impossible not to wonder if they were right.

Every evening as I kissed the man I loved goodnight, I'd look into his face and wonder if God really despised us this much. One of the last things I heard my stake president say after he told me I was excommunicated was, "If Heavenly Father still loves you, He'll give you AIDS to help you repent. It's so much kinder than letting you live in your sins for a lifetime, thinking you're not sinning. I'll pray that God gives you AIDS, for your own good."

He smiled and held out his hand warmly, as if he'd just said something comforting.

My hand stayed by my side, and his finally dropped as well, a look of confusion on his face. I turned and walked out of his office, and I never went to an LDS church again. Mormonism had always been my rock before, "the one and only true church."

Four years passed, in fact, before I ever entered any other church at all. A friend invited me to a meeting at the MCC in the Bywater, in an ancient red brick building along the levee. I didn't like the congregation, so a few months later, I tried a Dignity meeting with some gay Catholics. I didn't care for that, either. I attended a Reform synagogue Uptown on St. Charles and liked that well enough, but I was afraid to stop praying "in the name of Jesus Christ," even though I wasn't sure I even believed in Jesus Christ anymore.

I realized I was being superstitious, not religious. I attended a Methodist meeting on North Rampart in the Quarter and then an Episcopal service Uptown and a Hare Krishna meeting on Esplanade. At last I stumbled upon the Unitarian meeting. I'd been just about to give up my quest when I listened to a blonde woman with dreadlocks give a sermon on the importance of protecting the environment, and I decided to come back a second time. I'd been attending ever since.

"Really?" Dennis looked doubtful, almost mournful. "You're still attracted to me?"

"I want you, mister."

I grabbed my crotch, and Dennis's eyes lit up. He hurried over to the dresser and pulled out the two nametags I'd ordered a couple of months earlier. He slipped one on his shirt pocket that said, "Elder Top—The Church of Jesus Christ of Latter-gay Saints" and handed me the other to put on my pocket, "Elder Bottom," with the same fake Church name.

Dennis leaned forward to kiss me, rubbing against me and smiling as our two missionary nametags clicked against each other. Then, despite the costume, he took off his shirt and knelt in front of me, unzipping my pants as I rubbed his head, trying not to be distracted by the large black Kaposi's lesions on his shoulders and back. He didn't fuck me as I'd suggested but just sucked me off. I watched as his head moved back and forth, wanting to memorize every sexual encounter with him, so that I could replay them after he was gone. With a final thrust, I came, and then Dennis smiled and stood.

"Your turn?" I asked, pointing to his zipper.

He shook his head. "All I want is more Coke. I know it's a pain, but can you go to another store?"

I nodded and went to grab my cart again. We didn't have a car, and the Schwegmann's on Claiborne was the only store truly within walking distance, about nine blocks from the apartment. The next closest was a grocery on Franklin. I walked the five blocks to the bus stop, waited almost twenty minutes, and then boarded the 57. A few minutes later, I was at the store.

There were no three-liter bottles here of the off brand that Dennis preferred, but there were several two-liter bottles of regular Coke. I'd tried making this substitution for Dennis before with negative results. He wanted what he wanted, and nothing else would do. It could be annoying, but how could I deny him what few indulgences he had left in life?

If what the Church taught were true, there'd be no Coke in heaven. I'd never even dared try a sip until I went to my first gay bar.

I wondered if it were true that the Church owned lots of stock in Coca-Cola.

I pushed my cart along the pavement until I arrived at the bus stop. What could I try next? There was a Rouse's up closer to the lake. Since I was already taking the bus, I supposed it didn't matter how many blocks I had to go once I was sitting down. The bus jerked to a halt in front of me fifteen minutes later, and I dragged my cart on board.

I was the only white person in the vehicle. Whites in general were afraid to ride the bus in New Orleans, afraid they'd be murdered by all those "low-class" blacks who filled the seats. While I did get a few cold stares once in a while, obviously most other passengers ignored me completely.

Once, I'd run into my Sunday School teacher Theautrey on the Elysian Fields bus and said hi and shaken his hand. At the Unitarian church the next Sunday, he admitted he'd felt two conflicting emotions: one, surprise that a white person would acknowledge him in public, and two, embarrassment in front of other blacks that he was friends with a white person.

As a Mormon, I'd learned that blacks had been cursed with a dark skin for their lack of dedication to God in the Pre-Existence. While I'd grown up watching *Diff'rent Strokes* and *The Jeffersons* and didn't feel I harbored much prejudice, whenever I saw a news report of another black murderer or listened to the uneducated speech of blacks around me, I'd doubt just a little my belief that all people were equal.

Maybe it wasn't oppression and lack of opportunity that hurt this community. What if they really were inferior spirits? Even while listening to Theautrey teach a class on Sundays and feeling impressed with his knowledge, I'd doubt. Maybe he had some white blood, I'd think. Maybe that was why he was so smart.

I'd hate myself for thinking these things and then get mad at the Mormons all over again for filling my head with such nonsense. Gays weren't bad. Blacks weren't inferior. What kind of religion went around spreading such diseased teachings in the first place?

Then I'd wonder again if I was going to hell.

I climbed out of the bus across the street from Rouse's and headed for the store. I went straight for the soda aisle, ready to be finished with this interminable chore and get back home to relax. I worked all week at the public library under a tyrannical manager and then came home to a sick partner.

Saturday was my day to have fun, and I had to take my fun when I could get it. I tried to make these outings an escape from the confines of my apartment, but all I really wanted to do was listen to Roxette while putting together a thousand-piece jigsaw puzzle of Notre Dame or the Taj Mahal.

No three-liter bottles.

Why did Dennis have to drink so much? Was it his way of thumbing his nose at God?

I looked over the soda section a second time to make sure I wasn't missing anything. There was a section for three-liter bottles, all right, but there weren't any stocked. Was there an epidemic of cola addiction out there?

"Excuse me," I said, stopping a young black man with a nametag. "Could you check in back to see if you have any more of the three-liter bottles?"

The man looked at me, looked at the empty shelf, looked at me again with his lip curled ever so slightly, and headed off without a word. I waited fifteen minutes and then decided to try one last store, a new one that had opened next to the housing projects near Canal. This would be the last stop on my pilgrimage, regardless of the outcome.

I arrived thirty-five minutes later and pushed my cart quickly to the soda aisle. There was a lone three-liter bottle. An elderly woman looked as if she was contemplating it. I debated whether to snatch the bottle before she had a chance to reach for it but bit my lip and waited till she slowly moved on down the aisle. I put the bottle in my cart, added one more item from a few aisles away, and headed for the checkout.

Dennis was not going to be pleased.

Was I a bad partner for giving up before I'd accomplished what Dennis asked of me? The man was dying, after all. He'd be gone in only a few months. Couldn't I sacrifice just a little more for him? Perhaps this proved that fleeting gay relationships were a poor substitute for "true" eternal marriage. It was what I felt every Sunday, too, that my new religion was only a lackluster replacement for the real thing, no matter how much I told myself I preferred these services to the Sacrament and Priesthood meetings of before.

Could one be inoculated against the infection of self-doubt?

I dragged my cart off the steps of the bus twenty minutes later and pushed the metal cage ahead of me slowly, careful going over the cracked and uneven sidewalks of the Marigny. I passed the funeral home and the home of a gay hairdresser who was Clyde Barrow's cousin and then passed the home of a cute guy who routinely invited me to come in whenever he saw me walk by. I always politely refused, of course. He wasn't out today. I walked past the Lion's Inn gay bed and breakfast and finally made it to St. Roch.

The patron saint of the plague.

I unlocked the door underneath the balcony and headed up the stairs. "Kirk! I was afraid something had happened to you!"

"I could only find one more bottle."

Dennis stared at the bottle in disappointment and then managed a smile. "Maybe there will be more later in the week. I want you to spend the rest of the day with me. We have so little time left together. Tell me more of your mission stories from Germany. You know I like that."

Dennis sat down on the sofa eagerly, and I poured him a glass of cola. Then I opened my other purchase, my first bottle of red wine, and poured myself a drink, too. I brought both glasses over to the coffee table and set them down. Dennis picked up his and looked at mine for a long moment without saying anything. Then I picked up mine and took a sip. Not bad.

"Tell me again about that time you decked your zone leader," Dennis said, leaning back and smiling.

"Well, naturally, it was an accident," I began. I sat back on the sofa, too, and Dennis swung his legs up so that his feet were resting in my lap. I sipped my wine with one hand and rubbed his feet with the other.

I looked over at the man I loved, and wondered how I was going to fit the whole of eternity into the next few months. "It all started the day my zone leader told me in front of everyone that I didn't measure up to his expectations…"

I continued with my story, distracted by a new lesion on Dennis's leg. I began embellishing, just to add some variety, and Dennis grinned as I went on.

These are the good old days, I realized as I talked. One day soon, I'd look back and miss these times. I tried to memorize every detail of the room, the torn vinyl sofa we'd bought at Goodwill and had a friend deliver, the coffee table I'd carried two blocks from a garage sale, a mediocre piece of art Dennis had painted.

When I finished my story, Dennis asked for another, this one about the middle-aged German man who'd fucked me one day when I'd broken the mission rules and took a long walk on my own.

We both smiled as I began telling the story. When I finished, I poured Dennis another glass of cola, and I sipped more of my wine. Then I had Dennis tell me one of his own favorite mission stories, back when he thought it was a healthy thing to spread the teachings of the Church. We smiled and laughed and drank, happy for a few brief moments on the torn sofa.

In the back of my mind, I wondered where I'd packed my Book of Mormon, and if maybe I should read for a while after Dennis fell asleep.

When a Cold Wind Blows

"NOAA says snow Tuesday." Carolyn scanned in a book that had just been returned.

"Well, it's winter," said Todd, her coworker that Saturday. "These things happen."

Carolyn nodded but didn't feel comforted. She was from Phoenix, Scottsdale really, and not used to snow. She'd met her husband, Greg, when he'd come from Seattle to attend Arizona State University. He'd simply wanted a change of pace, but he'd also wanted an area with a decent percentage of Mormon girls. They married in the Mesa temple after graduation and, to Carolyn's surprise, moved to Seattle two months after that.

This had all been sixteen years ago. Of course, temperatures were temperate here compared to places like Salt Lake, and sometimes they didn't get any snow at all. Other times, they might get one or two days per winter. But every time snow threatened to fall, Carolyn felt vulnerable.

"It's like I'm being tricked," she told Greg that night over dinner. "Here it is mid-January. The irises are already starting to poke up, and now we get snow."

"I think the trick is your work assignment," said Greg.

"Oh, let's not talk about that anymore," Carolyn protested.

"You're full time at the Main Library," Greg went on, ignoring her, "at just thirty-two hours a week. And now you're being demoted to twenty hours a week. It isn't fair."

"Everyone's taking a cut," Carolyn said. "We decided that rather than lay anyone off, we'd all take a reduction in hours."

"So now *nobody* can afford to live on their salary. When you got this job, I thought, great, a City job, but civil service doesn't seem as secure as I once thought it was."

"Money, money, money," said Stacy, Carolyn's fifteen-year-old daughter. "That's all you guys ever talk about."

"And next year when you turn sixteen, we'll expect you to contribute to the family income, too," Greg told her.

"My job is to be a mother," Stacy replied.

"Well, you better not start *that* at sixteen."

"Greg."

"My job is to be personable and attract the right man."

"Then you better not have any more potatoes," Greg suggested, "if you expect a decent guy to marry you."

"Greg!"

Stacy pushed her plate away and huffed off. Carolyn was a little plump herself and quite aware of Greg's reaction to her body, and she ached to see that Stacy was following in her footsteps this early. Every Sunday, she walked in the chapel with her only daughter, embarrassed by the looks the

Laurels sent Stacy's way, and feeling guilty she was unable to conceive a second time and have the family of her dreams.

Yet she also felt just a little relief that additional pregnancies wouldn't add to her own weight. Carolyn had entered marriage thinking it was "for all eternity" and was discovering that eternity wasn't the issue—staying together in this life was the challenge. Nothing seemed to turn out the way she expected.

Just then, the phone rang, and though Greg sent her a disapproving look, Carolyn got up to answer. "Hello?" she said cheerily.

"Carolyn? It's Betty."

Sister Bradley was the Relief Society president and had told Carolyn on Sunday she had a job lead for her, since her income was about to be reduced so drastically. Carolyn hadn't wanted to discuss it on the Sabbath and had promised to call later in the week, but here it was Saturday and she still hadn't phoned.

"Hi, Betty, how are you? I'm sorry I forgot to call."

"Do you have a few minutes? I have Jim on the phone from Provo. He wants to talk to you about the job offer."

"Oh, okay."

"Hi, Carolyn," said a smooth male voice. He sounded like a radio announcer.

"How are you doing?"

"Fine."

"So what's the one thing you want in life?"

Carolyn wasn't prepared for an interview right off the bat and struggled for something to say that didn't sound stupid. "Security," she finally managed.

"What else do you want?"

Carolyn thought for a moment longer. "Not to have to deal with any mean people."

Jim laughed. "Well, if you join our team, you'll soon have financial security, and you'll be able to choose which people you deal with. How does that sound?"

"What exactly is your team? What kind of job is this?"

"We provide herbal supplements which help people lose weight."

"I take them," Betty interjected. "They work wonders."

"Basically, we'll be training you to train others," Jim continued.

"You can get in now on the ground floor," Betty interrupted again. "It's a great opportunity."

"And you're out of Provo?" Carolyn asked.

"We're very strong here in Utah, but we're expanding into Washington State right now. Still, we like working with other members of the Church. We feel we have an obligation to our brothers and sisters to help them reap the rewards of hard work combined with faith." He paused, but when Carolyn didn't say anything, he went on. "Let me email you a link to our website. You can look at our organization this evening, and perhaps we can talk again tomorrow."

"Oh, not on Sunday."

"Oh, that's right, it's Saturday now, isn't it? Can we talk again Monday evening?"

"On Family Home Evening night?"

"Just for a few minutes. We really need to act quickly if we want to get you on board."

"I guess talking for a few minutes on Monday will be okay."

Carolyn hung up and returned to the table. She hoped she'd be good at this, and that she could do it while still working at the library. Greg could be a jerk sometimes, but he was also a good man. He'd been laid off at Lowe's last month when he complained to his manager about Lowe's removing their ads from the show *American Muslim*.

Someone had called to criticize the company for supporting a program that showed good Muslims who weren't terrorists, and the company had caved. It was good that Greg had taken a stand.

Why he didn't go right away to Home Depot to get a job, she couldn't quite grasp. Now with only his unemployment check, and Carolyn's shrinking library income, things were going to get a little tight.

"Who was that?"

"Betty. She thinks she has a part-time job for me."

"Good."

They ate the rest of their meal in silence and then Carolyn took care of the dishes while Greg went to play on his computer. When Carolyn joined him in the office, he logged off and headed for the television. Carolyn took a few minutes to read up on Herbal Heaven. All its officers were high-powered salespeople, according to their bios.

Carolyn thought it odd that none of them seemed to be physicians or at least nutritionists. But it was a beautiful website, impressive. She wondered whether if she took a job, she'd get a discount on the products. She only had fifteen pounds to lose, but she did want to lose them.

And the majority of other Americans were overweight, too. There'd be a lot of people interested in the products. If it was a Mormon corporation, it wouldn't be like all those other weight loss companies that just offered snake oil. This must be the real thing. Betty said it was working for her. Carolyn thought about it for several minutes, made her decision, and then prayed to see if her decision was right.

She didn't experience that warm feeling she was supposed to get to confirm her decision, but she also didn't get that stupor of thought which was supposed to be a negative answer. She sighed, disappointed she wasn't in tune enough with the Spirit to hear, and joined Greg in the living room.

She wondered if she should check in on Stacy.

They watched *The Big Bang Theory* and laughed.

Sunday went well. It was cold outside, about 36, but only raining lightly, so Carolyn didn't bring an umbrella. She'd been surprised when she'd first moved here to see that most natives never used umbrellas when it rained. She'd quickly learned this was not only because the rain was usually light but also because when the rain was heavier, it was often accompanied by wind that made the umbrella useless in any event.

Carolyn and Greg sat about ten rows back during Sacrament. Stacy sat with her MIA Maid friends. Sacrament meeting was a bit dull, but Gospel Doctrine class was always fun, as was Relief Society. Carolyn wondered if Greg would ever move up to the High Priests Group or would stay forever in the Elders Quorum. Today in Gospel Doctrine, they discussed how Jacob had had to work for Rachel for fourteen years, being deceived after the first seven to take Leah as his wife.

"What does this tell us?" asked Brother Sampson, the teacher.

"That you can't trust fathers-in-law," said Greg.

Everyone laughed except Carolyn. Greg was always complaining that Carolyn's father hadn't helped pay their mortgage as Greg swore the man had promised. All Carolyn remembered hearing from her father was that he'd see that they were never homeless. She wondered if Greg was deliberately not seeking another job to test whether her father would start making the mortgage payments.

She almost thought about the job offer when she saw Betty later, but she cleared her mind and kept her thoughts on the gospel.

Sunday afternoons were the best. Carolyn had taken a little flak at work for not working on Sunday, but she volunteered to take every Saturday to make up for it. Now, with hours cut so drastically, she didn't think keeping the Sabbath holy would be a problem anymore. Sunday afternoons were for writing to the missionaries serving from her ward, for reading Mormon novels, and for having the elders over for dinner.

"This will be the last time for that," Greg said when the missionaries rang the doorbell later. "We can't afford to feed teenage boys every week." He looked over at Stacy. "Even teenage girls eat a lot."

"Hush, Greg," Carolyn whispered. "We want Stacy to enjoy being with upright Mormon men. You can't build up the moment and then snatch it away from her."

"We're building her up to believe marriage is important, but if we don't control her appetite, no man will ever want her. Is *that* fair?"

"There are plenty of fat wives at church," Carolyn returned. "Not every man is obsessed with looks over personality."

"I'm just saying."

"And she's not that heavy."

"Uh-huh."

Carolyn smiled brightly as she opened the door to let Elders Rasmussen and Ray into the house. They shook her hand and then Greg's, but they gravitated immediately after that toward Stacy. Carolyn stuck her tongue out at Greg when he wasn't looking.

Monday was cold and cloudy. It was a short day, just four hours of work, so Carolyn was home by early afternoon. She decided to call Betty and see if it was a good time to talk to Jim. Soon they were all in a conference call, and Jim went over some of the basics of what would be required. It didn't sound all that difficult. She didn't have to buy any of the products and then try to sell them. She'd have been awful at that.

"In fact," said Jim, "you don't have to invest anything at all. There's no risk."

"Well, that sounds good."

"But if you want to make *real* money…" Betty began.

"Oh, now, let's not go there," Jim said. "Carolyn's struggling as it is."

"What are you guys talking about?"

"It's just that since we're expanding into Washington State, there *is* room for investment," Jim explained. "$1000 now will turn into $20,000 within a year. But that's just for people who can afford it. That's not really what we want you for."

"But it would be nice to pay for Stacy's college, wouldn't it?" Betty pressed. "Or for her mission, too, if she's not married by then."

The comment irritated Carolyn. She was just about to ask Jim to get back to the original discussion when a thought crossed her mind. What if Greg didn't find another job? What if he didn't *want* to find another job? All the finances would be up to her. She did have a little over $3000 in a savings account she didn't tell Greg about. She could take just $2000 of that and have $40,000 back within a year.

It would almost finish paying off the house. It would be reckless to invest the entire $3000, and even giving up $2000 in their present difficulties seemed risky. But hadn't she heard the saying many times over the years—you have to spend money to make money?

And what was that other saying—when God closed a door, he opened a window? Perhaps this was that window.

"I'd like to invest $2000," Carolyn said boldly. Then she bit her lip. Shouldn't she have prayed about this first?

She'd pray tonight before she wrote out the check.

"Well, if you're sure," said Jim. "We have some things happening tomorrow that will make your investment even stronger if you can wire that money to us before 11:00."

Jim gave her the bank information she'd need, and they finished up their discussion. Carolyn decided to tell Greg only about the training part of the job, not the investment. If he thought money was coming their way, he'd never go to Home Depot, and she needed a husband who worked, regardless of how much money she brought home herself.

"It'll be great having you aboard," Jim said. "This won't be enough to retire on, but you'll still be doing well." He laughed. “Boy, I love helping other Saints. That’s the best part of this job. I feel like we’re preparing the way for the Millennium. Well, I’ll talk to you both again soon.”

He hung up, but Betty stayed on the line. “Carolyn, didn’t you say your father might help you guys financially sometime?”

“Yes?”

“Don’t you think you could ask him to loan you ten or fifteen thousand dollars? Maybe you really *could* retire then. Or at least not have to worry quite so much. Greg—” She stopped.

“I’ll think about it.”

“You’ll have to ask him tonight.”

“He still has Family Home Evening, too, you know.”

“Oh, Carolyn.”

Carolyn did think about it. She went to her bedroom and prayed first for confirmation about her original decision to invest her secret money. She waited on her knees for a good fifteen minutes but felt neither confirmation nor stupor. Perhaps it meant that the choice didn’t matter to Heavenly Father either way. She could invest and make money, or not invest and have her normal life: either path was acceptable to God.

If that was the case, then making money sounded like the way to go. Greg was out doing something, who knew what, so Carolyn took the opportunity to call her father while Greg couldn’t overhear. It took some convincing, but her father eventually agreed to wire $10,000 that afternoon so Carolyn would have it available first thing in the morning. "I always knew you'd be the strong one in that family," her father said.

"Oh, Dad."

"You're the one listening to that still, small voice, aren't you?"

The voice seemed awfully still and small sometimes. "I'm trying, Dad."

"After you pay off the house, you keep anything left over in your own account and don't tell Greg about it. It's up to you to provide for Stacy." He sighed heavily, and Carolyn felt both irritation and pride. "I was going to leave this to you when I died, but it's not much, and you need it now. I'm happy to help."

Carolyn decided she'd send Jim her own $2000 and maybe $3000 of her father's money. The rest she'd have as a buffer in case it took a while to start earning a return. Investing almost felt like gambling, and the prophets always warned against games of chance. Still, the Church itself owned stocks, so this had to be okay.

Carolyn thought about the warm, moderate winters of Scottsdale while preparing dinner. After the dishes were rinsed and put in the dishwasher, Carolyn joined Greg and Stacy in the living room for Family Home Evening. Carolyn offered an opening prayer, and Stacy gave a lesson about how it was always a risk to do the right thing, using Greg's situation at Lowe's as an example.

She also said that sometimes people were blinded by what they *wanted* the right thing to be. If Lehi had left Laman and Lemuel behind in Jerusalem rather than hoping in vain they'd repent, she said, the Nephites would have been a much happier people.

"Sometimes, love can trick us," Stacy said.

"What an odd lesson," Carolyn commented. "Why on Earth did you choose such a topic?"

Stacy glanced briefly at Greg but then turned to her mother. "I'd like to do my junior year in Scottsdale with Gram and Gramps."

"What?" Carolyn was stunned.

"I think it's a good idea," Greg said immediately.

"Wait, wait, wait," Carolyn protested. "Let's discuss this rationally."

"It's only January," said Stacy. "We have plenty of time to think about it. It's just that they're getting old, and I don't get to see them very much. I'd like to spend a whole year down there, and besides, it'll help me understand you better, Mom, to know your parents and where you grew up. It'll make us closer."

Carolyn felt she was being robbed or duped or something, but she agreed to think about it all more fully "later." She let the topic drop then, but Greg said something just as they were going to bed afterward that surprised her.

"I understand what Stacy means about thinking you were doing the right thing." Carolyn saw him looking absentmindedly at his wedding ring. "I thought getting a college degree was a good idea. But that only gave me years of student loans to pay back, and I still ended up with a crappy job."

Carolyn was tempted to say, "Did you really think a degree in Anthropology was going to get you a great job?" but held her tongue.

She'd have been happy if he'd taken even a poor job, if it had at least been in his field. He seemed so much happier back in those days, back when he believed in the excitement of discovery. Greg said there were lots of good jobs that simply required a degree of any kind, and he'd thought he could get one of those, but nothing had ever panned out.

Carolyn slept fitfully through the night. The furnace seemed to be acting up, and she felt cold even with the covers pulled to her chin.

In the morning, they watched the news and saw that the schools were closed because of the snow. Stacy was ecstatic and ran to her bedroom to go back to sleep. Carolyn called the library's inclement weather hotline to hear if she needed to report to work at 10:00 or not. "Yes, it's snowing," said the head librarian, "but we're still going to open today."

Carolyn was shocked. The library wasn't an essential service. Surely, they could have closed today. She was about to hang up the phone when she heard the end of the 90-second message. "Today is Monday, January 23."

Carolyn frowned. The message was dated yesterday. She looked at the phone in her hand and then remembered. There had been snow in the outlying areas yesterday and snow predicted for elevations of 500 feet or higher. Carolyn hadn't even bothered to call the hotline the day before because it had been so obvious there wasn't a problem. What if she hadn't listened to the entire message today? She'd have trudged through the snow to work only to find the doors locked. She'd have been irritated.

So *was* the library open today? Carolyn called the hotline back every fifteen minutes for the next two hours. The message was never updated. Now it was too late to leave for work in time to make it by 10:00. Carolyn decided she just wouldn't go in, if they couldn't bother to update the message. She felt terribly guilty, but the snow presented yet another problem.

How was she going to get to the bank to make the wire transfer?

Well, waiting a day or two wouldn't be the end of the world.

Greg sat in front of his computer most of the day. Hopefully, he was applying for jobs, though Carolyn had learned not to ask. Carolyn went to the bedroom and opened the curtains all the way and sat on the bed and stared at the snow. If you didn't have to go out in it, snow was rather beautiful. For the first couple of hours, the flakes were large, but after that, they turned into what looked like grains of sand.

Carolyn could see a ledge out the window, and she watched as the snow went from three inches to four inches to five inches deep. Five inches in Seattle. That was a lot. And she heard on the radio that farther south in the convergence zone, folks were getting up to a foot.

So much for those liberals complaining about global warming. Heavenly Father wouldn't let humans discover oil and coal and how to make an industrialized society that could help spread the gospel to the entire world, and then turn it into an environmental disaster.

If he was powerful enough to create a worldwide flood, if he was powerful enough to create the Earth in the first place, he could certainly handle a little carbon dioxide and a temperature range of two degrees. Liberals were godless people with no faith.

It would be so nice working in a Mormon company.

Around 4:00 when it started getting dark, Carolyn closed the curtains. She could imagine a person growing tired of snow if one saw it all the time, but for her, it was still a treat, as long as she could stay home. A couple of minutes later, just before she was about to join Greg in the living room, where he was watching television, the phone rang.

"Hello?" said Carolyn.

"Hi, it's Jim."

"Oh, hello, Jim."

"We didn't get your money today. Have you changed your mind about investing?"

"It's snowing here. We couldn't get out of the house."

"I see. Well, it's not that big a deal. I was able to hold off on what I was planning so we could still get you involved, but we'll need that money by tomorrow if you want to make the full return on it. Do you think you'll be able to get to the bank Wednesday?"

"I don't know. The bank is right next to the library, so if they call us in to work tomorrow, it'll be easy enough."

"Well, like I say, it's no big deal. There are plenty of other investors who can make the big bucks. It's just that Betty speaks so highly of you. I'd hate to see you miss out. By Friday, it'll be too late. Betty's already got half your ward investing, and I'm working with some of the other wards in the area, too. We're going to hit Washington State in a big way."

"She didn't tell me about anyone else."

"Yes, she's got the Spencers, the McCoys, the Andersons, and the Christies involved, and several more families as well. But really, if you can't make it, don't worry about it. Betty tells me you're very industrious. You'll do well with the training alone and make plenty enough money with that. There's no shame in being average. That's what most people are. It's what the word means."

"Oh."

Jim chuckled. "But you're not really average, are you, Carolyn? I can tell. You were meant for something more in this life. Didn't your Patriarchal Blessing say so?"

Carolyn was surprised. The truth was that her blessing did in fact say something about that. Something like,

"Heavenly Father has given you a physical bearing and a mental alertness that qualifies you for great achievement in this estate."

She'd always wondered about it. What really mattered was the *next* estate, but there was no reason not to enjoy life in this one, if that's what Heavenly Father had in store for her. Yet how did Jim know that? Was Jim exceptionally in tune with the Spirit himself?

Surely, patriarchs didn't just say the same thing to everyone. She'd read Greg's blessing, and his didn't say anything like that. Stacy wouldn't let anyone read hers, of course. Jim must simply be insightful, a true Latter-day Saint.

But if the stake patriarch himself was supposed to be inspired, Carolyn had often wondered over the years why this particular part of her personal prophecy had never come true. Was Herbal Heaven God's way of making sure it did?

"I'll be wiring $6,000 before Friday. Tomorrow, if I can."

"Excellent. Excellent. Heavenly Father is about to change your life. You're the last investor in the area. That makes thirty-two families in Seattle alone who are investing. We really are going to enter the market in a big way. There will be lots of money coming in by the end of the year."

Carolyn smiled. After she hung up, she looked out the window one last time. The snow was exceptionally beautiful. Why did something that beautiful always scare her so?

She wasn't sure why, but while she had the phone in her hand, Carolyn decided to call the McCoys and the Christies.

Sister McCoy mentioned how her husband had just had to take a pay cut at work, so they were investing $20,000 with Jim. Sister Christie told her that Brother Christie had been put on a list of possible employees who would face layoffs within the next three months. They were investing $23,000.

So maybe Carolyn could wire a total of $10,000. But would holding back on the last $2000 her father had given her be demonstrating a lack of faith? It was like the story of the man clinging to the roof of his house in a flood. "God will save me," he kept saying.

Yet he turned away the floating log that bumped against his roof, and the neighbor who came by in his canoe, and the helicopter from the Coast Guard, proclaiming loudly at each instance, "God will save me." When he drowned, he asked God why he wasn't saved when he had shown such faith. "Well, I sent you a log, and a canoe, and a helicopter. What more did you want?"

She would wire the entire $12,000.

Wednesday morning, Carolyn called the inclement weather hotline again. This time, there was a new message, saying that yes, the library was open today, and it gave the current date. While Carolyn was anxious to get out of the house, at the same time, she felt a little miffed. The snow was turning to freezing rain, and that didn't sound any more pleasant than snow to travel in.

Because she lived on a hill, the buses were on snow routes and had been diverted from her area. She could have Greg drive her to the light rail station, but the last thing they needed was to pay a huge deductible on their car insurance for an accident.

Carolyn had bought some Yaktrax the year before and put them on her shoes now. They served the same function as tire chains. She put on an extra sweater and an extra pair of pants underneath her thick coat, not that it was all that cold at 32 degrees, but to use for padding if she slipped down.

School was still closed, so Carolyn went to Stacy's room and kissed her goodbye before leaving. She saw ice already forming on top of the snow, making a sheen on its surface. She felt and heard the snow and ice crunching under her feet. She passed one car that had slid into the side of another on her way down the hill. She hoped a car wouldn't hit her as she walked.

When she finally arrived at the light rail station, she heard an announcement. "Light rail is suspended in both directions until further notice."

How annoying. Still, from here, it was only a matter of crossing the intersection to get to a bus stop, and that bus did appear to be operating. She saw one pulling off just as she started crossing the street, but she wasn't about to run for it. Carolyn could see icicles starting to form on the bottom of street signs, and one single man carrying an umbrella that had ice forming on the canvas. It cracked when he closed the umbrella at the bus stop.

Once downtown, the trick was walking up yet another steep hill to the library. What with all the delays, Carolyn didn't reach the front door till 9:51, a full six minutes late.

She felt terribly guilty but rushed inside and clocked in on the computer.

"What are you doing here?" Todd asked. "We're not opening today till noon. Didn't you hear the updated message?"

"No." Carolyn frowned. "So what are *you* doing here?"

"I didn't hear it in time, either. They only made the announcement twenty minutes ago."

"You mean, I killed myself to get here on time?" Carolyn stomped her foot lightly on the floor, the Yaktrax making a strong metallic click against the tile. "The weather's even getting worse. We might not open at all today." Be charitable, Carolyn told herself. Be a Christian. The head librarian had probably made an honest mistake.

"Well, go ahead and relax." Todd motioned to the stacks behind him. "Read a book."

Carolyn forced a smile. Then she had a revelation and stopped right where she stood. She could take the time to go over to the bank. Heavenly Father was simply helping her do the truly important errand today, not work, but the investment. This wasn't a trick, it was divine intervention.

She didn't bother to take off her coat but went right back to the door, telling Todd she'd return shortly. She made her way carefully to the bank, which still wasn't open even at 10:00, but she saw someone inside, so she waited on the sidewalk, and they opened at about 10:20.

Carolyn made the wire transfer, a little nervous, but afterward as she walked slowly back to the library, she felt an incredible sense of happiness. Finally, the Spirit was testifying to her. She'd made the right decision.

A gust of wind almost knocked her off her feet, but soon she was back in the warm library. It wasn't really her job, but she shelved a few books and straightened up some of the chairs. A couple of other workers joined them, and soon there were enough that they could open at 11:15. Only two other branches opened at noon, and no other branches opened at all. Their employees had simply refused to come in to work, even knowing they were ordered to come. The idea shocked Carolyn.

The homeless came in to warm up as soon as the doors opened, and Carolyn felt a sense of pride that she'd come in such bad weather. Other people depended on her. She helped a neatly dressed businesswoman look up some information in Value Line and the BBB Business Library, and she helped a high school student look up some articles on Paul Krugman.

But at 3:00, the head librarian announced they'd be closing at 4:00 for the day. It had started snowing again at 1:00, the predicted warming trend not arriving, and there was an extra inch of snow on the ground as Carolyn made her way to the tunnel to catch the light rail. Fortunately, the train was running again by this evening. She had a twenty minute trek uphill once she got off, and she passed three accidents along the way, but she didn't fall.

The following day was almost as bad, but the warmer weather finally did start to move in, and rain began melting the snow, at least on the streets. Plus, Carolyn didn't have to be at work until 2:00, so she didn't have any problems. The bus was going up her hill again. Some people lost electricity because of the ice bringing down trees on the power lines, but Carolyn's house was okay.

Stacy went off to school, and Greg sat in front of the computer again most of the day. Carolyn had Friday off, and she finished reading *Frankenstein.* Mary Shelley was a gifted writer, penning the first real science fiction novel. The icy finish made Carolyn pull the comforter up to her chin, and there was something about the conclusion which was decidedly unpleasant, but not enough people read the classics, and Carolyn didn't want to be one of the ignorant masses.

Saturday around 4:00, Betty called. "Hi, Carolyn. Have you heard from Jim?"

"No. Should I have?"

"Oh, it's just that he's not answering my calls. I thought maybe you'd heard from him."

"Well, he said he was just about to move forward with some big part of his project. Maybe he's too busy to talk right now."

"That's true. It's nothing urgent anyway. I'll see you at church tomorrow."

After dinner, Carolyn brought Stacy an individual piece of cake she'd purchased at Safeway. She slipped into her daughter's room without Greg noticing. She felt like a conspirator, and she wasn't sure she was doing the girl any favors, but sometimes, you had to indulge just a little bit or you felt too oppressed.

Carolyn watched some of the Florida GOP presidential debate with Greg. Newt Gingrich was such a jerk. Carolyn knew the only reason people weren't all flocking to Romney was simple prejudice. It was why Joseph Smith hadn't won the presidency back in the 1840's. But Romney had a real chance now.

Carolyn luxuriated in the thought that the country might finally be in safe hands. A Mormon would follow God and make the right decisions. She could *trust* him. There weren't many politicians a voter could really trust. Maybe with her extra free time now, Carolyn could do some volunteer work for his campaign. Perhaps that was why Heavenly Father had allowed her hours to be cut in the first place. He always had a plan.

Greg cooked breakfast Sunday morning, and church went well. Betty started to say something about Jim, but Carolyn steered the conversation back to the topic from Gospel Doctrine. In Relief Society, the teacher spoke about the problem of acting overly interested in investigators, only to abandon them once they became members. It was important that if they started a friendship they follow through with it. Lack of social connection was the number one reason new converts fell away, not a lack of faith in the gospel.

The evening was a little lonely without the elders coming over for dinner. Greg spent most of the time after the meal on his computer. Carolyn started fantasizing about paying off the mortgage but then picked up another Mormon novel and began reading, wondering if maybe she should try to take a walk with Stacy instead. But it was too peaceful to do more than lie in bed.

Monday was when she began to worry. At the library, Todd pointed to a news item he saw on Yahoo about affinity fraud in Utah. "What's affinity fraud?" she asked, not reading the article. It sounded anti-Mormon.

"It's when people trust someone because they share the same beliefs or culture. Like when Bernie Madoff defrauded lots of Jews. There were also some cases in the deaf community and among Evangelicals."

"So?"

Todd laughed. "So Utah had over $2 billion in affinity fraud in the last year or so. You don't have any family in Salt Lake you need to warn, do you?"

What Betty had said the other day came back to her. Jim wasn't avoiding their calls, was he? Surely, he was just busy. He'd said plainly he was about to start his big move into Washington State. Satan was so good at planting seeds of doubt. She prayed for Jim to be successful.

Then she phoned Betty during her break.

"Just wondering if you'd heard from Jim," she said.

"No, and I've left three messages with him. The Andersons and the Spencers can't get in touch with him either."

"You don't think…"

"I hope he wasn't in a car accident or anything."

Carolyn began feeling ill. It couldn't be true. It just couldn't.

But that article. She understood about Jews defrauding Jews. And Evangelicals defrauding Evangelicals. That all made sense.

But Mormons wouldn't do such a thing.

Paul H. Dunn had lied, but those were fibs really, and for the greater good.

Then Carolyn's hand flew to her mouth. *What if Jim had been given the Second Anointing?*

What was she going to tell Greg? What if he divorced her? And what was she going to tell Stacy? And Dad?

As soon as Carolyn arrived back home, she called Jim. She was going to keep calling until he picked up the phone.

But the phone made an odd beeping noise, and then a message came over the receiver. "The number you are calling is no longer in service. If you think you called this number in error, please hang up and dial your number again."

Carolyn ran to the bathroom and threw up in the toilet.

"You okay, hon?" Greg asked, knocking on the door.

"Yes, thank you," she managed from her kneeling position. She flushed but stayed on the floor another few minutes, her mind racing. She was going to have to apply for some full-time jobs. Perhaps this was the Lord's way of getting her a better income. Maybe—

She wiped away her tears. What was she going to tell Greg? What in the world could she possibly say?

It was all her own money, though, wasn't it? Maybe it was none of his business.

She looked at her wedding ring.

Carolyn thought again to the lesson she'd learned in church a couple of Sundays ago, about Jacob working fourteen years for Rachel. But then she remembered another part of the lesson, something that hadn't even registered at the time. Jacob had also practiced deceit himself, hadn't he? He'd stolen his brother's birthright. So maybe Leah was payback. God took revenge on the wicked. She started to smile.

Only Jacob wasn't wicked, was he? He was a Bible hero. And just what really was the result of his tricking Isaac and robbing Esau? His offspring ended up blessed throughout a thousand generations, and Jacob himself was blessed eternally.

So what was Heavenly Father *saying*? That fraud and theft were *okay* as long as you got what you wanted?

Carolyn felt sick again, but she breathed deeply and managed not to vomit a second time. After a few more minutes, she stood and washed her face in the sink. Then she put on a smile and headed out to the living room.

"You okay?" Greg asked again.

"Oh, I'm good. I might skip dinner, though."

"That's okay. I can heat up a pizza for Stacy and me."

"Thanks," she said, thinking about all those calories for Stacy.

“I have an interview tomorrow at Home Depot,” Greg added.

Carolyn put her hand on Greg’s arm.

He laughed. “I’ll probably have to start Wednesday.”

“Well, that’ll be good, won’t it?”

“You didn’t hear the latest weather report?” he asked. “More snow on Wednesday.”

Now Carolyn began to laugh. Greg laughed again as well, but when Carolyn continued laughing, even doubling over, he stopped and started looking at her in concern.

But she kept laughing, uncontrollably, for the next five minutes. Finally, Greg shrugged and turned back to the TV.

The Forest for the Trees

Helden threw his shovel and fire hose into the back of the truck and climbed into the cab of his F-150. It was early April in Snoqualmie and raining lightly, about 38 degrees this morning. It would soon rise to the mid-40's and reach perhaps 50 by late afternoon. Perfect weather for saving a life.

He had to drive for almost thirty minutes through the Cascade foothills to arrive at the house in question. The owners were getting rid of two trees to improve the view from their bedroom window. Both trees were Douglas firs, one of Helden's favorites. He would take spruce and dogwoods and hemlock and almost anything else, but he preferred the firs.

Preferred the firs. Helden smiled. It had a nice ring to it. Saving the salvageable. Reforesting the forest.

Helden said hello to the couple who owned the trees and had them show him which two they wanted removed. The husband watched him start digging but grew bored after five minutes and went back inside. That was the way it usually worked. Digging up trees wasn't a spectator sport, and it would take most of the day.

Helden enjoyed those first few minutes of being watched. He could feel his trim build and his sinewy arms and back on display, his slightly graying brown hair making him look distinguished even as his pants started to become splattered with mud. He felt important for those first five minutes.

Alice never watched him work anymore.

With all the rain the area had experienced in the past couple of weeks, the ground was soft today, which helped a great deal. Helden made a perimeter around the first tree, about two feet from the trunk in any direction. He liked to get as much of the root system as he could without making the tree too heavy to move. This fir's trunk had a diameter of about five inches, the largest he would attempt to move.

Anything larger he simply couldn't handle by himself. The tree was about thirteen feet tall, also about as large as he could attempt. There were people who killed even larger trees, and it gave Helden such a pang that he couldn't save those, but he could only do what he could do.

He dug in with his shovel again and again, always working quickly on days like this to finish before it grew dark. With two trees to salvage today, it would be a race against time. He remembered when he'd first decided on this plan of action. It was five years earlier after his neighbor cut down an acre of old-growth forest on his property adjacent to Helden and Alice's three acres. Alice had been the one to make the first comment.

"What happened to the owls?" she said one evening as she and Helden sat on their back porch. Alice was still trim, too, though her face looked more careworn than Helden's.

"They're gone," Helden had replied. "The Stevensons tore down their homes." There were still plenty of trees on Helden's land, but not old growth yet.

"That's awful. I liked hearing them. And who's going to eat the mice now?" She looked up into the sky as if expecting to see a rescuer approaching.

"Guess we'll need to get some cats from the pound."

"I suppose so. I like cats. But it won't be the same. I wish we could import some trees."

"We don't have the money. And you can't buy hundred-year-old trees."

"Couldn't you do something?" Alice asked. "You could go in the woods and dig some up."

"What good would that do?" Helden answered. "They need trees in the forest, too. The only thing that might help is to transplant trees people are about to chop down."

Alice looked thoughtful for a moment. Then she said slowly, "Maybe someone on Craigslist will ask for help chopping down a tree. Or offer someone to come take a tree. Maybe you could look."

And that was exactly what happened. Alice had a way of seeing that things got done. The new task made his complicated life more complicated, of course. Helden still liked singing in country/western bars on Saturday evenings, but if he spent all day Saturday transplanting a tree, he was certainly in no shape to sing half the evening into the late hours.

So he began alternating his Saturdays, one weekend saving a tree and the next still trying to jumpstart his singing career. He was forty-two back then, not the age to start a career, but he'd been singing in bars for over fifteen years by that time. They weren't the popular kind of country bars where one might be discovered, but Helden also didn't want to be out driving far distances late in the night when other people out on the road might be drunk.

Helden was never drunk, of course. He'd never had a beer in his life, or any other kind of alcohol for that matter. He'd been tempted on a few occasions, when it looked like the others at the bar were having such a good time. But he still wanted to be called as bishop, and you couldn't be a Mormon bishop if you broke the Word of Wisdom.

Alice had been ward Relief Society president a few years back, but the Church never seemed to want to move Helden up the ladder. It wasn't as if he wanted to become stake president or a General Authority in Salt Lake or anything, but bishop, yes, he did want to be bishop of his ward.

Helden had to cut through some of the thicker roots now with his shovel. He hated this part of the digging. Every time he cut a root, he knew the tree had just that much less chance of surviving the move. As it was, a full fifth of the trees he transplanted died. It was heartbreaking not only because of the labor involved, but also because by the time he'd spent that much time with a tree, it felt like a member of the family.

"It's unrealistic to expect every tree to survive," Alice had tried comforting him one day. "Even when you buy a plant from the store and take it out of the pot and put it in the ground, it sometimes dies."

Helden had shrugged. “I know. It’s just that I expect the tree to understand I’m giving it it’s only chance, and I expect it to put forth a little more effort. I expect it to *want* to live.”

Alice had laughed. “I’m sure it does. Most people who go to the hospital want to live, but not everyone comes out alive. It isn’t realistic to expect a miracle every single time.”

Realistic. The word was a favorite of Alice’s and one that irritated Helden to no end. It wasn’t realistic to expect to be called as bishop. It wasn’t realistic to expect to become a country singing star. It wasn’t realistic to expect to plant enough trees to counter global warming. But he *wanted* all those things.

Maybe it was like the tree wanting to live but not being strong enough to do it, despite the love and caring it was shown.

Helden dug some more, and when the pit around the tree was two feet deep, he wrapped his fire hose around the trunk and began pulling. This was always the hardest part of the entire enterprise, getting the tree to budge. He took a few breaks, drinking from his water bottle liberally, but the tap root simply went down too far. That was both a good feature and a bad feature of the tree. It helped prevent the tree from blowing over in the strong autumn windstorms western Washington faced every year, but it also made removing the tree from the ground extremely difficult.

In the end, Helden was forced to get his battery-operated saw from the back of the truck and reach far underneath the tree to cut the tap root. Every time he had to do it, he felt he was cutting off his own foot. If he could get at least two feet of the tap root to transfer along with the tree, the plant would have a chance at life. Including anything more would make dragging the tree over to the truck all but impossible. As it was, the fir probably weighed over three hundred pounds. It wasn't as if Alice could come along and help. At five foot two, she was like a tender sapling herself.

And she was home today comforting Chris. Helden and Alice had only two children, which made them practically childless by Mormon standards. Helden wondered sometimes if that was why Church leaders wouldn't call him as bishop.

Their oldest daughter, Patricia, had worked hard in high school and graduated salutatorian. She'd hoped for a presidential scholarship to Brigham Young and had been devastated when she was forced to attend college here in Washington instead.

"It doesn't mean you're a failure," Alice had comforted the girl at the time. "It's unrealistic to expect the best the world has to offer. Second-best is still pretty good. It's not as if you have to accept eighty-third best."

But Helden thought perhaps that was in fact what it meant. Instead of graduating from BYU, Patricia had dropped out of college in her third year and married a non-Mormon boy she'd met in class.

Helden wondered if *that* was why he hadn't been called as bishop. It wasn't even as if it gave him good song-writing material. What country music fan wanted to hear a forlorn song about their daughter not marrying in the temple?

Chris's problem was that he'd applied to five Ivy League schools. He wanted to become a world-class historian. He wasn't expecting a scholarship. He was quite willing to take out student loans. But yesterday, he'd heard from the last of those schools that he wasn't accepted.

He, too, could go to college in Washington State. It wouldn't prevent him from being great. But the boy felt he'd just been told he was always going to be half-rate.

Helden could hear Alice now. "It isn't realistic to expect to go to Harvard or Yale. There are a million college students in this country. They can't all fit into the best five schools. You can make your mark even if you're not there."

Helden stopped tugging and wiped his brow. Only she wouldn't have said Chris could still make his mark. Instead, she'd say something like, "It's unrealistic to expect to make a mark in this world. There are almost seven billion people on the planet. You're just one person, no matter how special you are. One person can't really make a mark."

Helden finally had the tree cut off from all its continuing roots. He tugged and pulled and dragged and tugged some more, and finally he had the tree in the back of his pickup, hanging well over the edge. He had to pee, but filthy as he was, he knew he couldn't ask the couple to use their bathroom.

He went off behind a bush and then pulled his lunch out of the cab. He always ate lightly on these days. His body needed the nourishment of a good meal, but you couldn't work that hard without getting sick if you ate very much. Helden allowed himself one turkey and mustard sandwich and some Gatorade. He rested for fifteen minutes, and then he walked over to the second tree and began digging in a circle a couple of feet from the base of this one.

"Did you really have high hopes for such a long shot?" Alice had asked Helden when he auditioned for The Voice. Not making the cut had hurt, but hearing her say that had hurt even more. Yes. Yes, he did have high hopes. What was wrong with having high hopes? The Church taught him that he had to be perfect, that he could reach the Celestial Kingdom, that he could become a god one day. Was it asking so much just to be able to record one song?

"You know that *I* always enjoy hearing you sing," she'd said that evening.

But more often than not, he'd see her working on her grocery list as he strummed his guitar. She'd look up and smile as he sang, but it wasn't quite the same thing as having a real audience.

Helden found himself taking longer breaks while working on the second tree. Sometimes, he worked so hard on these transplants he worried he might have a heart attack. Would it count for him or against him in heaven if he died while trying to improve the world? Would it be enviable martyrdom or self-indulgent suicide?

Fortunately, he'd arranged the order of these extrications correctly. This second tree had a diameter of only three inches. It would be much easier to remove than the first tree. And it was only ten feet tall. A difference of three feet would tremendously lower the overall weight. Helden would be more likely to include enough of the root system of this one to keep the young tree alive.

A few hours later, Helden was ready to get out his saw again and cut the tap root. He stood looking at the tree in its hole and willed it to be strong. "You've got to *want* this," he said firmly.

He didn't feel silly talking to trees. He believed they could hear him and understand him. In the past five years, Helden had transplanted over a hundred trees. He was almost to the point of needing to purchase more land.

Yet when he thought of all the vast acres of property just in his one small town which needed trees, and how no matter how hard he worked, he'd never be able to reforest more than three or four more acres in his lifetime, he felt the same way he felt every time he raised his right hand to sustain another new bishop.

He thought back to when he was a kid in town, and on some sunny days, he'd see earthworms drying up on the sidewalk. He'd pick them up and toss them on the grass so they could dig themselves back into the earth and live. The other kids made fun of him. Then one day he read a story about a boy who did the same thing with starfish that had washed up on the beach and were drying to death in the sun.

There were several hundred of them on the beach, and the boy went along, tossing as many as he could back into the ocean. But another boy stopped him and asked why he was bothering, saying he could never save all of them. "What difference does tossing twenty starfish back make?"

The boy looked at the starfish in his hand and said, “It makes a difference to *this* one.”

Helden took out his saw and cut the tap root. He could practically hear the tree screaming in pain. “It’s for your own good,” he said softly. “Really, I’m helping you.”

Was that why Heavenly Father kept Helden from succeeding? Was this some spiritual form of pruning? Helden felt he was busy, busy, busy *doing* all the time, yet never getting anything done. Why wasn’t wanting and trying and praying and struggling enough to make something happen?

After another thirty minutes, Helden had the second tree in the back of the truck alongside the first. He tied them both down and attached red flags onto the ends. He still had to get them in the ground at his place, too. He might get one in today, but the second would have to be done on the Sabbath.

Helden hoped Heavenly Father understood. He rarely missed church, and he knew missing tomorrow would do nothing to help his chances of becoming a bishop, but you had to do what you had to do. Ox in the mire and all that.

Helden enjoyed the long drive back home. It was soothing to sit for such a long time and listen to the radio. He wished he sounded as good as Keith Urban.

As he drove back up the driveway to his house, Helden saw a couple of the cats dart out of the way. They’d only live ten or twelve years out here in the country. They’d never “accomplish” anything, but they certainly seemed content with their lives. Was ignorance the secret to happiness?

Alice came out to greet him, leaning over to kiss him without getting herself dirty. He remembered that saving the trees had been her idea in the first place, and he smiled at her. He was forty-seven now. He could probably keep this up for at least another thirteen years, maybe longer. That would easily be another two or three hundred additional trees. Helden knew the Jewish saying, "If you save one life, it's as if you saved the world."

He wondered if trees counted.

"What time will you be ready for dinner?" Alice asked.

The holes had already been dug for the new arrivals. "Give me an hour," he said. That would be enough time to put one in the ground. By then, it would be close to 7:00. Technically, at this time of year, there would still be enough light to get the second tree in, but Helden felt he had to spend some time with his family as well. Chris would still be feeling bad, and Alice needed her share of attention, too. You couldn't cut off all ties to your family just to feed your dreams.

Clouds had rolled back in after a few hours of sunlight in the late afternoon, and it was drizzling again. That always made it feel later than the real time anyway, so he'd be ready to stop for the night before long. Helden had dragged the smaller tree halfway to its hole when he heard some rustling beside him.

"Hey, Chris," he said, a little surprised as he turned around. "What's up?"

"Mom suggested maybe I ought to help you this evening," he returned. "She said that way maybe we could get both trees in the ground tonight, and you wouldn't have to miss church tomorrow."

Helden looked at the boy, wearing an extra pair of Helden's rubber boots. The boy usually didn't want so much as to help weed the garden. Helden of course didn't particularly mind his lack of helping with such chores. Chris had always been studying. He was smart and knew his history, and he was good at it. Helden never felt that Chris was obliged to share the same personal dreams. His son had hopes of his own.

"Are you sure?" Helden offered Chris a handhold on the tree, and they began pulling together.

Chris shrugged. "Mom pointed out there might not be much need for history if we didn't save the planet first."

Helden smiled a little uncertainly.

"I've still got a year before my mission," Chris continued. "I might be able to take out a student loan, but there's no mission loan I can take out. I've only saved a thousand dollars from my part-time work during high school. Maybe I can earn a little more money on the weekends working with you."

It wouldn't be much. Helden never charged people any more than they'd have to pay to have the trees cut down. Sometimes, he hardly charged anything at all, so happy simply to take the trees for free. But it would certainly be pleasant to spend a little quality time with his son. If the boy wasn't up to eight hours of hard labor, it would be okay if he rested more than Helden needed to.

"You know," Helden said, "there's no reason you can't get your undergraduate degree locally and then apply to one of your favorite universities for graduate school."

"Mom said that, too."

Helden smiled. Alice truly was a good woman. Father and son soon had the tree in the hole and began shoveling dirt in around the roots. The drizzle would really help. The tree would probably survive. He and Chris walked back through the brush to the truck and grabbed the larger tree next.

Helden was really too tired to continue, and even Chris had probably done enough for his first day, but they plowed on, and within another forty minutes, the second tree was standing tall as well.

"Thanks, Chris. That tree will have a better chance since it made it into the ground tonight."

Chris grinned. Helden clapped his son on the back, and they walked back to the house slowly. They both undressed in the mud room. Helden had put in a small shower five years ago at Alice's suggestion to make sure he didn't drag any dirt into the house. He motioned for Chris to go in first, and he watched as the boy walked into the stall. How had such a little boy become a man so suddenly? Even with all his book reading, he looked strong and firm.

Helden wasn't sure anymore if Heavenly Father was going to spare the world by ushering in the Millennium. He hoped if that didn't happen, people like Chris would be strong enough to battle all the problems they'd surely face in the coming years.

He wondered if he could write a good song about a father and son planting a tree.

After a few minutes, Chris came out and toweled off while Helden took his turn, and soon they joined Alice around the kitchen table for dinner. Helden enjoyed the feeling of relaxation after such a difficult day. He looked about at his family and wondered if any one person ever truly connected with another.

He thought about how an aspen grove in Colorado was the single largest organism known, ten thousand trees or more all connected by their roots. It's what the Church tried to do with genealogy and temple work, he supposed, but sometimes, even his immediate family felt distant.

Helden considered whether he could write a song about that but figured such a feeling wasn't new material. They continued eating and talking of this and that, nothing in particular, until Alice brought out the dessert.

"The stake president called today," she said, putting a piece of apple pie in front of Helden. His heart jumped.

"Yes?" he said.

"He had me come in for an interview this afternoon. They want me to be the stake Relief Society president."

"Wow," Helden managed. "That—that's great. Did you accept?"

She nodded lightly. "I think it'll be fun."

"Well, you'll definitely be great at it," he said. Chris murmured some nice words as well.

Helden chewed slowly and looked at Alice out of the corner of his eyes. How could she ever be a compassionate counselor when everything always came so easily to her?

Then Helden had a revelation. Just how good a counselor would *he* be if he was the type of person who resented seeing his wife happy?

He was never going to get a good song out of that dilemma, either, he realized. Helden sighed, but when Chris turned to look at him quizzically, he forced a smile and continued eating.

After dinner, Helden and Alice sat out on the back porch, listening to the drizzle falling softly on the leaves. Helden debated if he should skip church the next day anyway, even with no real excuse before him.

What could one honestly expect out of life, he wondered? He had a good job, a decent family, a good home. Even Patricia's husband was a nice fellow, whether or not he was LDS. No one committed adultery, no one was on drugs, everyone was kind to one another.

If only…

Alice leaned over and rested her head on Helden's shoulder, taking his hand in hers. "I'm really glad they called you to be the stake Relief Society president," Helden said quietly. "You should have everything you deserve."

"I have you," she replied into his shoulder. "My man who believes it's worth trying to make a difference in the world, even when the world won't cooperate."

Helden felt a lump forming in his throat, and he blinked his eyes dry. He stared at the crescent moon coming out briefly from behind the clouds and then becoming hidden again.

Helden held onto Alice's hand tightly, and she held back onto his. They sat there in silence another twenty minutes, not moving even when they heard an owl hooting softly in the distance.

The Last Four of Your Social

"Orca Credit Union. This is Janet. How may I help you?" Janet was tired, and it was only 8:15 in the morning. "Please, Heavenly Father," she sent up a silent prayer. "Help me make it through the day."

"I'm locked out of my online banking," said a woman on the other end of the phone.

"I can help you with that," Janet responded cheerily. She knew members could hear if she had a smile in her voice, and she wanted to get good member service surveys. Janet had been in the Call Center in downtown Seattle for four months, her first "real" job after graduating from the University of Washington.

She could hardly believe she was twenty-one now and still single. She wondered sometimes if she should go on a mission for the Church, but Mormonism focused so much on marriage and family, and she figured she'd better get married while she was still at her prettiest.

"Please, Heavenly Father," she prayed, "help me find a righteous man."

Perhaps tonight at the Single Adult dance. Janet would need to take a nap when she arrived home and rest up before going to the stake center.

"All right," Janet said. "I've reset your online password. You'll use your member number as your user ID, just like usual, but the first time you log on, you'll use the last four digits of your Social Security Number as your password. Then it'll prompt you to change it to something more secure."

"Thank you."

"Have a great day."

Janet had barely pressed the button to hang up the phone when the earpiece beeped in her ear again. "Orca Credit Union," she said, smiling. "This is Janet. How may I help you?"

"What time does the Rainier Branch open today?" asked a man with a thick Indian accent.

"All our branches open at 9:00 today," Janet told him.

"Thank you."

"Have a great day."

Janet hung up and then immediately pressed the button to answer the next ring with her standard cheerful opening. Last night, Janet's phone had rung at home around 7:30 as she was watching television. She'd picked up the phone and said automatically, "Orca Credit Union. This is Janet. How may I help you?" It had been her mother on the line.

"Are you sure that job isn't taking too big a toll on you?" her mother had asked worriedly.

"I'm a big girl," Janet had replied. "I'll eventually be manager of the Call Center, and then I won't have to answer the phone every sixty-five seconds."

"But won't you have to deal with all the really nasty problems then?"

Janet frowned. "I suppose so." She wondered if eight nasty problems a day was better than a hundred minor problems. In her first week at the Call Center, she'd begun reaching over a hundred calls a day. Of course, their calls were timed, so she was supposed to keep each one under two and a half minutes, but sometimes, that simply wasn't possible.

Just the day before, an Ethiopian woman had kept her on the phone for almost twenty-five minutes, the woman's baby wailing loudly in Janet's ear the entire time.

It was almost 9:00 now. Janet had only had one break between calls, a period of about eleven seconds that had seemed heavenly. But the phone was beeping yet again. "Orca Credit Union. This is Janet. How may I help you?"

"I need to check my balances."

"Sure thing. Can I get your member number?"

The man offered his number.

"And the last four of your Social?"

The man gave those as well.

"And your mother's maiden name?"

Once Janet had asked the necessary questions to verify the man's identity, she read off his balances in checking and savings. "Is there anything else I can do for you?"

"No, that's it."

"You have a good day."

"Please, Heavenly Father," Janet prayed, "send me more easy calls like that." She closed her eyes briefly to send the prayer heavenward. "Orca Credit Union," she said cheerily, answering the next call. This was someone wanting to transfer funds from their checking to pay their Visa bill. The call after that was to transfer from a woman's savings to her checking, and the call after that was to reset a man's online password.

"How can I help you?" Janet asked the following caller.

"I'd like to refill my prescriptions," an elderly woman said softly. Janet explained carefully that the woman should probably call her pharmacist, and then she offered up another brief prayer, "Please, Heavenly Father, don't let me ever become senile."

Finally, after several more calls, it was 9:30 and time for Janet's first fifteen-minute break of the day. She removed her earpiece and set it back in its cradle. The power would go out if the headset wasn't recharged at every opportunity throughout the day, and it was pure hell having to use the regular telephone to answer calls.

Janet took a sip of water from the glass she kept on her desk and then headed for the bathroom. After that, she found a chair in the building's large meeting room that no one was using. She didn't like going to the dining area because there were always other people there, and after talking every second of the day, the last thing she wanted to do on her breaks was talk some more.

She leaned back in her chair and sighed, sending up another silent prayer to heaven. "Please, Heavenly Father, help me have a good time at the dance tonight. Please help me look good. Help me be friendly so guys will be attracted to me. Help me not have to dance with any weird guys. Help me have fun talking with my friends. Help me not spill anything on my dress. Help me pick exactly the right outfit to attract just the right guy. I want to do the right thing by staying active in the Church and by getting married in the temple. Please help me find the right man so I can do these things."

Janet kept resting her eyes, but she was afraid of falling asleep, so she checked her watch every couple of minutes to make sure she wasn't late getting back. All too soon, fourteen minutes had passed. She sighed again and headed back for her desk in the Call Center. The instant she logged back in to the queue, her phone beeped. "Orca Credit Union," she said, making herself smile. "This is Janet. How may I help you?"

"I have $300 in my checking account," said a man with a Filipino accent, "but only $200 is available. I need to make a purchase. Can you see what's going on?"

"Sure thing. May I get your member number?" After verifying the man's identity, Janet clicked on his checking account, went to Maintenance, went to Holds, verified that there were no management holds or check holds, and then moved on to card holds. "It looks like Shell put a $100 hold on your card. Did you recently purchase gas?"

"Yes, but not $100 worth. I bought $33 in gas. And that's already been taken out. Why do they need to put a hold on my account?"

"I'm afraid that's just their policy. We get this question every day. I can tell you the hold is due to come off at 2:46 tomorrow. They haven't actually taken that hundred dollars. There's just a hold on it. And it'll be available again tomorrow."

"But I need it now. Isn't there anything you can do?"

"I'm afraid there isn't. I can tell you that next time you get gas, if you go into the store rather than pay at the pump, they usually don't put the hold on your funds."

"Well, that doesn't help me now. Can I talk to a supervisor?"

"Sir, I can assure you, we get this request every day. I know for a fact there's nothing we can do. I do apologize. I know it's very frustrating."

The man hung up without another word, and the very next second, Janet's phone beeped again. "Orca Credit Union," she said, still smiling. "This is Janet. How may I help you?" She thought about the green dress she might wear tonight. She started to pray for help finding her green barrette when she got home, but then the caller began talking, and Janet put Heavenly Father on Hold. She'd cleared the practice with Him when she started the job back in December.

"Three days ago," the woman said, "there was a charge on my account for $44.78 from Fred Meyer. Can you look at the detail?"

Janet verified the woman's identity and then clicked on the account, went to History, then clicked on the transaction in question. "It was done at the store in Renton," she said.

"Well, I *know* that. I have access to online banking myself. What I want to know is what I bought there."

"Excuse me?"

"Can't you click on the transaction and see what I bought?"

"I'm afraid not."

"Well, what am I supposed to do?"

"Don't you have a receipt?"

"No."

"Can you call the store?"

The caller sighed heavily. "Well, if you won't help me, I guess I'll have to." She hung up.

Janet shook her head. Why did people ask for unreasonable things all the time? Wasn't the job hard enough without idiots calling in, too? "Please, Heavenly Father," she prayed, taking Him off Hold, "help me win the Publishers Clearing House so I don't have to put up with people like that every day." Then the phone beeped in her ear again.

The next ninety minutes continued in much the same fashion. Janet reset the online password for seven more people. This was by far the most common request they received at the Call Center. Several other people had problems with Bill Pay, there were several more funds transfers, and then one caller needed Janet to put a stop payment on an ACH, saying a payday loan company was taking money from his account after he'd already paid them back.

It was odd really that Janet could pay close attention to every call and yet still have part of her mind free to pray. It was kind of like conferencing in a third caller. She believed in the command to "pray always" and probably prayed a couple of dozen times a day.

Of course, many times, Heavenly Father didn't answer her prayers. She'd asked all throughout high school for God to soften her parents' hearts so they'd be willing to send her to BYU for college. She was sure she'd not only get a great secular education there, but she'd learn more about how the Church functioned in a predominantly Mormon setting. And she was certain to meet a good man at BYU, a returned missionary for sure.

But after what must have been literally thousands of prayers on the subject, Heavenly Father still had Janet's parents send her to UW. It was certainly a good school, and it obviously saved her parents thousands of dollars, but still. Why hadn't God answered her prayers? Didn't He say, "Ask and ye shall receive?" What was the point of praying if you didn't get what you prayed for?

"Orca Credit Union," Janet said, smiling brightly. "This is Janet. How may I help you?" This would probably be her last call before lunch. Tracy was already five minutes late getting back. As soon as she returned, Janet could leave. Oh, good, there was Tracy now. Janet prayed this would be a short call.

"I need to transfer money out of my savings to my checking," a woman said, "but I couldn't do it online."

"Let me see if I can help you with that."

"Well, you'd better be able to help me," the woman said, laughing. "I need that money."

Janet pulled up the woman's profile and verified her identity, and then she pulled up the screen in Statistics that showed what she was looking for. Yep. The woman had already made six Reg D transfers this month.

"I'm sorry," Janet told her. "There's a federal regulation that limits the number of online or by phone transfers you can make in a month from a given savings account. It's a dumb rule, but we got stuck with it and have to enforce it. I'm afraid at this point, your only options are to make the transfer at an ATM or to go into a branch."

"But I can't do either one of those. I need that money right now so I can make a purchase online."

"I'm afraid there's no way around it," Janet said. "The computer simply won't allow any other Regulation D transfers for you this month. I couldn't override it if I wanted to. If there's a Shared Branching location closer to you, you could make the transfer there as well."

"Oh, good grief. What's the good of calling the Help Desk if you can't help me?"

Janet pulled out her earpiece and set it in the tray and locked her computer. It was only 11:36. The days were so, so long. Every single second of the day, she had to listen to people constantly demanding things. Even when she could deliver, it was exhausting. "Please, Heavenly Father," she prayed, "please make 4:30 come quickly."

Janet took another sip of her water, headed to the bathroom, and opened her Greek yogurt for lunch. It was Blood Orange, her favorite. She managed to sit on the far side of the dining area from two other people who were eating and thus avoid any discussion, but as soon as she was done, she hurried back to the empty meeting room to sit by herself.

"Heavenly Father," she prayed silently, "help me know if this is the career path you want me to take. Help it not have to be for very long, whatever career I choose. Help me find a good man and get married and have children and be a good mother. I know that's the career you really want for me. Help me do my part to make sure that happens. Help my future husband make enough money so I can stay at home with the kids. Help my friends or my family meet the right guy and recognize he's a good fit for me and set us up on a date. If there's a returned missionary in Seattle on business right now, help him hear about the dance and show up tonight and come to church on Sunday. Please help things work out well, and soon."

Janet tried to doze a little bit, to truly rest on her half-hour break, but people kept passing the meeting room and seeing her inside and popping in. "Find yourself a nice, quiet spot?" they'd all ask. The same question from everyone, as if it were original. She'd smile and nod back.

But the minutes flew by, and soon it was 12:05 and time to head back to the Call Center. Maybe tonight would be the night Heavenly Father finally answered her prayers. Janet looked around at the other employees in the room. She wondered briefly what their prayers were.

Were they all perfectly content with their lives as they were, or did they all want something more, too? How many people just in this one room were sending up prayers to God right now? The idea intrigued her, but she logged back onto her computer, put her earpiece back in, and signed back into the queue.

"Orca Credit Union. This is Janet. How may I help you?"

"I'm locked out of my online account. Can you reset my password?"

"No problem. Can I get your member number?"

This next stretch was the longest, a full two and a half hours without a break. Janet answered call after call, with not even one second between them. Most were for online password resets and questions about Visa transactions or funds transfers. One woman needed to raise the $2000 limit on her debit card to $2500 just for the day, so she could purchase airline tickets. Something like that always required a manager's approval, and Mike had been working on another difficult case right then, so Janet had been on the phone almost fourteen minutes before the request could be taken care of.

Rotten for her numbers, but it was the only break she had for a long while. Every single time a member would hang up the phone, it would beep in her ear again not one second later. The onslaught was relentless, but Janet continued to smile all afternoon.

"Orca Credit Union," she said, ten minutes before her next scheduled break. "This is Janet. How may I help you?" She closed her eyes. "Please, Heavenly Father," she prayed. "Please, please help me."

"I live in Oregon now, and I just realized I'm not getting my statements anymore. I need to update my address."

"All right. Let's see what we have in the system. Do you know your member number?" Janet verified the member's identity and read off the address currently in the system.

"Yes, that's the old address. I want to update it."

"I'm not allowed to update it over the phone," Janet explained, "but we do have a few options. Do you have access to your online banking?"

"No, I never use online banking. I don't trust computers."

"All right. Can you fax over the address change with your signature so we can compare it to your signature on file?"

"No. I don't know anyone with a fax machine."

"All right. You can always send a signed letter with the information and we can update the address when we receive the letter."

"I can't wait that long. I need to update my address *now*."

"Well, I'm afraid the only other alternative is to go into a branch and take care of it in person."

"I *told* you I'm in Oregon."

"Ma'am, there are only four ways to update an address. I'm afraid you'll have to choose one of those options."

"This is *completely* unacceptable. Can I speak with a manager?"

"Ma'am, these are the only four options. Are you sure you can't find any business in your city that has a fax? Most banks and credit unions and photocopy places have one."

"I don't have time for all that. If you can't help me, I'm going to close my accounts."

Janet looked at the balances. No loans, no credit card, and only five dollars in both the savings and the checking. "You're certainly free to do that, ma'am. To close an account, you can go into a branch, or you can send us a letter, or you can send us a fax—"

"God help me!"

"But of course, we'd only be able to send the funds to the address we have on file, so—"

The woman hung up.

The phone beeped again, and Janet pressed Answer. "Orca Credit Union. This is Janet. How may I help you?" But only part of Janet was listening to the man on the line. That last woman's inadvertent prayer had caught Janet off guard.

Suddenly, Janet realized working in the Call Center was exactly the job she was supposed to have.

Mormons were in training to become gods, weren't they, and what would a god be doing all day but answering calls? Billions of people sending up petitionary prayers every second of the day. Not even a five-second break between calls. Constant. Never-ending. Endless.

The man on the phone was an RV dealer. One of the credit union's members was there presenting a cashier's check for $119,000 but there was no second signature on the check. Was that necessary for a check of such a large amount to be valid?

"Oh, I'm afraid it is," Janet said. "I do apologize. The teller must have forgotten. We issue large amounts so rarely. But the member will need to bring the check back to one of our branches to be countersigned. I'm terribly sorry for the inconvenience."

"I understand. I'll tell the customer."

The man hung up and Janet's phone beeped again. "Orca Credit Union. This is Janet. How may I help you?" Smiling, smiling, smiling all day long, no matter what. She could understand now why God sometimes became so testy in the Bible. Maybe that also explained some of His seemingly arbitrary, occasionally rather mean rules.

"I have three charges for returned checks, and I don't think it's fair," a woman complained. "Can you reverse those?"

Was this like repentance? Playing God all day was absolutely exhausting, but maybe if she thought about it in the right light, it could be fun, too. Of course, sometimes, she felt more like Santa Claus. People would call with a list of things they wanted, and she was expected to give it to them simply because they asked, whether they actually deserved that or a lump of coal instead.

But was *she* treating Heavenly Father like Santa as well?

Janet felt her stomach lurch as she reconsidered all her prayers. She'd thought she was doing the right thing by praying constantly, but what if Heavenly Father was sick and tired of hearing her? It was like Isis, the woman who called every single day that Janet had worked here. And with a total of eight Call Center reps, for Janet to be hearing from this woman every day meant she had to be calling multiple times a day.

Maybe Heavenly Father *hated* hearing from her. Maybe He rolled his eyes. Maybe He laughed and gossiped with His godly wives about her. Maybe He in fact cared, but there was nothing He could do. Maybe there were federal regulations up in heaven, too. Perhaps He was giving her useful alternatives, and she was simply being obstinate and childish not to accept them.

Janet looked at the woman's account. The woman had clearly written two checks while knowing there was no money in the account. The first check had tried to go through twice, which was the norm, so she'd acquired two NSF fees for that check, and the second check had gone through once and was sure to go through another time. Since none of this was the credit union's fault, Janet couldn't reverse the fees.

It may well have been unfair for the bank to penalize the poorest people, but that was out of Janet's control.

Was she perhaps training to become a god while working for an unethical company?

Had Heavenly Father done the same thing? Was *that* why some of his rules seemed so mean?

"You're going to end up with still another fee," Janet told the member calmly. "I can either place a stop payment on the check before it tries to clear a second time, which would be $25. Or we can let it attempt again, and there will be a $28 NSF charge."

"Are those my only options?" the woman asked sharply, clearly frustrated. "Isn't there anything else I can do?"

"You could always deposit money into the account."

"Oh! I hadn't thought of that." She was serious.

Janet tried not to laugh. "I pride myself on thinking outside the box." Was that too snarky a thing to say? She sent up a quick prayer for forgiveness.

The phone beeped again. Janet took herself out of the queue and answered this one last call before her afternoon break. "How may I help you?" she asked cheerily.

"I'm locked out of my online account. Can you reset the password?"

And suddenly, Janet had another revelation. While it was a bother to be resetting passwords all day long, in the end, it clearly decreased Janet's workload. Once a member was in their own account, they could do their own transfers, check their own balances, update their own information, send out their own Bill Pays, pretty much take care of themselves.

Was *that* what Janet should be praying for? The ability to tap into the positive energy of the universe and then take care of her own problems?

"Heavenly Father," she prayed silently, "is this what you want me to do?"

If it was, would He even be able to answer such a question?

Janet hung up her earpiece and headed to the bathroom. Then she sequestered herself in the empty meeting room again. She wanted to pray at greater length to discuss these new possibilities with God, but she was afraid now she'd irritate Him. Yet she was afraid *not* to discuss it, too.

She remembered hearing a talk at church many years ago about a father who asks his son to perform a certain difficult task. The boy tries to do it one way and fails. Then he tries another way and fails. He attempts to perform the task over and over in a variety of ways and finally ends up crying, saying he can't do it. Then the father says gently to the boy, "There's one thing you haven't tried yet."

"What?" asks the boy, sniffling.

"You haven't asked me for help."

Janet never did fully understand the moral of the story. Wasn't it a good thing to work hard and try to do things on your own? Or was she supposed to just ask Heavenly Father for help every time she needed it and let Him grant her wishes? If it was the latter, Heavenly Father didn't seem overly anxious to do His part.

So maybe the story was wrong. Maybe the boy needed to read an instruction manual. Maybe he needed to try one more approach to the problem before giving up. Maybe giving up was an acceptable response to some problems to begin with.

Janet looked at her watch. 2:44. Time to head back. Would this day never end?

The moment Janet inserted her earpiece again and logged back into the queue, the phone beeped. "Orca Credit Union. This is Janet. How may I help you?"

The member was doing her taxes and realized she couldn't find her 1099s. Janet looked up the numbers for her. "You earned $16.23 in interest last year," she said. "Anything under $10 doesn't get reported. Did you need me to mail you the actual form as well?"

"Yes, thank you."

Janet hung up and the phone beeped again. This time it was a man going to Sweden for two weeks who wanted to put a travel notice on his debit card so it wouldn't be deactivated for suspected fraud when he did transactions out of the country. The next caller needed to order checks and couldn't figure out how to do it online. The member after that was interested in a car loan and wanted to be transferred to Lending. And the person after that needed his online password reset.

Finally, at 4:11, there was a lull of seventeen seconds between calls, and Janet took a long sip of water. Only nineteen more minutes till her shift was over. "Please, Heavenly Father, please help me."

She shook her head, feeling like an idiot. She hoped the Singles dance would go well this evening. It had been a long time since she'd had any real fun. She thought again about the possibility of serving a mission for the Church. Maybe she'd be sent to London or Berlin or Tokyo or someplace else interesting.

But if God wanted her to tap into the positive energy of the universe and take care of her own issues, maybe she should consider something like the Peace Corps instead. If she had to take care of herself, that meant God wasn't taking care of the teeming masses of poor people in Third World countries, either. That was probably up to her, too.

And really, what would look better on a resume'? A safe eighteen-month mission for the Church, or a two-year stint in Brazil teaching people hygiene? Both might be good for her soul, but one might help her more in getting a satisfying job, if she never did meet that one perfect man. Maybe her future really was entirely in her own hands. *She* had to give *herself* worthwhile life experiences.

The phone beeped. "Orca Credit Union. This is Janet. How may I help you?"

"I just wanted to call and say how wonderful you all are. Everyone at the branch I go to treats me well, and you guys are always so great on the phone. Is there someone I can talk to just to let the company know how I feel?"

A prayer solely of gratitude. Janet sure didn't send many of those heavenward. "Just a moment," she said, "and I'll transfer you to the manager."

"Thank you so much."

Three more calls, and finally, it was 4:26. Janet smiled for real and took herself out of the queue for the last time that day. She quickly printed out her closing paperwork and put it in the interoffice envelope to Electronic Services, and then she logged out of the time clock and off the computer. She stood up and stretched. She sure hoped that nap would revive her so she'd be presentable by the time the dance started.

"Heavenly Father," she began silently but then stopped herself and laughed. "Oh, never mind." Adjusting was going to take a while. She shook her head, looking back for just a moment at the phone. Then she put on her jacket, picked up her purse, and headed out the door.

Playing the Card

"Hey, Brady." Lucas slapped the table. "A King of Hearts. You're off to a good start." He flexed his right arm to show off his muscles. Lucas loved this game.

Brady smiled and then dropped to the floor and started doing push-ups. When he'd completed thirteen, he jumped back up and sat down at the table again and pointed to Lucas. "Your turn now."

Lucas picked the next card from the top of the deck and waved it in front of Brady's face. "A Three of Clubs." He stuck out his tongue.

"Wimp," Brady said as Lucas lay on the floor and did three sit-ups.

Lucas and Brady had been friends for over thirty years, since they'd first met as Mormon missionaries in Rome. They were both from Boise, though they hadn't known each other before becoming missionaries, and when they returned home, they decided to keep up their friendship. One of the things they did together was meet regularly and play cards.

While card-playing was technically against the rules of the Church, they adapted their play to make the game an endurance test. Hearts and Diamonds indicated push-ups, and Spades and Clubs indicated sit-ups. The two men would go through a deck one card at a time, doing the corresponding number of exercises indicated by the face value of the card.

It was kind of like a spelling bee. Whoever couldn't complete the current card's exercises was eliminated, and the other player won.

They used the card-playing as a device to keep a conversation going. Rather than say, "Let's talk," they'd play, and during the course of an afternoon or evening, they'd also discuss work and politics and family life and everything else. Brady would complain about his "oppression," of course, but Lucas talked about real troubles, all the things that seemed intent on keeping him out of the Celestial Kingdom.

Who better to ask about how to avoid hell than someone who was destined to go there himself? Still, despite their occasional philosophical musings over the years, they mostly kept their talk light. That seemed the best way to stay happy.

The friends had gone through only half the deck today before Brady started complaining about a pain in his side. "You're not going to quit this early, are you?" Lucas grinned. "You really are getting to be an old man."

They were both fifty-one. Brady was trim and firm, though his salt and pepper hair still gave away his age. He usually ended up taking off his shirt a good while before the game was over. Lucas, on the other hand, had a bit of a pot belly and a bald spot on the crown of his head. He never took off his shirt in front of Brady anymore.

Brady didn't smile at his friend's joke. "I've been getting this pain a lot lately," he said. A shadow crossed his face.

Lucas leaned forward immediately. "Have you seen a doctor? Are you all right?" Though he accepted Brady's homosexuality, Lucas was still an active Mormon, after all, and couldn't help but think that at some point, God was going to smite his friend. Lucas tried to invite Brady to church socials and dinners once or twice a year, hoping against hope Brady would feel some spark of the Spirit and return of his own accord before it was too late.

Lucas still bargained with Heavenly Father occasionally that if he could bring back this one soul, Heavenly Father would finally stop testing him so severely all the time. Just the other day at the office, for example, that jerk down the hall—

"It's not Kaposi's sarcoma," Brady replied with a sad smile. "That's usually visible on the skin. I don't have AIDS, Lucas."

"Oh, of course, of course. But are you all right?" It wasn't homophobic to be concerned, was it?

Brady's smile faded, and he rubbed his side slowly. "I guess I have to tell someone," he said, sighing. Lucas knew Brady had split with his last partner two years ago and so had no regular confidante. Lucas couldn't even remember how many partners Brady had had over the years. Was it four? Five?

Lucas was still with the woman he'd married six months after returning from Italy. His three children had all married in the temple as well. Though he and Brady had discussed homosexuality at length many times during the last few decades, Lucas still couldn't understand why someone would *want* to be gay. It was so much nicer to have a family than to be alone. Even Brady must realize it, the way he'd talked

Lucas out of having an affair with Rebecca at work the time Lucas confided those stray thoughts to his friend.

"The results came back a couple of days ago," Brady continued. "It's cancer." He looked at Lucas challengingly.

Lucas didn't quite know what to say. He couldn't really say he was surprised. Actions did have consequences, obviously. After a long moment, he finally offered, "Is it treatable? What's the prognosis?"

Brady forced a smile. "I guess I'll find out for sure what Heavenly Father really thinks of gays before long."

"What do you—?"

Brady shrugged. "It's already stage four. Doctors never want to give you a real timeline, but I've read everything I can find on the internet. I probably have about three months."

"Three! I thought people always had six months from the time they found out." That would have given Brady more time to repent. He wondered if he could anoint Brady with the consecrated olive oil he carried with him at all times and bless him to live an extra few months, on the condition that he read the Book of Mormon again. Wasn't that the real reason he'd stayed friends all these years, to be there at the end and make sure Brady died a good Mormon?

"Depends on when they find out."

The two men were silent for several moments. Lucas had watched his mother die of breast cancer almost ten years ago, and all four grandparents plus several aunts and uncles had gone on before. Death wasn't always a sad event for Mormons, though. They understood it meant only a temporary separation from loved ones, that everyone would be together later for eternity.

Lucas normally would only bother investing in relationships he knew were eternal. But it was different with Brady. When Brady was between partners, Lucas occasionally invited him to share Family Home Evening with his family. He would sometimes spend an evening with Brady watching an R-rated movie, something he'd never do at home, to prove he was enlightened.

He'd even sent letters to senators and representatives a few times to ask them to vote in favor of gay rights. Lucas did honestly believe that in the secular world, gays should be treated equally, but that didn't mean he didn't understand that things would be different with Heavenly Father. God couldn't accept sin with the least degree of allowance. Lucas loved Brady, but he knew he'd never be with him on the other side if Brady didn't repent.

"When were you baptized?" Brady asked out of the blue.

"What do you mean?"

"Do you remember the exact date of your baptism?"

Lucas frowned. Naturally, he'd been eight years old at the time, like all Mormons who were born into the covenant. But the exact date? It was probably a couple of weeks after his birthday. "Does it matter?"

Brady smiled. "When I was fourteen," he said, "my Teachers Quorum instructor wrote several dates on the blackboard and asked us what they were. The other kids in class just looked at each other in confusion. None of the dates seemed like anything we'd learned in school. But I raised my hand. 'I know what one of them is,' I said. The teacher didn't look convinced but asked me which one. I said, 'February 5, 1970. That's the day I was baptized.' All the other boys stared at me in awe, and even the teacher looked impressed. February 5 was always a special day for me as a boy. I couldn't imagine not knowing the date of my baptism into the Church."

Lucas felt embarrassed. "Why are you telling me this?"

"I'll always be Mormon, even if I was excommunicated twenty-five years ago."

"I'm so sorry, Brady." Lucas didn't know exactly what he was sorry about, but he felt such pain to look at his friend's face. "What can I do?"

At this, Brady smiled. "Actually, there *is* something you can do for me."

Lucas now felt uncomfortable. Was Brady going to ask him to join a protest rally for gay marriage? Lucas had seen first-hand from Brady's life that gays were not good at marriage. Yes, he supposed they deserved the right, but it was hard promoting something that was wrong, even if people had the right to be wrong. "What is it?"

"What do you think of Senator Richardson?"

Lucas frowned again. "He's a good senator. Nice guy. I've seen him at stake conference. He goes to church regularly when he's in Boise. Why?"

Brady had a disgusted look on his face. "Did you send him the letter I asked you to?"

Lucas wasn't sure. He usually sent all the letters Brady asked him to send, but he didn't pay that much attention to whom he was addressing them. It would be different, he supposed, if he really cared how the politicians would react. He only sent them to show Brady that Mormons could be loving. He nodded.

"The guy's an asshole. He talks about family values all the time, though he divorced his first wife because she couldn't have kids, and that one housekeeper filed a suit against him for sexual harassment."

"Which was eventually thrown out," Lucas reminded his friend.

"He's behind all these anti-abortion bills—"

"Because abortion is a sin."

"And behind the bill to ban contraception."

Lucas was quiet on that score.

"And behind the push for a Constitutional amendment to ban gay marriage."

"Yes, well…"

"And he's against workers' unions, and against a minimum wage, and against Social Security, and against Medicare."

"He believes in personal responsibility." The way Brady phrased it, it almost looked like Richardson was a jerk, but you had to put things in perspective. The senator simply believed that children should take care of their aging parents, that people should work hard and honestly for what they got, that people shouldn't have sex until they were ready for children, things like that. All perfectly understandable principles.

"Maybe this isn't going to work," Brady said glumly.

"What?"

"I need you to help me bring Richardson down. Destroy his career."

Lucas's mouth fell open. "Why in the world would I want to do that?"

Brady looked him straight in the face. "Because he's evil."

Lucas was immediately irritated. "You gays are always complaining about being demonized, and now you say he's 'evil'?"

It was the same when gays complained about how "hateful" Church leaders were when they condemned homosexuality, when every time those leaders insisted they loved gays. It was the gays who said hateful things about the Church.

And Lucas had put up with it all these years like a good missionary, just on the off chance one day Brady would see the light. Without any guarantee at all, Lucas had offered his friendship.

"I sucked his dick last week."

Lucas stared at him. "I don't believe you."

"We're going to go over to his house later. He's out of town."

Lucas shook his head as if to clear it. "I still don't understand. Just why would we go over there, and why would I want to destroy him? If he's gay, don't you want to help him?"

Brady looked disgusted again. "Collaborators always do well *during* the war, but after it, they lose their position. I already know he'll go to Spirit Prison when he dies, but I want him to pay *now.*"

The conversation was becoming tiresome. Lucas didn't understand what Brady was after, and he began to wonder if whatever cancer his friend was suffering from was causing so much mental stress the man was having a nervous breakdown.

"I'm going to need to get back home soon," he said. "Got a lot of things to buy for tomorrow. It's a special day for Megan, after all." Megan was such a good wife to have, always calm and quiet and dependable, not odd and demanding like Brady. Lucas wondered how he'd managed to stay friends with Brady all these years. Turning the other cheek was one thing, and going the second mile another, but had he perhaps put up with *too* much?

"Do you remember the time Chase had appendicitis?" Brady asked. Chase was Lucas's oldest son and had been eleven at the time of the attack. Lucas and Megan had been at a T-ball game for their next oldest son, Barry, and had their youngest, Tad, with them as well. But Chase had complained he didn't feel well and had asked to stay home. Even knowing he was too young to be left alone, Lucas had done just that.

But he'd left for the game without his cell phone, and when Chase began feeling worse later, he'd called Brady for help. Several months earlier, Megan had had to take care of her mother who was dying of uterine cancer, so she'd been away in Spokane for over three months. Brady had been between boyfriends at the time and had offered to move in with Lucas and lend a hand with the kids. It had been a tremendous help.

So Chase had called Brady, who'd rushed over and carried him to the hospital, where an emergency appendectomy had been performed. Brady had signed the medical forms using Lucas's name, just to make sure everything was done as quickly as possible, and Lucas had always been grateful.

Still, he wasn't sure Brady wasn't a little manipulative as well. Why else bring up that story at a time like this?

Brady stood and retrieved a card from a nearby shelf. He handed it to Lucas. "I got this in the mail yesterday," he explained.

Lucas opened the envelope and found a Mother's Day card addressed to Brady and signed, "You'll always be a second mother to me. Love, Chase." Lucas looked up at Brady in confusion.

"I never told you," Brady said softly, "but ever since I helped you with the kids that year, Chase has been sending me a Mother's Day card every May. I have seventeen of them now. I've saved every one."

"What is it you want from me?" Lucas asked in resignation. Was he going to make him say something positive about Brady's lifestyle at his funeral? Was Brady actually going to ask him to write a letter to the Prophet and not just to random politicians?

"I know you don't believe in assisted suicide," Brady began.

"Oh, you can't ask me that!"

Brady reached across the table and put his hand on Lucas's. "I'm asking for more than that."

"What?" said Lucas dully. He almost wished *he* could die rather than listen to any more of this conversation.

"We're going over to Senator Richardson's house tonight. I've told you they're out of town. We're going to open the panel to the crawlspace, and then you're going to strangle me, and you're going to bury me underneath his house."

Lucas stared in absolute horror at his friend, his heart racing. "Are you mad!?" Brady had held his side earlier, but the tumor must be in his brain. It *must*.

"I have some lime you'll put over my body. They'll be gone for two more weeks. And you'll wait three or four months after that before you call the police anonymously."

Lucas continued staring in shock and wonderment at his friend. Was this all some kind of sick joke? He felt he might be going mad himself.

"The forensics will be tough. I've watched *CSI.* After you strangle me, you'll want to hit me over the back of my head strong enough to crack my skull. I've bought special clothes for you in case any fibers get caught on anything. You'll have to burn all that afterward. And you'll strangle me with a rope so if the body is discovered too soon, your hands' measurements won't be around my throat."

"But—but Brady—"

"Richardson is evil. And he's going down. I'll be dead in three months anyway. I have a will leaving some of my belongings to several friends. Staying here three months longer won't change that."

"But to implicate an innocent man in murder…"

"Innocent?" Brady laughed. "Didn't you hear about Jerry Simpson?"

"Who?"

"The eighteen-year-old in Richardson's ward. Richardson gave a talk about the evils of homosexuality, and the next day, this young man waiting for his mission call hung himself in his back yard."

"What does that prove?"

"You'll need to act normally during dinner tonight," Brady said, "and around 11:00, you'll come pick me up."

"What possible excuse would I give Megan?"

"Tell her I have cancer and I need to talk."

"Sheesh." Lucas stared at the floor, unable to look Brady in the face. "I can't possibly do what you're asking." It was certainly terrible that boy had died before his mission, but suicide was a sin that the sinner was responsible for and no one else.

It was a shame, though. Lucas had had such a great time on his own mission, back in the days when Brady had been righteous. They'd sure had some good times together. They'd been the elite of the Church back then.

"Heavenly Father ordered Nephi to kill Laban for the good of the people," Brady said softly.

Lucas's brows furrowed. "That was different."

"And think how much better off they'd have been if they'd killed Laman and Lemuel, too."

"Brady—"

"I've fasted about this."

Lucas tried not to look dismissive. What good was the fasting of a homosexual? "I'm not doing it."

"I have an idea," said Brady. "Why don't we see what the cards say? You'll pick the next card and go from there."

"What did you do?" asked Lucas. "Stack the deck? Is there an Ace of Spades next?"

"Shuffle the cards yourself and then pick."

"God doesn't speak through a deck of cards."

"He will if He needs to convince you and has to do it in a way that can also be interpreted as coincidence."

"This is ridiculous. I'm going home. You need to get some therapy. I can see if the bishop will talk to you, even though…"

Brady scooped up all the cards and handed them to Lucas. Lucas felt stupid, but he started shuffling them anyway. He could see where this was leading. If Hearts came up, Brady would ask him to do this terrible thing out of love. If Clubs came up, he'd say, "See, you have to club me." If it was Spades, he'd say, "The symbol for death" or "You have to bury me with a spade."

There'd be nothing to say if Diamonds came up, he supposed, but there was only a twenty-five percent chance of that. This was just more manipulation on Brady's part.

He finished shuffling, took a deep breath, and pulled out a card. "Four of Hearts."

Brady smiled and put his hand on Lucas's. "See? The fact that you chose a card proves you *want* to hear from God that it's okay. You *want* to help me."

"That's preposterous. I—I—"

"I'll take all the responsibility myself. I'll tell Heavenly Father to punish *me* if this is a sin."

"You can't just *take* the responsibility. Only Jesus can do a thing like that. I'm going now."

"Pick another card."

Lucas knew he should stand up and walk right out of the house. All these years he thought he loved Brady, but Brady was more of a sinner than he'd realized. Lucas needed to leave.

"Pick a card," Brady repeated.

Lucas pulled up another card. It was a Ten of Hearts.

"Pick another one."

Lucas chose a Seven of Hearts.

"Pick another."

It was a Jack of Hearts.

The two men looked at each other. Lucas could feel Brady's eyes boring deep into his soul. He felt naked and exposed. He wanted to cover his face and blunder his way to the door. He watched in horror and confusion as Brady moved over to kneel beside him as he sat, as Brady held his hand, as Brady moved forward and…

The kiss lasted a full two minutes. It started out static, with just lips touching, but that alone was electric. Lucas's lips hadn't met anyone's other than his wife's in years. At first, Lucas didn't know what to think. Then Brady's lips parted slightly, and Lucas felt the first moisture start to part his own.

Despite how inappropriate it all was, he began to feel the slightest stirrings in his groin. It was just a natural biological reaction, of course. The fact that it could occur with another man was intriguing. Then Lucas felt Brady's tongue force its way into his mouth.

His struggling erection almost hurt as it pressed against his pants. He wanted to shift to give it more room. Instead, he let his tongue find its way into Brady's mouth, too. It seemed a sin not to give his friend this little token after all these years.

The kiss alternated between soft and sweet, hard and passionate. Lucas hadn't had a kiss like that with Megan in a very, very long time.

Finally, it was Brady who pulled away. He looked Lucas steadily in the eye.

"I-I'm not gay," Lucas whispered.

"But you do love me."

Lucas sighed heavily. "Yes. I love you. But this?" It wasn't in the least fair to ask anyone such a thing. Life always conspired to destroy him. There were illnesses and weaknesses and demotions and transfers to other departments and bosses who humiliated at every opportunity. There were demeaning callings at church and neighborhood kids who ruined his lawn. There was the news on television and all the awful things of the world which seemed to grow worse and worse no matter how faithfully he paid his tithing or supported the missionary effort.

Life tried relentlessly to make Lucas cranky and irritable and depressed and selfish and mean, no matter how much he tried to bury his head in the sand and think positively. Every day was a battle to remain a decent human being.

And he had. Was he going to throw it all away now on the whim of this son of perdition? Perhaps Satan had planned this all along, to make Lucas think he was doing a good deed by staying friends with an avowed homosexual, only to use that against him and drag him to Outer Darkness along with Brady. Satan was conniving. He could take thirty years to bring his plan to fruition.

How ironic that it had been Brady who'd kept Lucas sane during all his battles at work and in the ward. Brady who always had a kind word to say, who always made Lucas laugh, who made him believe that fidelity meant something.

Lucas felt as if he'd just discovered Megan had been cheating on him for the past fifteen years, and he'd only now found out.

"I've got to go." Lucas stood up, took one long, last look at his friend still kneeling at his feet, and turned toward the door. He could never see Brady again. It was a sin to abandon a friend in need, certainly, but he had his own soul to think of.

Standing there, Lucas remembered the time in Rome when he really wanted to move up from District Leader to Zone Leader. There were a few other elders who were being considered for the promotion, and Brady had come up with an idea to help.

"Politicans buy votes, don't they?" he asked. He took an extra hundred dollars out of his savings account and paid two different young men to be baptized, to boost Lucas's stats.

Lucas had been shocked at the idea at first, till Brady explained that the contract required the men to attend church regularly for three months and then they'd be given a second $50 payment each. Brady had said that the men would do it out of crass self-interest, but they'd eventually feel the Spirit and stay at church for the right reasons. The two men had still been attending Sacrament long after Lucas had been called as Zone Leader. Brady had been there for him, maybe even sinned for him. Brady truly loved him.

Lucas reached for the front door and paused briefly, wiping away a tear. It really was goodbye. This must be what it was like for couples on Judgment Day when one spouse is chosen for the Celestial Kingdom and the other only gets the Terrestrial, and they know they'll never see each other again throughout all eternity.

If Lucas went ahead with the plan, though, he could at least be with Brady again in hell.

Lucas wrenched the door open savagely. He'd have to repent of even considering such a thing.

"See you next Saturday?" Brady called out from the living room.

Lucas stepped outside but then turned and looked back into the house for a long moment. "No," he finally called back. "I'll see you tomorrow. You're coming to church with me."

There was a brief moment of silence. Then Lucas heard Brady call out from the other room. "I'll be ready by 8:30."

Lucas stood on the doorstep a moment longer, smiling. Church tomorrow, and then cards again next Saturday. There were still three more months, after all. Plenty of time to be together. And to think. And to act. Lucas might yet baptize Brady.

Gays, he thought.

He reflected again on Senator Richardson and remembered now that he had in fact heard about that poor kid in Richardson's ward. The guy truly was a bastard. Someone *should* make him pay. It just wouldn't be him.

That was Heavenly Father's job anyway.

He'd done the right thing by asking Brady to church. Even Brady was happy about it. Lucas could still hear the smile in his friend's voice.

He walked briskly to his car and headed back for home.

Broken Wisdom Teeth

"Did you hear?" Luana leaned over conspiratorially. "Shari and Katrice got fired."

"Why?" Miranda asked. "What happened?" Katrice was one of the few people who were nice to her. It wasn't fair.

"That guy Aaron in room 103. He told the director they were smoking pot with him, and the director asked the girls to take a drug test, and they refused."

"Why did they refuse?" Miranda knew that Katrice didn't smoke pot. They'd discussed it when Miranda mentioned wanting pain medication one day.

"They were offended. Wouldn't you be?"

"Yes, but I wouldn't want to lose my job over it."

Luana walked off to check on another patient, and Miranda finished entering some information in the computer. She rubbed her jaw, where her wisdom tooth was really hurting. Why in the world didn't Katrice simply take the test? What a stupid way to be fired.

Walking home across a couple of miles of no-man's-land after work, Miranda kept an eye open for any muggers. The Westbank of New Orleans was mixed, a decent neighborhood here, an awful one there. She never knew what shift she was going to be called in to cover, so sometimes she had to make the trek in blazing heat and other times in the dead of night. It was almost midnight when she reached her apartment today.

She put an ice cube at the base of her orchid and looked at the firm white bloom, sighing. Then she opened the fridge and took out a piece of bologna and some bread. She was down to 184 pounds now, well below her maximum weight of 203, which had horrified her to no end. She still had a lot to lose, and at the age of fifty, her metabolism sure wasn't cooperating. But she only put mustard on the bread tonight, no mayonnaise. She was trying.

As she chewed, her jaw hurt. Damn that tooth.

Miranda was PRN at the nursing home. She didn't have any dental insurance. You'd think she qualified for Medicaid, she fumed, since she was already on Disability because of the schizophrenia, but for some reason, they told her she couldn't get it. If she was really as crazy as they said, she'd tie a string around her tooth and pull it out herself.

But she was on meds now and not crazy anymore. She looked at her orchid, and at the blank TV screen, and at her refrigerator.

It sure was boring not to be crazy.

She picked up a romance novel she'd been trying to get through for weeks now. *On a White Horse*. It was about a waitress in a cowboy town who meets a customer who really likes her. He pretends to be poor, and she resists falling in love, but eventually she gives in, and then he reveals who he really is. Miranda used to love these kinds of books, but now that she was no longer delusional, they simply didn't have much appeal. She read four pages and put the book down again.

She wished she could have gotten some kind of group therapy, a chance to meet other people, to talk freely. But the only group they offered her was one with drug addicts—poor, uneducated people she had nothing in common with. So she was left meeting her psychiatrist once every two months, alone. He was good, she supposed, but it simply wasn't enough.

She thought about calling some of her old Mormon friends, back from her days in the Single Adults group at church. That had been twenty-five years ago. It was remarkable really that they still kept in touch, especially considering her awful behavior as her schizophrenia grew more and more pronounced.

Why hadn't they abandoned her? The parents who'd adopted her were long dead, and her boyfriend of several years had died of ALS a few years back, a decade after he'd married another woman. She hadn't had Visiting Teachers from church in twenty years.

But she still had friends. Jerry, and Tammy, and Ed, and a few others, too. How could it be?

Was it possible they actually *liked* her?

They'd put up with her wild stories all these years, but now she found she could hardly ever call them. What did she have to talk about, if there were no FBI plots against her? If the girl at Burger King really wasn't putting toenails in her Whoppers? If the Relief Society president at church wasn't sending out nude postcards of Miranda sitting on the toilet to scare off the single men in the ward?

She felt bad she'd tortured her friends with her bizarre complaints all that time, but she felt even worse now to bore them to tears with her thoroughly uneventful life.

She turned on the TV. An infomercial for facial cream. Miranda sighed and turned the channel. Not an infomercial this time, just a regular, tedious commercial for Honda. She'd saved up $700 over the past year to buy a car, but seeing the price for a shiny new one was depressing. She hit the Off button.

She wanted to take a walk and use up some energy so she could fall asleep, but it was after midnight now. She wasn't *that* crazy.

Miranda decided to do some push-ups. She couldn't do real ones, of course, like men did, and even girl push-ups on her knees were hard. So she did a modified version, leaning against her kitchen counter at a 60-degree angle and going down to meet the counter. Mark, her gay friend in San Francisco, said she couldn't really call those girl push-ups. He called them fairy push-ups.

That kind of joking used to bug her. She hated anyone thinking she was a lesbian because she wasn't married. And it irritated her that a terrible sinner like Mark could have a good life after leaving the Church, when she'd suffered for years trying to reconcile her sex life with LDS teachings. She was only having sex to catch a man, wasn't she, and she had to catch a man to get married in the temple, which was the highest goal a Mormon girl could aspire to.

But despite all the terrible things she'd said to Mark over the years, he'd stayed her friend. He was the one who finally talked her into getting help. He must like her, too.

Miranda thought she understood what Sally Field had meant at the Oscars.

All those years Miranda had felt alone, had almost gloried in it. And all that time she could have enjoyed her friends instead. What might life have been like if she'd never been sick? If she had simply managed to get on meds sooner? She might have had a real life.

Now that she'd exercised, Miranda felt hungry and wanted a piece of bread. Maybe some toast with butter.

No. She drank a full glass of water instead to try to fill her stomach. She was still hungry, though, and drank half a glass more. The water made her tooth throb, so she took an aspirin. She looked about her apartment slowly, searching for something, though not sure just what. Finally, she sighed again, heavily, then undressed and went to bed.

Miranda worked the next day as well, and the biggest problem for most of her shift was learning the new computer system the company had installed. That, plus being short-staffed, made the day hectic. So when Aaron, the guy in 103, asked to be left alone to smoke outside, Miranda assented readily. She didn't want anyone thinking she was out there smoking pot.

The problem was what happened fifteen minutes later. Aaron couldn't maneuver his wheelchair back through the door and rammed the doorframe repeatedly as he tried to get back in. By the time any of the nurses saw what was happening, the frame was ruined.

"Who left Aaron outside by himself?" Jessica demanded. She was the shift supervisor.

"Well, I did," Miranda admitted, "but he asked me to."

"He's in a wheelchair and can barely use his arms. What were you thinking?"

She was thinking about all the extra work Jessica was making her do because the director had fired Shari and Katrice for no reason. She felt a flare of anger rising inside her, the way she used to always feel when she thought her previous boss was making up complaints about head lice to put in her file to get her fired.

The familiarity of that anger was comforting, but Miranda took a breath and said softly, "I'm sorry. I won't do it again. You can deduct the cost of the repairs from my paycheck."

"No, no, we won't do that, but I will have to put it in your file. Just be more careful in the future."

And that was that. Miranda was still angry at Aaron, who she suspected had damaged the door deliberately, just to be an asshole, but she still had her job. She'd had this one for eleven months now, ever since her meds had stabilized her mood. After losing seven jobs over the previous four years, she was doing pretty good. She went back to her desk and focused again on inputting information with the new program.

Miranda took a moment during her lunch break to check her appointment calendar. There wasn't much on it. A meeting with her NAMI social worker and another one for her first annual review coming up. But it was the dental appointment she wanted to think about. Two more days until she could have her wisdom teeth pulled out.

She'd had one pulled when she was in her early twenties. Why they didn't take them all at the same time, she didn't know, but she was going to have the remaining three removed this Thursday. It would be terrible to lose all the money she'd saved up for the car, but if that forced her to keep walking everywhere, maybe she'd lose a little more weight. Perhaps this was God's way of looking out for her.

As her shift drew to a close, Miranda started brushing her hair. Tomorrow, she'd color it so her roots would be brown again before her dental appointment. She'd always had luxurious hair. Luana noticed her brushing and smiled. "Boy, you must have really been pretty when you were young."

Miranda's hand froze over her hair. Had she really just heard that? Her particular manifestation with the schizophrenia had always been auditory hallucinations. She was continually thinking people were saying horrible things to her.

"Thank you," Miranda said, putting the brush down. "I used to be smart, too."

"Oh, well, you're *still* smart."

Miranda smiled.

She was home by 7:30 that evening and thought how pleasant it would be to watch some primetime television. The advertising drove her crazy, of course. She wondered for a moment if it was infuriating things like commercials which drove people over the edge.

Or was it politics? She saw a report about some state—was it Arizona?—that wanted to outlaw cursing. What was truly amazing was that there weren't *more* crazy people in the world.

Miranda had just sat down on her sofa in front of the television with a sandwich when there was a tremendous crash, and she dropped her tray on the floor. "What the—?"

She stared at her kitchen. Half the ceiling had fallen in. There was sheetrock and water everywhere. If she'd been in there…

Miranda called the landlord, who came quickly and determined that the bottom of the water heater upstairs had rusted out. He would get someone over in the next few days to fix everything and make sure no mold started growing. "You gonna be okay?"

"At least it wasn't the bathroom," Miranda said, "or the bedroom." Maybe this would cut down on her calories, too. She wondered if it were her battle with weight over decades which had made her crazy. There seemed to be no end to the maddening things in one's life.

But it was liberating not to be thinking it was her bishop who had rigged this to eliminate her for trying to have an affair with a Mormon doctor. It really wasn't a sign that the CIA was after her for feeding stray cats. How awful it had been to believe all those things for so many years. For a moment, she felt sorry for that old Miranda, but then she smiled at herself in the bathroom mirror, happy with the new one.

It was just after 9:00 now, a little late for taking a walk, but she decided to lose a last 120 calories before the day was over. She hurried the last little bit of her walk, sensing someone following her, but she slept well that night anyway.

The following day, Miranda worked yet again, almost unheard of since she was just PRN, but the nursing home, of course, was still short-staffed. "Now, I can't make over $1000 a month," Miranda reminded her supervisor. "You're going to have to hire someone else to take Shari's and Katrice's positions."

"We're interviewing today," Jessica said. "I understand you're off tomorrow, but on Friday, we'll need you to help train the new girl."

Train? thought Miranda. What a bother. It wasn't as if she'd get paid extra for it. But then, it might be something she could put on her resumé. Sometimes, she felt Jessica was deliberately holding her back so she couldn't become more valuable as an employee and go somewhere else that paid better.

Miranda certainly didn't want to stay at the nursing home the rest of her life. What if she grew old here? Would she just go from being an employee to being a resident? There was no one else who was going to take care of her.

She'd be at the mercy of all the incompetent, mean staff. Miranda shuddered and went to go check on Aaron, who'd pushed his call button again.

"Can I help you?" she asked sweetly as she entered his room.

"Yes," he said, pointing to his crotch and smiling. Miranda turned around and left the room without a word.

The rest of the day passed uneventfully. Mrs. Smith in 109 snapped at her once for no apparent reason, but Miranda understood that old sick people were unhappy. She was really quite good at ignoring things like that. Luana offered Miranda some hard peppermint candy near the end of her shift, which Miranda thought slightly insensitive, considering her teeth, but the offer seemed to be made sincerely enough. Miranda wondered if she had bad breath.

The next morning was the big day. Miranda got ready for the dentist and walked three miles to his office. Damn the pathetic bus system on the Westbank. Sometimes, she wondered if the transit director put a pin in the map where Miranda lived and deliberately routed every bus line far from her.

She shook her head. No need to be paranoid, she thought, smiling.

"Good morning, Miranda," Dr. Gonzalez said cheerily as he came into the room where she was sitting on the dental chair. "You're looking good today."

Miranda smiled, glad she'd fixed her hair especially nice. It would be too wonderful if she could marry a dentist and be a stay-at-home mom. She wasn't too old to adopt, was she? Her parents had certainly been old.

Dr. Gonzalez picked up a huge hypodermic and started injecting her, just a few jabs, but they seemed to last a long time. Then he pulled the first tooth, in her upper right jaw. It didn't come easily, and Miranda felt wrenched halfway out of the chair. Then she heard a clink as he dropped the tooth into a metal basin.

How disgusting. Miranda wondered if a patient could look attractive with blood oozing out of her mouth. At least her pretty hair was still showing.

Next came another series of injections, lots this time, as Dr. Gonzalez deadened both her upper left and lower left jaw. He seemed to have even more difficulty with the second tooth, muttering about it being broken. He pulled and pulled, and after Miranda felt surely he must be done, he went back in and pulled again. Was he taking out more than just the one lower tooth? Was he trying to force her to buy dentures?

The procedure didn't hurt, but Miranda couldn't help but see the blood on Dr. Gonzalez's mask. She had a fleeting thought that maybe he was trying to damage her mouth so she'd have to come in for further work, giving him more money. Then, just as she heard another clink in the metal basin, she heard him whisper to his assistant, "We'll see what she looks like after all this is done."

Miranda wanted to get up from the chair and run out of the office, but she calmed herself down. She understood what was happening. She hadn't taken her meds the last few days because they made her too sleepy at work. *You're hearing things*, she told herself. *It's all in your head. It's going to be okay.*

She'd take her meds tomorrow, and she'd be fine again. She felt a little sad to realize she could never miss even a single dose. It must be like being a diabetic, she thought. You had to have your insulin every day. At least she realized what was going on, though, not like all those years before when she'd thought everything was real.

She still wondered sometimes if the EEOC had hidden a camera in her apartment so they could put a nude picture of her on the internet. Just because you were paranoid didn't mean someone wasn't truly after you. Was that picture the reason why the dentist had agreed to have her pay only $600 for removing three wisdom teeth?

Extracting the last tooth was excruciating. It, too, was broken, and instead of pulling one tooth, it felt like the dentist was pulling three. One last bit seemed fused to her jaw, and Dr. Gonzalez practically put his foot on the chair to give him leverage. Miranda felt sure he must have damaged her jaw in the process. He was sweating, and so was the assistant.

Finally, finally, it was time to go home. Miranda could hardly talk, but she thanked the dentist and went to the bathroom before leaving. When she looked at herself in the mirror, she was horrified. She was sweating, too, and despite her bib, there was blood on her shirt, ruining it. But the worst part was that her mouth was so heavily novocained that the entire left side of her face was drooping as if she'd had a stroke. She looked like a monster. And she'd have to walk three miles home looking like this.

Miranda straightened her shoulders and started out the door. There was no pain, what with all the anesthetic, but she wondered if the dentist had pulled out every last bit of her broken tooth or not. Had he just given up before he finished, because it was too hard? There was something about the look in his eyes that made her suspicious. Maybe he'd damaged her nerves, and he knew she'd look like this permanently.

The first mile wasn't too bad. It was mostly a good neighborhood. But as Miranda drew closer to her own, the area changed. More blighted and abandoned houses. More empty lots filled with weeds. More black people.

She wasn't prejudiced, of course. Even the Church let black men have the priesthood these days. But she'd been mugged once before. You didn't forget things like that.

Well, it had been a white man who'd broken into the house when she still lived with her father. A nude white man who barked like a dog. Miranda's father had shot him dead on top of her.

That was all *real*. It had made the front page of the newspaper.

Miranda should have brought a walking stick so she'd have a weapon if she needed one. She tensed when she saw a black teenage boy approaching her. Oh, my god, this was it. He came closer and closer, his eyebrows furrowing as he neared her. He was going to attack.

"Ooga booga!" Miranda lunged toward the boy with her drooping lips and bloodied shirt. He took off running.

Miranda smiled in her head, though her lips wouldn't cooperate.

Back home, Miranda took a nap. She enjoyed being able to work part-time on call and just relax all the rest of the time. Sure, sometimes it was boring, but that was better than feeling one's every waking moment was spent at work. She picked up her romance novel and read for over an hour. She wondered if she should bring Dr. Gonzalez a thank-you gift in a couple of days, when she was looking pretty again.

The next day, Miranda had to train Laveatra on the computer. It was annoying, mostly because Miranda had so little experience with the new program herself. But Laveatra was quick on her feet and didn't cause too much trouble. Still, it would have been nice to have been able to take some pain medication before coming to the nursing home. Miranda's jaw was killing her.

Mrs. Smith made a couple more nasty comments today, but most of the other residents behaved themselves. Miranda had a pleasant lunch with Luana, and Jessica said she was interviewing one more applicant for the remaining position. Miranda was feeling good and thought maybe she'd made the right decision not to take her meds again this morning.

She certainly couldn't afford to be sleepy at work on a day she had to train someone. And really, wouldn't her body develop a tolerance to the medication, make her immune to its good effects, if she took it every day?

Besides, those pills were for crazy people, and she obviously wasn't *really* crazy. People were always trying to make her look bad. Perhaps she should only take them once a week for a while and see how that went. They did seem to help her lose weight.

"I've got to go to Aaron's room," Laveatra said after Miranda came back from lunch. "I'm afraid to go in there by myself. Will you come?"

Miranda nodded. She'd always been willing to go the extra mile. Too bad no one had ever done that for her. But she believed in the commandment, "Do unto others." She wanted people to be nice to her, so she was going to be nice to them. If other people wouldn't return the favor, God surely would at some point.

Miranda stood off to the side while Laveatra waited on Aaron, mostly letting her mind wander, just there to offer moral support. But then as Laveatra leaned over Aaron as he lay in bed, Miranda heard him whisper to the new girl, "Don't get too close to her. She's been targeted for elimination."

Miranda's mouth fell open. Aaron was a Jew, wasn't he, she realized suddenly. He was probably with the Mossad. But why would they be after her? What had she ever done against Israel?

Then she gasped. *Dr. Khalid.* But that was three jobs ago.

She had another sudden thought. Had the Mossad been behind her kitchen ceiling collapsing? Had that been a *murder* attempt? Was the Mossad trying to *assassinate* her?

"That'll teach her for flirting with an Arab," Miranda heard Aaron whisper to Laveatra.

Miranda ran out of the room and down the hall. How could he *say* that? How *could* he? It just wasn't true. Dr. Khalid had always flirted with *her*.

Miranda ran into the bathroom and sat on the toilet, crying. Just when things had started going so well. And now people were being mean to her all over again. What was *wrong* with them? Why couldn't people just be *nice*?

She had to admit, she was thinking much more clearly now that she was off those meds. That must be part of the plot as well. To keep her mind all muddled. She'd toss the rest of the pills down the toilet when she got home. She'd just have to walk extra to lose weight now.

Miranda gave as little instruction as possible to Laveatra the rest of the day. The girl hadn't shown that she was in on the plot, but Miranda knew Laveatra would want to be part of it soon enough, and Miranda had to try to keep some control over her. She walked home slowly, too tired to worry about getting mugged, yet still looking over her shoulder every couple of minutes out of habit.

She moaned when she walked in the door, forgetting that it was going to be such a hassle to prepare dinner. If only she had some appetite suppressants, she thought. She remembered a pill called AYDS way back in the early 1980s. The company had quickly changed the name when associating AYDS with rapid weight loss was no longer a selling feature. Miranda wondered if the pills had *caused* the terrible epidemic that followed. You certainly couldn't trust pharmaceutical companies.

Miranda put a Lean Cuisine in the microwave and ate it quickly, but she was still hungry afterward. She thought about having another frozen dinner, but she didn't want to gain back all the weight she'd just lost. She glanced toward the bathroom door. Would it kill her to take her meds just one more time? But what if it were those pills that were making her crazy in the first place?

It was just so hard to know what to do. Had the Church put Mark up to talking her into seeing a psychiatrist? Miranda wondered if all those people from the old Single Adults group were just being told by the bishop to keep tabs on her. They were only pretending to be her friends.

If Miranda could just get down to 180 pounds, she was sure Dr. Gonzalez would ask her out. And if he didn't, Miranda could always get another job at a hospital where she'd run into *real* doctors every day.

Maybe she'd take the pills and then go on an hour-long walk. It was cloudy out now, not too hot, and still light. And she'd take her walking stick this time.

Miranda got down on her knees and prayed about it, and she decided to take the risk. She simply had to lose weight if she was going to attract someone rich. She walked decisively to the bathroom, grabbed her pills, and swallowed them quickly before she could change her mind. Her jaw was still hurting, so she took a couple of aspirin, too.

Damn those broken wisdom teeth. But they'd be okay in a few days. And she'd be pretty again soon. She let out a huge breath of air, picked up her walking stick, and headed out the door.

Killing Them with Kindness

Immunology was the only class I made a C in while working on my undergraduate Biology degree. I made A's in both Organic Chemistry courses and a B+ in Biochemistry, but Immunology was complicated.

So it's odd, I suppose, that I ended up as an HIV researcher.

It's not that I felt an overwhelming impulse to help cure the disease. My brother Bill was gay and died in the early 1990s of AIDS. I felt it was God's retribution for his leaving the Mormon Church. It was obvious, though, that lots of people were going to catch the virus, and if I studied HIV, I'd have job security for a long while.

When I told my wife Jenna about my motivation, she said I was a cold fish. I felt bad about that until a few years ago, when I took part in a blind study and discovered I had the AA genotype for the rs53576 DNA sequence of the oxytocin receptor gene.

Okay, okay. I know you don't know what that is. I didn't either at first, but I do feel I finally need to express myself here in this open letter. The fact is that while often a given trait is the product of multiple genes, this one DNA sequence seems to be largely responsible for a person's ability to feel kindness or empathy. The study I was in basically just tried to determine whether a complete stranger would be able to detect if someone else had the gene.

People with GG have the empathy gene. People with AA do not, and people with AG have one copy of the gene. Participants were asked by their spouse to listen to a story about an incident of suffering in their life. Then other study subjects were asked to watch the listener's reaction to their spouse's story.

Nine out of ten observers could quickly tell who had the AA genotype. They saw almost immediately and quite clearly that those listeners couldn't be trusted to care. On the other hand, six out of ten participants who seemed especially social to observers were found to carry the GG genotype.

Further discussion showed that, in general, those with the AG or AA genotypes had more negative personalities and felt less bonding with their children.

It was a revelation for me. I suddenly understood why I preferred working late to spending time with my family. I understood why I didn't like mentoring graduate students. I understood why I didn't want to accept teaching positions at church, why I never considered volunteer work, why I rarely gave to charity.

It wasn't my fault.

Of course, that conclusion wasn't fully satisfactory as an answer. Bill probably had a genetic component to his homosexuality, but it had still been his duty to overcome it and lead a righteous life. People had genes influencing their tendency to become alcoholics, but it was nevertheless a sin to drink, and they had an obligation to live appropriately regardless. So I still *needed* to be kind, even if it didn't come naturally.

How else could I earn the Celestial Kingdom and rule entire worlds?

But I began to wonder. If Jenna had the GG genotype, as seemed evident by her behavior, was it any great accomplishment for her to be nice? Wasn't that like saying it was a wonderful achievement for someone with a high IQ to pass a spelling test? Or for someone who wasn't color-blind to be able to distinguish red from green?

Maybe *only* those people in Alcoholics Anonymous were righteous for not drinking. Maybe *only* people with AA genotypes were good when helping someone in the Elders Quorum pack and move. Perhaps it was better not to have the gene. Only then could we truly "overcome the natural man" and merit the Celestial Kingdom by our vigilance.

But I *wanted* the world to be a better place. So did the fact that I desired this despite my genome prove I was truly a good man? Or was it like an autistic person trying to cope socially by telling himself, "He's crying—that means he's sad," without ever fully understanding the concept?

I didn't get any particularly warm and fuzzy feeling for wanting the world to be a happier place to live. I simply thought it might be a way of ushering in the Millennium. Once everyone was kind, a thousand years of peace seemed inevitable. Even if I didn't really give a damn about what people were feeling, something inside me wanted them to experience love.

And you couldn't truly feel love if you didn't care about your fellow man. I suppose in a way it was like a stage mother who could never fulfill her own dreams and therefore pushed her child to become a star so she could live vicariously through her. I did feel empathy for *me*.

It was as if I had two diverging lines of command running through me, and believe me, I struggled for many months over what to do with this knowledge.

Then I had another revelation.

HIV was such a terrible infection because it was more than simply a foreign entity living inside a human body. It inserted itself into the very DNA of its hosts. The HIV became *part* of the host. That's why it was so difficult to eradicate. It was like trying to cut out the gene for lipid formation, a code which existed in every cell of the body, whether that code was actively being used by a given cell. HIV even crossed the blood-brain barrier, making it a perfect vector for my plans.

I figured out a way to splice the GG genome into a culture of HIV, tricky since the virus was composed of RNA rather than the typical DNA. By working closely with the medical team developing an HIV vaccine, though, I was able to place my altered virus into their vaccines undetected.

Tens of thousands of people were lined up to be inoculated, once the vaccine was approved, so in one fell swoop, I was able to insert the empathy gene into the DNA of vast numbers of people. Even better was the knowledge that given the nature of how HIV was spread, those numbers would soon be increasing exponentially. Tracking down who was infected would be like trying to count the stars at night.

So even with my inferior AA genome, I managed to do the kindest thing anyone had done since Jesus Christ atoned for our sins. Surely, this qualifies me for the highest degree of heaven, whatever society thinks of me at this point. I know the liberal media has maligned not only me but also the LDS Church, blaming it for my actions.

People should instead be praising any possible doctrines that led to my epiphany. And praising the cool detachment with which I interpreted those teachings to make some very difficult decisions.

After the vaccines were delivered, I decided to do one more kindness, another victory over my Telestial genome. I was going to deliberately infect myself as well, so I could finally listen to Jenna without growing bored. It would be like bringing my own body closer to a perfected state by myself, without having to wait for the resurrection. And maybe once I was a GG, I'd be able to do more research and find a cure for cancer and Alzheimer's and other mortal conditions.

But then I wondered if it would take me away from the lab and make me spend more time with my children. That seemed a real possibility. Perhaps I should just keep working. Maybe *some* people should stay AA. "There must needs be opposition in all things," I remembered from the Book of Mormon. Perhaps that included alleles, too.

I suppose I was playing God, but I figured it was like lion cubs playing together, having fun as they clawed at one another but really learning how to behave as adults in the process. I was just showing our own God that I was ready for the challenge of godhood.

But I realized my own kids had gotten an A from me even if they did get a G from Jenna. So I inoculated both of them as well and gave them two G's. It was the least a father could do. Sure, the modified vaccine carries the most lethal version of the virus, but it was the only one I could get to splice correctly. Obviously, there are plenty of meds out there to keep everyone alive, at least for several years. And I only killed one police officer when they came to arrest me.

I'm writing this letter the night before my execution in the hopes that some newspaper will print it. *Deseret News*, at the very least, but I'd prefer the national audience I truly deserve, even an international one. I can't win the Nobel Prize posthumously, of course, and the committee probably wouldn't know whether to award it in Chemistry, Biology, or Peace in any event.

From my vast personal experience in the lab, I think there are plenty of other scientists out there who share my genomic AA inferiority, so it is primarily you I'm addressing. Many of you are atheists, but I testify to you that God promised we can make "weak things become strong unto us," and I steadfastly encourage any of you with a healthy intellect and a discerning soul to continue my work making weak genomes into strong ones to save the human race.

I suppose we could always simply *teach* people how to empathize, but don't you think my way is easier? The gospel teaches us that Satan's plan was to *force* people to be good, which was inherently flawed, while Christ's plan was to let them choose and then atone for any mistakes, certainly an improvement. But *my* way is better than either of those proposals. With my plan, people still have free agency, but they'll *want* to choose kinder actions. It's a win/win situation.

So I gladly go to my death a martyr. My last request is for all of you to help spread my strain of HIV everywhere you can. Well over 200,000 people were inoculated before anyone discovered what I was doing, and they'll undoubtedly spread the virus more on their own. Or even just procreate and pass the genes to their children.

Beyond that, I quickly discovered that HIV vaccines weren't the only vaccines which could be contaminated with my new version of the virus.

Perhaps I shouldn't have let that slip, but I also probably have the gene for ego. No one's perfect, after all. Not yet. Anyway, I did it for the betterment of mankind. Because I'm like Gandhi, and like King, like Christ himself, those with the AA genotype feel they must do everything they can to try to stop my work.

The next step forward will be to find the gene sequences that create naysayers and fear and people who would rather destroy than uplift. I wish I could have done more work.

But I've done a tangible good in the world, and I'll sleep well tonight.

I wonder, though, if one could do some useful gene splicing with convicts on Death Row, so that at least they'd be resurrected later with good genes already in their system. What kind of reformation could we bring about if all convicts for any crime at all were injected with GG their first day in prison? If politicians were empathetic? CEOs? Boy, I wish I simply had more time to do all the wonderful things that are coming to mind.

I can't help but think of that little fish emblem I've seen on the back of some cars, with four tiny feet underneath and the word "Darwin" written inside the fish.

Maybe once I'm gone, some nice young entrepreneur will start selling double helices to glue onto those cars. And maybe one of them will have my name on it, too.

The Occupiers

I voted for Ronald Reagan in 1984, as did most other faithful Latter-day Saints, but by the time the next presidential election came around, I was a determined liberal. What had changed during the intervening years was that I had come out of the closet, and in the process, come to the conclusion that the authoritarian, restrictive Church I belonged to was not, in fact, “the one and only true church” on the planet.

Once I began questioning, I realized there were lots of “causes” out there largely ignored by Mormons that were important to me. Women did deserve equality. I no longer believed Blacks had been fence-sitters during the Pre-Existence. America was no more “chosen” by God than the Roman Empire had been in its time. Abortion did seem like something the woman should decide for herself.

Although I disapproved of things like meth and heroin, I also felt the “war on drugs” was designed more to disenfranchise African Americans from voting rights than anything else. I was none too happy with the privatization of prisons, either, for that matter. Or the effort to privatize schools and public utilities and everything else.

Still, despite my newly opened eyes, I continued to move through life in a relatively conservative fashion. I taught college English for fourteen years and liked it well enough, but universities were only taking me on as an adjunct, which meant I taught more than the regular faculty but received no benefits and less than half their pay. It obviously struck me as unfair, yet I was slow in coming to the realization that our entire economic system might be corrupt. I simply moved on to another job.

I enjoyed being a teller at Pacific Northwest Credit Union in Seattle. Customer service was right up my alley. Taking in checks and balancing a cash drawer were simple tasks, and the occasional difficult customer was easy enough to ignore. But life began to change around 2009. The job description started to shift.

Rather than be concerned with customer satisfaction, we were increasingly told that sales were all that mattered. Yes, a bad member survey rating would count against us, but a good one did nothing in our favor. The only thing that truly registered come annual evaluation was whether or not we reached our ever higher loan goals.

I went through loan training and began processing loans in addition to opening new accounts and still working the teller line. But loan applications were miserable, and even worse was trying to interest people in applying in the first place. I worked at the City Hall branch, the smallest branch in our entire system, and because of our location right across the street from City Hall, we mostly had visits from the same hundred and fifty people over and over again.

Terry Lee, for instance, came in every single day, sometimes twice a day. Tom Masterson also came in three times a week during his lunch break. We were his social outlet at work. Naomi came in to get money orders once a week. Bob came to completely cash out his check because he didn't trust financial institutions. Mary came to deposit checks into her daughter's account. We knew almost everyone by name because our clientele was so limited. How could you ask the same person thirty times if they wanted a loan?

"I got a 2.69 on my annual review," said Anna, my coworker. There were just the two of us at our branch. Our manager was stationed at another branch nearby. "I'm on probation. If I don't make my loan goals this month, I'm going to be fired."

"That's terrible. You've been here thirty-one years, Anna. You're good at your job."

"Not anymore, Garth. The job is sales now. And I suck at sales."

"Well, I can't be far behind. I've only made my loan goals twice in the last six months."

"I've never made mine even once."

Anna never did get fired, despite repeated threats, but things grew increasingly stressful as our loan goals not only didn't decrease because of our limited clientele but rose by $5000 each month. On some days, we waited on only three or four people apiece in an hour, but we were expected to rake in $35,000 in car loans each month, and then $40,000, and then $45,000.

I did get almost fifty home loan referrals one quarter when our rates were at forty-year lows, but even though that must have led to millions in loans for the credit union, none of that counted toward my personal loan goals. Whenever I made my new member goal for the month, or my new checking account goal, or my financial investments referral goal, I would email my manager to tell him, and he'd reply, "Now do the same with your loan goals."

He'd never thank me for reaching any of the other goals, only tell me I wasn't doing enough in the really "important" category.

"So tell me about your credit union," said a middle-aged woman who came into our branch a few weeks ago. She was a non-member, unknown to us, and just asking questions. This almost certainly meant she was a secret shopper, here to evaluate us. I made sure to smile pleasantly.

"We started in 1932," I said, "during the Depression. We're owned by our members, not by stockholders, so our obligation is to the members. We're not like big banks. They get 75-80% of their money from fees, where we get maybe 12%."

"Did you get a lot of new members during Bank Transfer Day the other week?"

"We got eight new members at this branch, which is a lot for us. Our main branch a couple of blocks away got nineteen."

"That's great. I hate banks. They created this housing mess we're in now and screwed up Wall Street but good. And then *they* get a bailout, not the little people who really need it."

Hmm, maybe she wasn't a secret shopper. Still, she left without opening any accounts, so I never knew for sure. We occasionally got someone from the plaza down below, where Occupy Seattle was headquartered for a while before moving up to Capitol Hill near the community college. But even after the move, there were a few tents which remained on the plaza. One day, a young man about twenty-five came in to open an account.

"I need a checking account so I can help buy things we need at Occupy Seattle," he said.

"Do you have a valid, unexpired ID?" I asked.

He handed it to me.

"And is this your current address, Alan?" I always asked that first because anti-terrorist rules meant that without proof of a current address, we couldn't open any accounts. He said it was, and I ran the OFAC list and saw he wasn't on it, always a good sign. "Looks like you're not a terrorist," I said, smiling.

"I was in the Army," he replied. "Got out four years ago. Nobody wants to hire a vet. We have too many problems." He shrugged.

I next pulled Chexsystems to see if Alan owed money to other financial institutions. He did, $65 to Bank of America and $432 to Wells Fargo. Both entries listed "account fraud" as the conclusion. There was no point in running a credit report and continuing with the screening process. He'd already volunteered that he knew his credit was bad in any event.

"Alan, what happened at Bank of America and Wells Fargo?"

"My card got stolen. That was all settled at the time."

"Well, you'll need to get a letter from both institutions stating that before we'll be able to move on."

He didn't get mad. He just looked resigned and said, "Living on the street is pretty hard."

"I thought this was your current address?" I pointed to the driver's license. If the current address wasn't a physical address, he'd have been ineligible for membership in any event.

"That's a maildrop. I've been on the street for four years. But I'm doing something good now. I'm a medic with Occupy Seattle. I was a medic in the Army."

I shook his hand as he left, and when he was gone, Anna said, "Gonna wash your hands?"

The incident left me feeling uncomfortable. Usually, when I met a panhandler on the street who asked for money, I'd say, "Not today, pal, but good luck," hoping he'd feel less ignored if I at least acknowledged him, but truthfully, I had the typical reaction to the homeless.

"Go away, kid, you bother me." W.C. Fields discomfort, but for the unhoused.

These people had done something wrong and were on the street most likely because of an alcohol or drug problem. It was pointless to give money to them, though I did give to a couple of local charities for the poor like Farestart and The Millionair Club. I was still rather Republican in my attitudes.

Yet my own finances were pretty iffy. I made $15.90 an hour, the most I'd ever made at any job, and I'd bought a house for the first time two years ago when I was forty-eight. I'd only managed to buy it at all because my grandmother had left me enough for a down payment when she died a couple of years before that.

If with all that help I could still barely function, how did that make me superior to folks who never had the same breaks?

My partner Derek and I lived in a 1950 ranch in Columbia City, a poor section of Seattle, and the house was falling apart. The tax appraisal showed that the building itself was only worth $65,000 while the land around it was worth another $70,000. But we still owed $73,000, and with no earthquake insurance to be had in the region, we could lose the house without warning and still owe all the money. As it was, I only managed to save $25 each month. Every last cent of the rest went to bills.

Derek was a small contractor and only worked maybe one week a month. He had no health insurance, so I paid for that through the credit union. He was sensitive about his financial situation and hid the bills from me. "Don't take this out of my hands," he said once when I complained. "I need to have some responsibility to feel like a human being."

But I came home one day to find our cable and internet cut off because he hadn't paid the bill, and the next day, I looked through his mail and found a cut-off warning for the water. I took the bill and paid it without saying anything, but I also found the electric bill, postmarked three weeks ago, so

I asked Derek if he was going to be able to pay that the next day.

"I'll take care of it," he said gruffly and changed the subject.

The following day, I saw that the bill was still unopened, so I put a note on his desk when I left for work, asking again if he could pay the bill that day. The bill was gone when I got home, but Derek never said a word about it, so I didn't know if the electricity was going to be cut off or not at any moment.

It was an uncomfortable way to live, and this wasn't the first time we'd been through this scenario. My one credit card was maxed out at $19,000, an outrageous and embarrassing amount, but when someone was pretty much the sole breadwinner for the family, there wasn't much choice.

That plus the remaining $22,000 on my student loan had me feeling overwhelmed. I worried I might have to declare bankruptcy, but even then, you couldn't default on a student loan, and I didn't want to include the house in any proceedings, so that would only eliminate one bill and yet still destroy my credit.

"I have something to tell you," Derek said one evening. I knew it was bad news by his tone. We'd been partners for three years. My previous partner of eighteen years had died six years back of stomach cancer, and Derek had split with his partner of seventeen years four years ago because that partner had become an alcoholic.

"Yes?"

"I owe the IRS $450,000."

I stared at him, my mouth hanging open. "How is that even possible?" I asked. "You make less than I do."

"I couldn't pay my taxes five years ago, and I got a penalty. I haven't been able to pay ever since, and the penalties and fines keep getting bigger. The IRS scoops money out of my account any time I have over a hundred in there, so when I try to pay bills, there's always a zero balance. I started out owing $7,000, and now it's up to almost half a million."

"Derek, I've known you for three and a half years. Why didn't you ever tell me this before?"

"It's embarrassing."

I'd always believed in taxation and still did, very much a Democrat on this issue. Society couldn't function without an infrastructure, and that had to be paid for through taxes. Still, it struck me as unfair to take every penny out of a man's account, despite whatever he owed. If Derek didn't have me to pay the mortgage, he'd be homeless. How could the IRS ever expect to get any money from him then?

"Well, you can start putting your earnings into my savings account," I suggested, "and then we'll use that to pay our utilities." I expected that to the IRS the money would then look like my own income and I'd have to pay taxes on it myself, but so be it.

"It makes me feel useless to have you do everything."

"But it'll still be your money."

He sighed. "I guess we don't have any choice." He looked at the floor. "That's assuming I ever make any more money, of course."

I'd tried to talk him into getting a job at Lowe's or Home Depot for months, thinking that would be up his alley, give him a steady income and pay his health insurance, too, but now I understood why he'd resisted. He could work forty hours a week and still not have a cent to show for it. If he was going to be poor in any event, he may as well be doing something he liked.

I called my dad and hinted at our money troubles, trying to feel him out. The hints must have been obvious, though, because he finally said, "I love you, son, but I won't support you in your lifestyle. If you want to repent, I can maybe help you out, but otherwise, you have to face the consequences of your actions."

I emailed a friend in Colorado about Derek's revelation, and Jeremy said, "Kick the bum out. You've got to think of yourself. Find a partner who can pull his own weight."

Breaking up, of course, wasn't even an option. Everyone came with their own set of faults. I rarely helped with the gardening, for instance, and I wasn't that great in bed. Derek had resisted my suggestion for a legal marriage in another state, and now I understood his reasoning there, too. If we were married, I'd be responsible for all his debts as well as my own. His turning down my proposal had been because he loved me.

Browsing online, I was drawn to an article about finances and read some startling statistics. A full 48% of

Americans were either low income or in actual poverty. I remembered hearing that someone, perhaps Henry Ford, had said you had to pay your employees enough to buy your products, but I wasn't sure that was something employers believed anymore.

I kept reading and saw that 18% of homes in Florida were now vacant because of foreclosures or other problems related to the collapsed housing market. 19% of adults between the ages of twenty-five and thirty-four in this country lived with their parents. 41% of Americans were having problems paying off medical debt. I thought again about how Obama's attempt at creating universal healthcare had failed. I began to wonder for the first time if Derek and I were going to be able to make it.

I wanted to give a presentation on these statistics at the weekly business meeting at the main branch of the credit union, the teacher in me itching to share. But I could already imagine the other tellers nodding off, the branch managers rolling their eyes.

With all of this on my mind, I was unprepared for what happened at work the next day. "I got a 2.86 on my annual review," I told Anna. "I'm on probation, too."

"What do they expect from us?"

"More."

And the next day, "more" is what we got. Our HR director came to the City Hall branch to talk to each of us alone. "We're closing this branch in two months," Hsin-yi told me quietly in our tiny kitchen. "We can offer you a teller position at either the Downtown branch or the Rainier branch, Garth, but you'll still be on probation. Or you can take a severance package. We'll pay you two weeks' salary for each year you've worked here. For you, that's six years, so that'll be twelve weeks of pay. We'll give you a week to make your decision, but don't tell anyone about this yet."

I was dumbfounded but quickly did the math. Twelve weeks of pay would come to about $8266, probably around $6000 after taxes. That would keep me going two or three months if I couldn't find a job right away.

"There will be other changes, too," Hsin-yi continued. "The Lynnwood branch will be getting rid of the teller line altogether. We'll get a 'recycler' that both takes in money and dispenses money. The only thing the employees will be doing is opening new accounts and processing loans."

"No more customer service," I said.

"Giving people loans is service."

I nodded. At our last all-branch meeting, our senior finance officer had spoken about how we'd lost a great deal of money in bad loans because so many people had been laid off in the last couple of years. The only way to make that up, she said, was by doing more loans. It struck me as odd that the credit union believed the way to make up losses was by repeating the action which had created the losses. It felt like we were doing more and more what had almost brought down the big banks in the first place.

I made a mental note to check out the documentary *Inside Job* from the library. I'd heard about its scathing indictment of banks and Wall Street but had thought the subject too boring to watch. Maybe I ought to rethink that.

"Once we see how that works, we'll be instituting the same model at other branches," Hsin-yi went on, but I was barely listening. All I could do was translate her previous comment in my head: "Putting people further in debt is service."

There were more comments about why the credit union would soon start timing how long it took us to do transactions, how much paper each teller used, how long we spent in the bathroom.

I knew I'd be taking the severance package, but I still wanted to wait the full week before giving my official answer. I went home that night and told Derek, who was reluctant for me to leave, saying plaintively, "I want more financial stability in my life!"

I laughed and said, "So do I!"

I went online and looked up jobs with the City. Despite a huge number of layoffs in the past two years, which I'd seen first-hand at my branch as dozens of regulars announced their last day of work, there were still a few job openings. I applied for a temporary, year-long position working with the tax assessor.

Then I applied for a position at Harborview Medical Center dealing with the personal effects of people who'd just died. Neither seemed a glorious career, but they also didn't seem like jobs that would entail quotas.

Over the next few days, I applied for another temporary job, this one with King County, something to do with voting. I also applied for a dozen jobs at various medical centers as a receptionist. The pay would be less, and it had the potential to be fast-paced, but it didn't look like it would involve sales.

I looked at some opportunities at Amazon, but they all seemed to mention "team goals," and that scared me off. Another job at a medical facility scanning documents also specifically stated that employees would be responsible for a certain number of pages a day. That in itself didn't sound unreasonable. It was just that I was sure the actual number required *would* be unreasonable.

Boeing didn't need anyone in customer service. Elliott Bay Bookstore wasn't hiring. The public library wasn't hiring. I tried an office position with the University of Washington. Another position came up at the City, for an Elder Abuse Advocate, and I applied for that as well.

But three weeks passed, and I didn't hear back from a single one of the applications.

Anna was feeling good. Her husband worked in a lab at Harborview, so she could get added to his health insurance, and he made enough that, while it would be difficult, they could get by on his salary alone. She was fifty-nine, too young for Social Security, but she decided she'd just stop working when the branch closed. "Twenty-six more working days," she said today, smiling, after one of our few crotchety members stopped by. "Nothing bothers me anymore."

Things still bothered me. The City Hall branch was located right across the street from Police Headquarters, so we often had police officers coming to our branch. Today, we had Ron, who would've been cute if he hadn't put hair plugs in his bald spot. "How're you doing today?" I asked as he sat down at my desk.

"Oh, getting grief from the media again. You know how they like to portray the police."

I thought back to the time a year or so ago when a local police officer had shot and killed a Native American wood carver. The wood carver had been walking with his knife, and the police officer yelled at him to drop it. Only the man was deaf and didn't hear.

"What happened?" Anna asked from her desk. She wasn't waiting on anyone, and she thought Ron was cute despite the hair plugs.

"It's that old woman who got pepper sprayed at Occupy Seattle. I'm sure you've seen the picture."

"Yes," I said.

"It wasn't like she was an innocent bystander or anything. She was a *protester*. She got what she deserved."

"I wish they would all go home," Anna said. "Such a nuisance."

"So you're not part of the 99%?" I asked, forcing a smile.

"They don't represent *me*," said Ron.

I wondered if I'd be out there with them in five weeks. I'd written to the unemployment office, telling them my exact situation, not fired, not exactly laid off, but pressured to resign from a position whose job description had changed.

Would I be eligible for benefits? They wouldn't tell me, only saying "You can always apply."

What would I do if I couldn't even get unemployment? Would we lose the house? Would one of Derek's friends take him in and one of my friends take me in? Certainly, no one would take in two people. What if no one would "adopt" us at all? Maybe we'd be on the street in just a few months.

I'd looked at job descriptions for tellers at other credit unions. They all mentioned the importance of sales as well. It looked like this was the way the industry was evolving. And I knew I didn't want to go to a bank. There were no adjunct teaching positions open, either.

As I sat on the train on my way home that evening, I wondered if God was punishing me. Maybe I hadn't committed the sin of alcohol abuse or drug use, but was Heavenly Father upset with me for leaving the Church? I'd thought I'd come to terms with this years ago, but I suppose in moments of crisis, one always doubted.

Perhaps it was punishment, though, for not doing more while I had the chance to help the other unfortunate people in the world. I never gave to those "starving children" campaigns. Or to the Peace Corps or other groups like them. I did give to Doctors without Borders occasionally, but maybe I just hadn't given enough. Derek volunteered with the Food Brigade, bringing food to the elderly once a week. He did real *things*, while at best I gave a few dollars.

Perhaps it wasn't God at all, though. Maybe it was just that the people in power were not nice people.

I took a shower after dinner and made love to Derek. It might only be a few months before I no longer had the opportunity to shower. As we sat on the sofa eating sugar cookies afterward, I felt an overwhelming sense of indulgence. Wasn't it decadent to be eating sugar cookies when so many millions of other Americans were homeless? When so many millions were unemployed and even more underemployed?

It seemed like the same kind of indifference that Mitt Romney had displayed the other night when he made his $10,000 bet with Newt Gingrich. Or his boasting about his time at Bain Capital, declaring that his experience putting people out of work and closing companies to destroy lives, all in the name of making money for the rich, qualified him for the presidency.

Perhaps I deserved to suffer, just so I could understand what other people felt. I'd thought being cast out by the Church had made me sensitive to the plight of the "other," but it turned out I could be just as cold as everyone else.

Yet if that were so, what hope was there that the 1% with all their economic and political power would ever be sensitive to the needs of the rest of us?

We weren't simply numbers. Each one of those millions and millions of people had a story as important as mine, most of them almost certainly more poignant. They were without a doubt all-consuming to each one of those millions. Everyone was the center of their own universe, and millions and millions of universes were becoming black holes.

But it was indeed almost an astronomical calculation, like trying to count the stars. The sheer magnitude of the endeavor made people cut off their emotions, just as I did by turning the channel when Sarah McLachlan started singing about abused animals.

I couldn't let myself become depressed. It would make a job search that much harder. I had to keep up my spirits. "Let's take a walk around the block," I suggested.

"It's cold."

"We need to work off those cookies."

The next day at work was slow, and I chatted amicably with most of our members. Being pleasant was the fun part of the job, remembering whose son was turning two, who'd just returned from a trip to Hawaii, whose daughter was studying fashion at college. People were not only impressed but also flattered when I remembered their member number and pulled them up on the screen even before they had time to hand me their card.

Kerry, a police officer from across the street, came in just before noon. "How's Central?" I asked. The Central District was his usual assigned area.

"Some jerk mentioned the investigation the Department of Justice is doing for our alleged police brutality. Made me want to beat the crap out of him."

I couldn't tell if he was joking or not.

Mary came in a little later. She was a Shared Brancher who always acted superior. I'd once heard her talking in favor of the Tea Party, so I usually kept our interaction professional and didn't try to engage her any further. Today, I made the mistake of asking her, "Anything fun going on in your life?"

She gave me a funny look and then said, "I'm disgusted with this primary campaign. None of the good candidates are getting any airtime."

"Uh-huh," I said non-commitally. There were still about ten GOP nominee hopefuls competing with each other, two of them Mormon, and almost all of the prospects horrifying to consider as president. With corporations able to act as "people," just a handful of puppet-masters like the Koch Brothers could fund an entire party by themselves.

I'd read a report the other day that said something like six or seven of the richest Americans funded 90% of all right-wing candidates. That was the same day I'd seen another article saying the six heirs of the Walmart empire had a net worth equal to that of the bottom 30% of all Americans put together.

That meant 93,000,000 people. The Right was complaining about the Left trying to foment class warfare, but when you had people like Newt Gingrich suggesting we rewrite child labor laws because poor kids needed to become janitors and take care of their own schools, I had to wonder where the country was headed.

I didn't pursue the conversation with Mary, and fortunately, she didn't offer any more opinions. The exchange still left me in a bad mood, though, which is probably why I was more receptive for what happened later.

Nora came in around 2:00 to deposit a check from the Socialist Party. She didn't come in often, so I really didn't know her very well. "Socialist like Sweden?" I asked to make conversation.

"No, that's social welfare. Socialist like Trotsky."

"Oh." Wasn't he some character in the movie *Frida*? I smiled uncertainly.

"You doing anything Saturday night?" she asked.

"Well…"

"Why don't you come to our Socialist Christmas-tree-decorating party?"

Normally, I would have resisted a similar invitation, but now I considered the importance of networking. And since Derek and I didn't have a tree of our own, why shouldn't we join in for twenty minutes?

Two days later, Derek and I stopped by Nora's house in Leschi. The walls were packed with books, but it was hard to read any of the titles because of all the people gathered. I hoped at the very least Derek would be able to drum up some business for himself when mentioning his occupation, but it also seemed a bit obnoxious to be thinking of money among a group of Socialists.

"Hi," said a woman about sixty-five, offering her hand. "I'm Nan."

"Garth," I replied.

We chatted for several minutes, and I learned that she was originally from New York, where she'd lived in Hell's Kitchen in 1970. "I had some artsy friends, and one of them filmed a short movie. He wanted to use my apartment as the set. I didn't understand why until I saw the film. It was about alienation." She laughed. "My place was pretty dreary."

She went on to say she'd married and moved to London with her husband, where she'd worked in the welfare office. She began studying the women's rights movement, and she and her husband eventually moved into a group home with ex-convicts.

"I thought it was a great idea to mix stable people with ex-convicts. I figured we could model good behavior for them." She shook her head. "My husband left me before I realized it really didn't work very well. But it was in London I first learned about socialism. Lenin was a great man, not like Stalin who was a monster. But Trotsky was a true man of the people."

I nodded politely. I had grown tired of the progressive promises Democrats often made, only to "compromise" with Republicans and almost never deliver. They knew liberals had nowhere else to go. Of course we'd keep voting for them despite their failures. What other choice was there?

Looking about at the thirty or forty people gathered in Nora's house, I wondered if something like this was my only alternative. But they weren't even socialists in the way I thought of the term. They were Communists. What good could possibly come of something like that?

I remembered 4 Nephi in the Book of Mormon, after Jesus came to visit the Americas. The verse in chapter one went something like, "And they had all things common among them; therefore there were not rich and poor, bond and free, but they were all made free, and partakers of the heavenly gift." And living in this manner, the Nephites and Lamanites enjoyed almost two hundred years of complete peace amongst themselves.

That is, if one believed any of that nonsense to begin with. Still, it was a major point in Mormon scripture, and yet Mormons seemed completely against any idea of socialism on any scale. Even though everyone who went through the temple to get their endowments had to swear to give all their possessions to the Church, in preparation for living the United Order. Mormons were no longer required to live that form of communism, as they had briefly in the nineteenth century, but they had to swear that they *would* if requested.

Having made that oath myself, and having believed in the eventuality of fulfilling it, I had to wonder if this small group had "the answer."

"How are you going to get people to accept socialism?" I asked.

"Well," Nan said, "it'll only work if lots and lots of countries put the principles in place at the same time. One country acting alone ends up like Cuba. They've got some things right, but they can never survive the onslaught from countries like the U.S."

I could feel the polite smile on my face fading. Didn't that mean it was hopeless? You could never get "lots" of countries to agree on much of anything, certainly not on something this radical. Even if the principles were sound, they could never be put into practice, so what good were they?

I felt a weight settling on my chest.

"Time to decorate the tree," Nora announced from across the room. She went around offering boxes of ornaments to people. "The person who puts on the biggest lefty ornament gets a prize."

"Is it this one?" A man lifted a huge tin foil hammer and sickle.

"No, that's for the top of the tree."

I dutifully put three small ornaments on different branches. Derek put up a couple as well. Then I saw the woman next to me find the "biggest lefty" ornament. It was a burning American flag.

I felt decidedly uncomfortable. What if some undercover spy were filming this? I could be blacklisted from holding any job at all, just like happened in the 1950s. These people were only trying to make the world a better place, but that kind of action had repercussions. Martin Luther King had been trying to do the same thing. So had Robert Kennedy.

Derek and I made our excuses and left a few minutes later, and on the short drive home, I looked at the poor African Muslims and the Latinos who made up so much of our neighborhood, still walking outside even at 8:30 on a cold December night. What could I do to make sure they had a part in the American Dream? What power did I have to help *anyone* achieve that, even myself?

"That wasn't a very good Date Night," Derek commented as we pulled up in front of our house.

"Maybe we can watch an old episode of *Dick van Dyke* on Me TV."

"Something quintessentially American?"

"Something lighthearted."

"A fantasy?"

I nodded and climbed out of the truck, momentarily buoyed by Derek's banter. For a construction worker, he was very dedicated to an intellectual life. We watched college lectures from The Teaching Company once a week. Our latest series was History of the English Language, a course I'd enjoyed studying as an undergraduate. Something I'd heard a few weeks ago came back to mind.

After the Norman Conquest in 1066, England had been ruled by French-speaking Normans for a couple of hundred years. So many different countries over so many centuries had been ruled by small elite groups. It suddenly occurred to me that just because certain people were in power didn't mean they had the best interests of their subjects at heart.

Was even America occupied by occupiers, I wondered?

Derek put his hand on my arm to stop me. "What?" I said.

"Someone's at our front door."

I looked, and a second later, a man stepped out of the shadows. "Oh my god," I said.

"You recognize him?"

"It's a homeless guy from City Hall."

We walked slowly up to the man, and he moved forward to meet us. "Hey," he said.

"Hi, Alan. What are you doing here?"

"I followed you home from work." He looked from me to Derek.

"Why did you do that?"

He shrugged. "Because you have a home. I thought I might see if I could sleep in a bed for a change." He looked at Derek again.

I suppose I should have felt uneasy, threatened even, but his request seemed like the most natural thing in the world. "I'm losing my job in a month. We might be joining you on the street before long."

"Then you'll need someone to teach you the ropes." He saw Derek and me looking at each other. "I'll have sex with both of you," he offered.

"You don't need to have sex with either of us," Derek replied calmly.

I looked again at Derek and could see the acceptance in his eyes. "No drugs," I said.

Alan shook his head. "I don't do drugs. I'm just fucked up is all."

I nodded. Who wasn't fucked up in this world? Of course, I couldn't help but wonder if this guy would kill us during the night, or rob us, or even just give us bed bugs, and I certainly realized the arrangement couldn't go on forever, whether or not I found another job. I simply felt I had to do *something* that the ordinary, conservative Garth would never have tried before.

And possibly I was just repeating the mistake that Nan had made almost forty years ago. I *wanted* it to make a difference, though, to feel like I was a good person despite my failings. But would bringing in a homeless man even temporarily really make the world any more just?

It was like asking if adding a single grain of sand to a beach would change it in any way, while storms were gouging away tons of sand every day.

But if adding that single grain was the only thing under my control, I had no choice but to act as if that grain mattered.

I leaned over to kiss Derek, and next I moved forward and shook Alan's hand. I watched as he and Derek shook hands as well. Then I took out my key and unlocked the door.

Vomiting on Command

When I was six, my seven-year-old sister talked me into sneaking into the closet under the stairs. That was where our mother kept the baby aspirin, St. Joseph's, I believe. Ellie opened the bottle and took one of the tiny pinkish-orange pills.

"Mmm," she said, offering me the bottle. I took one of the pills as well, and then she took another. Then it was my turn again, and I took my second baby aspirin. I felt very naughty, but the pills were so good, just like candy.

Right after Ellie ate her third aspirin, we heard footsteps on the stairs. We'd thought our parents were asleep. They'd gone to bed right at 7:00, after all. We had no concept, of course, that they might be having sex. The only other incident that might have tipped us off was once when we heard our mother screaming in the bedroom. On that other occasion, Ellie and I bravely went to the bedroom door and knocked.

"What is it?" my mother asked nastily a moment later, grasping her nightgown tightly around her bosom with her right hand.

"Is Daddy trying to kill you?" I asked, my voice shaking.

"Maybe," she said abruptly, closing the door in our faces.

And that was the end of that. As far as I knew, our father never physically abused our mother, so we'd probably simply overheard a very loud sex game. Of course, any understanding about this was years away for me. All I knew was that we were about to be discovered under the stairs. And somehow, even having heard the steps, we were unable to put the bottle away quickly enough.

"What are you doing?" our mother asked in alarm. She grabbed the bottle out of Ellie's hands. "Walter! Come here!"

Our father was only a few steps behind Mom, so he soon joined us in the tiny half bath. Mom showed him the bottle, and his eyes narrowed. He grabbed me first, jerked open the lid to the toilet, and forced me to lean over the bowl. "Vomit!" he ordered. "Vomit it up!"

I was terrified but unable to vomit on command. Dad thought it might encourage me to cooperate if he whacked me a few times on the behind. I started crying but still couldn't throw up. He switched to my sister and went through the same routine with her. She didn't cry, though. She was a tough girl.

"Vomit, or we're going to take you to the hospital and have them pump out your stomach!" Mom threatened.

Dad turned back to me and pushed me over the toilet another time, spanking me yet again. "How many did you take, George?" he asked. "How many?"

"J-just two," I whimpered.

"Ha!" he said. "How many? I'm going to stick my finger down your throat!"

"Two!" I insisted.

Eventually, our parents gave up, spanked us one last time, and sent us to bed. I only say all this to help put things in perspective. This one incident was the full extent of my drug use. In my whole life, I never delved any more deeply into substance abuse than that.

While in a sense this aspirin episode was traumatic, the fact that it was essentially the *only* traumatic episode of my childhood also emphasizes the absolute innocence of that period in what was really quite a typical upbringing. I grew up in a traditional Mormon family and expected to create a traditional family of my own one day.

My sister Ellie started smoking as a teenager, ended up pregnant at sixteen, and after the bishop married her and her boyfriend in our living room, dropped out of church altogether. I, of course, obediently went on my mission to Sweden for two years, graduated from Brigham Young University, and married my wife Natalie in the Los Angeles temple.

But that synopsis doesn't quite tell the whole story. Natalie, it turned out, was divorced. My mother told me not to marry a divorceé, while my dad whispered to me secretly that maybe it would be a good idea. The truth was that I hadn't met anyone in college, I felt the clock ticking away, and the pickings at stake dances were getting slimmer.

Natalie seemed genuine, and this seemed a good quality for someone I was going to spend several trillion years with. She had two sons, aged four and five. Her ex-husband, Beau, was given custody of the oldest boy, Reid, and Natalie was given custody of the younger boy, Damon. I felt conflicted joining a family already in progress, wondering if this somehow disqualified me from having an eternal family of my own, but the bishop assured me that if I had faith, "Heavenly Father will take care of the particulars."

Natalie and Beau had also had a temple wedding, and later a temple divorce, and Beau was still as active in the Church as Natalie was. Fortunately, they now lived in separate wards, but their relationship, while civil, was always a bit strained.

"Hi, George," Beau said the first time I met him, four months after starting to date Natalie. He had a leering grin on his face. "I've heard a lot about you."

"All good, I'm sure," I replied, trying to sound casual.

"You know, Natalie doesn't like it from behind."

I stared at him. Natalie hissed, "Beau!"

Beau laughed. "She still tells me everything," he said, grinning. Natalie and I of course at that point had never had sex yet, waiting to be sealed in the temple together first, but we'd talked openly about what we wanted out of sex.

"Well, now she has someone else she can confide in," I returned.

"Women always need a friend, George," he replied.

"I'll introduce her to my sister." I knew women needed to talk more than men did, but I felt uncomfortable knowing Natalie was still on such intimate terms with Beau despite their shared history. As it turned out, Natalie never did feel all that comfortable with Ellie, but she did at least start shifting her emotional friendships to other women in the ward.

The first night I slept over, after Natalie and I returned from our honeymoon, Damon knocked on our bedroom door at least three times. "Mommy, something's wrong," he kept insisting, looking over at me suspiciously. Finally, Natalie let him in the bed with us, and he slept between us every night for a week, kicking me repeatedly throughout the night while pretending to be asleep.

I had deliberately not had Natalie move in with me the night of our marriage, thinking it would be better if we let Damon get used to the idea of us as a married couple before we uprooted his home. I'm not sure it worked all that well, but after three months, Natalie and I chose a house together, and we all moved in a few weeks after that.

In those first couple of years, we tried various arrangements. Natalie would get Reid to join us on one weekend, and Beau would get Damon to join him another weekend, so both boys could be together.

Other times, we would simply trade off the boys and each get the other parent's boy on a given weekend. On some holidays, we'd have both, and on other holidays, Beau would have both. No arrangement worked perfectly.

One parent always felt he or she was being slighted and that the other was receiving preferential treatment. Often, I was the bad guy for either wanting both boys or for agreeing too easily to let Beau have them. All in all, it was a continually sticky situation, not at all what the warm, fuzzy lessons about family I'd learned while growing up at church had prepared me for.

"You're walking funny," Beau said to Natalie one day while dropping Reid off at our place. This was about ten months after we moved to the new house together. He looked at me with narrowed eyes. "You never let *me* do you from behind." The boys, fortunately, had already gone off to play.

"You're going to need to let that drop," Natalie said.

"It's just that if *we* could have done that more," he continued, "we might still be together."

"I'm walking funny because I have a corn on my foot. That's all there is to it. Please stop obsessing about me."

"I date other women!"

"And are you this charming with them?"

"They like me just fine!"

"Good," I said, interrupting, "then you don't need to fantasize about *my* wife anymore." Beau looked at me for a long moment, looked at Natalie again, and then walked back to his car. I wondered what life was going to be like sharing my wife's body with another man, even if it was only in his mind.

Beau had known Natalie intimately for years, after all. When I made love to her now, I could still feel him present in Natalie's thoughts. Was she comparing me to him? Would she still be thinking about him even after we were together twenty years? Three thousand? It was not the kind of intimacy I'd expected from marriage. Beau's naked body was in my mind as well, and I was not in the least bisexual.

To tell the truth, though, we had more problems with the boys than with their father. One especially annoying habit that Reid had when he visited was his ability to vomit on command. The first time he did it, I was grilling hot dogs on the barbecue out back. "I love hot dogs!" Reid said happily, stuffing an entire one down his throat in less than thirty seconds. "My dad makes the *best* hot dogs."

He looked at his mom, smiled mischievously, and then vomited the hot dog all across the kitchen table. Damon screamed, Reid laughed, and I knew instantly he'd done it on purpose. I swatted him on his behind, but rather than cry, he just glared at me. "You're not my father! *My* father's a good cook!"

This went on for years, on almost every visit for the longest while, but still every couple of months thereafter. Reid would start to act like he was accepting me, and then he'd say something like, "Dad told me you're only after Mom for the *sex*," and he'd throw up again.

I asked him after one of these outbursts what he knew about sex, and he glumly admitted he didn't know anything. As far as food triggers, it didn't matter what I prepared or how much Natalie told me the boy would like a certain meal. He threw up whether it was hamburgers from McDonalds, chicken nuggets from a box in the freezer, or Heaven forbid, a real meal like chicken parmesan or Asian noodles with vegetables.

And every time he did it, it would remind me of that one incident in my own childhood when I was ordered to vomit on command, and I would feel such a bittersweet nostalgia for that simpler time that I would start questioning my decision ever to marry Natalie in the first place.

Then little Larissa came along, and although it sounds cliché, and though it really wasn't fair to the boys, our having a child together did seem to make a difference. I felt more connected to Natalie, and by extension, to both of the boys, who I'd thought I was already loving as much as any father could.

This nevertheless created new awkwardness for us all. Even when Beau had both boys, he still didn't have Larissa, so he never had the full complement of children and began resenting the fact that this seemed to push him into second place.

"The boys know they're only a partial family when they're with me," Beau would complain. And this also meant Natalie and I no longer had our occasional weekends completely to ourselves to focus on our own relationship.

"You guys could at least let me *watch* you have sex," Beau said one day after dropping Reid off. The boys were in their room and Larissa in her crib. "I'm still single, you know, but staying celibate while waiting for the *right* girl to come along is pretty demanding."

"If you want to get married in the temple again, you can't say things like that," Natalie said.

"But it's not as if I haven't already seen you," he insisted. "What would it hurt? I wouldn't be participating. It would be like…like pornography."

"Gee, thanks."

"But it's not pornography to look at the woman you had sex with for years. I wouldn't have to confess to the bishop or anything."

"Thanks for dropping Reid off," I said then, motioning for Beau to leave. Would this man always be a thorn in my side, I wondered. Even if his crass obsession with sex kept him out of the Celestial Kingdom, would he have eternal visiting rights? If by chance he repented and became a model citizen here and a god on the other side, would I still have to share Natalie and the boys with him forever?

Having that kind of intrusion repeatedly even from someone I might eventually learn to like didn't sound like the kind of thing that would spark my singing, "Love at Home" every Monday night throughout eternity. I wondered again if I'd made a mistake marrying a divorced woman.

So this was pretty much the way the first few years of our marriage went along. Some days were good, some were bad, and some seemed both good and bad at the same time. There were certainly days when I thought I might end up divorced myself, and my second wife would have to put up with an even more complicated relationship than I had, involving multiple extraneous characters.

Then came the moment when everything changed.

Reid came over again for a weekend with us, and the boys played computer games while I grilled hamburgers outside. Natalie played with Larissa, who was now almost eighteen months old. Reid by this point was ten and Damon almost nine.

Beau, naturally, had been the one who baptized Reid when he turned eight a couple of years earlier, but Damon had requested I be the one to baptize him when he reached that special age. This created another strain on the family dynamics, of course, but things had been going well the past few months.

So I was unprepared for what happened when I set the hamburgers down on the kitchen table. "Are you sure these are cooked enough?" Reid asked, looking at the burgers suspiciously. "We can get sick from undercooked meat, you know."

"They're all well-done, just the way you like them." I smiled back at him.

"This one looks a little pink," he said, sniffing with a disgusted look on his face.

"Now Reid," said Natalie.

"It's okay," I said. "Reid, if you don't want to eat, you're perfectly welcome to go to your room and entertain yourself there while we finish dinner."

"Starving a kid is child abuse," he shot back. "I can have my real father report you."

"Now Reid."

"Why don't you just try the hamburger?" I suggested. I wanted to say, "For Heaven's sake, stop being such a bratty baby!" but I smiled and added sweetly, "And if you vomit, you're going to be the one to clean it up."

Reid glared at me then and grabbed a burger and shoved it into his mouth. It was all I could do not to roll my eyes, but I didn't want to act as immaturely as my son was behaving. I turned to Damon and smiled impishly as I took a big bite of my own hamburger, and he did the same. I thought that was the end of the tantrum, but a moment later, Reid slapped the table with his hand, making his glass topple over.

"Reid," I said warningly. Then I saw the look in his eyes.

"Oh my god!" Natalie shouted.

"Reid!" I said. "Are you choking?" I jumped up from my chair and rushed around to the other side of the table, grabbing him and trying my best to give him the Heimlich maneuver. He was clutching at his throat and Natalie was screaming, which made Larissa start wailing, and Damon, well, I don't know what Damon was doing. All I could do was focus on Reid.

I squeezed Reid around his diaphragm three times, but nothing happened. He went limp, and Natalie screamed again. Then I squeezed one more time, and a hunk of food shot out of Reid's mouth. At that point, he still didn't seem to be breathing, so I laid him on the floor and quickly checked to make sure no more food was in his mouth before starting CPR. Natalie was on the phone with 911, and within 60 or 70 seconds, Reid was breathing again but still unconscious.

Oh my god, I thought, the boy had brain damage. What were we going to do? Natalie called our neighbor, Gladys, who rushed over to take care of Damon and Larissa. Natalie rode in the ambulance with Reid, and I drove the car to the hospital, only a few yards behind the ambulance the entire way.

The good news was that Reid woke up in the ambulance and seemed more or less normal by the time he arrived at the hospital, perhaps just a little groggy. The doctor decided to keep him overnight for observation, and it wasn't until Natalie and I were finally left alone with Reid that my head snapped up and I almost shouted, "Beau!"

"Huh?" asked Natalie.

"We need to call Beau! Oh my God. He's going to be furious we didn't call already." I pulled out my cell and dialed. When I explained what happened, I made it sound as if we'd just arrived at the hospital, but I knew Beau would find out eventually.

Beau was there in fifteen minutes. We left him alone with Reid for several minutes. Natalie wanted to stay in the room, but I was afraid she'd let slip the time issue, and I wanted to be the one to explain it to him. When he came back out into the hallway, I nodded for Natalie to go back into the room. She didn't need my permission, of course, and was already through the door before Beau was out.

"So what happened?" Beau asked quietly.

"Reid was goofing around," I said, "and he took too big a bite of hamburger and choked. I tried the Heimlich maneuver, but I've never had to do it in an emergency before, and it took me too long to get the move just right. I'm really sorry. And there's something else." I explained how we hadn't even thought of calling him till the emergency was completely over and the doctor had left. "I can't tell you how sorry I am I didn't call you on the way to the hospital."

Beau was silent a moment, looking at the floor. I couldn't tell if he was too mad to talk, if he was about to hit me, or what. "It was good you didn't call on the way," he said slowly. "You might have gotten into an accident."

"Yes, but—"

"But it would have been nice if you could have called as soon as you did get to the hospital. You certainly had time while walking from the parking lot to the emergency room."

"I'm really sorry, Beau."

He looked through the little glass window in the door at Reid in his bed. "Which one of you finally thought to call me?"

Now I felt even more awkward. It was no great achievement for me to have been the one to remember him as an afterthought, but I didn't want to put a further strain on Natalie's relationship with Beau by admitting it had in fact been me.

Beau looked back at me and nodded. "You're all right, George."

"Well…"

He shook his head. "You were 100% involved in Reid's care and didn't think of anything else. That's being a real father. And when you *did* finally have a chance to breathe, the first thing you thought of was me. You're all right." Beau offered his hand, and though I felt stupid, I took it. In a silly way, I felt I was meeting him for the very first time.

"Beau…"

"I'm sorry I've been such a pest all these years. All that talk of sex. It was just to annoy you, you know. I didn't mean any of it." He looked up at me like a little vulnerable boy. It was the same expression Damon often had on his face.

"Go on in there," I said. "We don't want to reinforce Reid's behavior by giving him too much attention, but what else can we do?"

"I'll have a talk with him." He smiled. "Give us five minutes, and then you come back in the room, too. We're all family."

I stood out in the hallway looking at the door and feeling very much left out and included at the same time. I had a headache from all the tension but had already swallowed two aspirin and was afraid to take any more.

I couldn't help but wonder who would get these two boys in the hereafter. Would our eternal family forever be a stepfamily? Would we have to deal with the awkward dynamics of a multi-parent family on an eternal, permanent basis? Or would it simply be like the show *Survivor*, where whoever made it to the end and gained the Celestial Kingdom would be the winner?

Of course, unlike the TV show, all three of us were theoretically eligible to make it all the way, so those other questions remained unanswered. Even if in the Celestial Kingdom we were all "perfect" beings, the eternal family we would be forced to be part of would still be unlike anything ever discussed in Priesthood meeting.

I missed my mother. I would have to give her a call in the morning before church.

Through the little window, I saw Beau waving at me, and I pushed the door open, plastering a smile on my face. "You do realize you'll have to clean up the mess you made?" I said, wagging my finger at Reid.

"I won't do it again," he said softly. "And no more vomiting, either."

"We'll see about that," I said. "You haven't had hospital food yet, have you?" As a child his age, I'd followed my parents blindly, with absolute faith that everything would work out okay. As an adult making my own family, there was no such confidence in the future, whatever my bishop might have said.

But it was up to me, I decided, to build that kind of trust in my own children, whatever our family structure. "Lima beans suspended in green jello," I added. "You'll never be the same."

"Now George," said Natalie.

Beau laughed, and then Reid laughed, and finally Natalie and I joined in as well.

The Ruins of His Faith

Ralph boarded the ship at the Mississippi River in New Orleans. He was forty-seven years old and single, so he was going on a Singles cruise in the Gulf. An LDS Singles cruise, to be exact. It wasn't enough to find an acceptable woman. He needed to find an acceptable Mormon woman.

He'd never been on a cruise before, never felt the idea to be especially appealing, but it had been long enough since Heidi had left him that he had to start doing whatever it took. The bishop had told him he needed to get married again if he wanted to make it to the Celestial Kingdom.

What Ralph wanted more than anything else was to die, but he simply couldn't allow himself to do that until he was married.

He looked at his watch. It was 4:13 pm. Ralph had memorized I Corinthians 10:13 when he was in Seminary classes as a teenager. The verse explained that God would never tempt anyone above that which he was able to bear. It was a promise.

And it seemed that ever since he'd memorized the passage, whenever Ralph felt tempted to do something wrong, he'd look at his watch, and it would read 10:13. He was never sure if his internal body clock was making him look or if it was truly God gently reminding him that He cared.

For superstitious people, thirteen was an unlucky number, but for Ralph, it always made him think of this verse. Even today, the thirteen in the 4:13 was a reminder of the promise. God wanted him to be strong. He wanted him to marry. God would provide a way for Ralph to do both.

"Welcome aboard," said a smiling young woman. She was an employee of the Sapphire Dream. She smiled at everyone.

Ralph made his way to his cabin. To be a part of the Singles Cruise, he had to accept one of the package rooms. That meant either three to a room, four to a room, or five to a room. Since he wasn't here to make friends with other guys, he'd picked three to a room, but that still meant he needed to put up with two other people. He scowled when he saw that one of the others was already in the room.

"Hi!" said the young man. He looked to be in his mid-twenties. He reached over as Ralph entered and offered his hand.

"Hi," Ralph muttered back.

"I'm Andrew," said the young man, smiling pleasantly. "Where are you from?"

"New Orleans."

Andrew laughed. "Really? I'm from Chicago. I guess I just figured people would be here from all across the States."

"Don't you have Singles wards up in Chicago?" Why was Andrew coming down here to steal one of the few women available now for Ralph? Finding a woman might be the only thing that would keep Ralph from falling away from the Church. He *needed* to find someone.

"My cousin from Salt Lake went on one of these cruises last year and met her husband on the cruise. Even Mormons from cities with lots of Mormons want some variety once in a while."

Ralph forced a smile. He'd thought about moving to Salt Lake himself, but why would a forty-seven-year-old man be any more of a catch there than here in New Orleans?

Ralph opened his suitcase to begin unpacking. He'd brought several shirts to wear with his jeans, and one suit. All the shirts were light-colored, but only dark suits were in style, so he dreaded the one formal dinner and dance.

He'd been afflicted with dandruff since he was a child. Head and Shoulders didn't help. Selsun Blue didn't help. Tar shampoos didn't help. Washing his hair every day didn't help, and neither did washing only twice a week or once a week. He'd tried everything.

What girl worth marrying would be interested in a guy with disgusting dandruff? He knew he was being petty, that there were plenty of people who suffered a lot more than he did, but Ralph couldn't help but wonder sometimes if there was even a God at all, if the Universe could be so unfair. A dead-end job as an accountant, no friends to speak of, a house half-eaten by termites. Was a miserable life worth living if there was no one to love him?

Another young man pushed open the door and entered the room. "Hi!" he said. "I'm Ben. Looks like we're roommates!" Ben put his suitcase on the bed next to Ralph's.

"Who gets the bed to himself?" asked Ralph. "There're two beds and three guys."

Everyone looked at each other, and Ralph could see Ben regretting his decision to put his bag on Ralph's bed. "Oh, well," Ben began, "I don't see why you can't have a bed to yourself. You're…you're…"

"I'm old," Ralph finished. "And I'm fatter than either of you two."

"No…" Andrew protested, raising his hand as if to stop traffic.

Ralph weighed 170 pounds. He wasn't grotesquely obese, but he knew those extra fifteen or twenty pounds made him undesirable. Both Andrew and Ben looked perfectly fit. Why they hadn't already found women back home, Ralph didn't know. Kids these days never seemed satisfied with anything.

Just like Heidi hadn't been satisfied. Only she hadn't been a kid.

"I'm happy to have a bed to myself. Thanks."

Andrew and Ben looked at each other. They were silent a moment as they all continued unpacking. When Ralph went in the bathroom to brush his teeth and check his hair, he could hear them starting to talk again in the next room. Ralph stayed in the bathroom several minutes, patting his hair for a while to knock out the most blatant particles of dandruff, and then painstakingly picking out the few remaining persistent flakes.

It was something he had to do several times a day. He'd absentmindedly scratch his head at some point, and an hour later pass in front of a mirror and realize that for all that time, he'd had a bright neon flake glowing prominently on his head. It was just as mortifying as realizing you had spinach in your teeth, only this could happen not only during a meal but at any point during the day.

By the time Ralph came out of the bathroom, both Ben and Andrew had left the room. Ralph wanted nothing more than to lie on the bed and read a book. He'd brought two on the trip, *The Hunger Games* for relaxation and *The Immortal Life of Henrietta Lacks* to stimulate his mind.

But he was paying good money for this cruise, and short of traveling across the country visiting Singles ward after Singles ward, this was his best chance at finding another wife, so he didn't want to be a hermit. Regardless of the reasons the bishop gave, Ralph was tired of spending his evenings and weekends alone.

Coming home to an empty house every evening was like being convicted of treason day after day. He wasn't good enough to be loved. The repeated verdict relentlessly chipped away at his soul.

It wasn't long before the ship left the dock and started its way toward the mouth of the Mississippi. Ralph went up on deck and stood at the railing to watch what was left of the Ninth ward pass by. After that came several other small towns and some marshland, and eventually, they were out in the Gulf of Mexico.

"It's beautiful, isn't it?" said a woman about forty, pausing just long enough as she passed to point toward the last bits of land.

"Not particularly," said Ralph. "I think Mexico will be prettier."

The woman stopped and laughed. "You're not one of those 'the grass is always greener' types, are you?"

Ralph looked at her and wondered if she was part of the LDS group who felt she could therefore take liberties or just a shamelessly bold woman. She had shoulder-length brown hair and wore shorts that were short enough to prove she wasn't wearing Mormon undergarments underneath.

A gentile then, but she seemed pleasant enough. Ralph supposed there was no harm in talking to her. "Life will be better once I get a raise," he said. "It'll be even better than that when I retire. It'll be better when I meet the woman of my dreams."

The woman nodded in playful thoughtfulness. "I see. Life'll be better for *me* once I win the lottery. Once I become President of the United States. Once I win the Pulitzer for the article I'll be writing about this cruise."

"Well, if you're going to be *unrealistic*…" Ralph began.

The woman moved up next to him along the railing. "My name's Terri. I really am writing an article for *The Times-Picayune*. Do you mind if I talk to you a while?" She offered her hand.

Ralph was still a little unsure but shook it. "Are you going to make fun of me?"

“If I do, I won’t use your real name. Fair enough?”

Ralph almost smiled. He didn’t know what appealed to him about her, but it felt good to be engaged for a change. “I’m an open book.” He wasn’t really, but if the old way of doing things hadn’t generated any success, maybe this trip was a chance to try something new. May as well practice on this woman before meeting up with the Mormon girls later.

“Excellent.” Terri opened her bag and pulled out a small notepad and a pen. “Are you traveling alone?”

“I’m part of the LDS Singles group. We’re Mormons.”

Terri raised an eyebrow.

“We’re going to the ruins of Chichen Itza to reflect on the Book of Mormon.” He watched as Terri scribbled away. “And while we’re there, we hope to hook up with each other and end up in the temple.”

Terri frowned. “Just one woman apiece?”

Ralph almost curled his lip at the ignorance of the question, but Terri seemed sincere. “Just one. Isn’t that enough?”

Terri shrugged. “I’ve had two husbands already. Neither one was enough for me.” She smiled again. “But this is about you. Go on.”

“I want a wife. And I can’t find one in church in New Orleans. So I’m hoping I’ll meet someone out here.”

“Ah, the romance of the sea.”

"Something like that. I go to regional Singles conferences once in a while, too. Only a couple so far." He offered a short explanation about what they were like—no one liked boring old men—but admitted he didn't know quite what to expect on the cruise.

"Any hanky panky aboard ship?" asked Terri. "You mentioned hooking up?"

Ralph shook his head, almost sadly. "No, we have to obey the rules of the Church while we're here or we can't participate with the group. That means no sleeveless dresses for the women. No smoking or drinking or sex for anyone."

"No drinking? Really? On a cruise?"

"No drinking." He wanted to add, "No masturbating, either," but he wasn't willing to be *that* much of an open book.

Terri asked him a few more questions, saw a young couple walking by oblivious to everything else, and then thanked Ralph quickly and headed off after the couple. Ralph shrugged and turned back to the Gulf. He really did need to try adapting his personality while out here. He had five days to experiment.

If no one liked the old Ralph, maybe there was a reason. It couldn't *all* be the dandruff. He stared out at the calm water and wondered just what he needed to change. He wasn't sure which parts of his personality were turning people off. Hopefully, it wasn't twenty-three or twenty-four different parts.

Maybe not already knowing meant he was insensitive. Perhaps he should do something about that. He strolled around on deck for a while. Almost everyone else seemed to be in pairs or groups. He wondered if he'd make any friends with the other LDS Singles while he was out here. That wouldn't be such a bad idea, he supposed.

He certainly hadn't made a very good start with his two roommates, and there didn't seem to be much possibility of making it up to them. It wasn't as if he could turn down their bedcovers to show how nice he was being.

Just as Ralph was about to head below deck and start reading one of his books, he saw a young woman, perhaps twenty, stooped over and staring at the deck, her arms outstretched as if about to take flight. "You okay?" he asked.

"I lost my contact."

Ralph leaned over, too, and started searching. This caused her to finally look up at him, and Ralph heard her breathe out heavily with a sound of disgust. "Don't worry about it," she said. "I've got another pair." She turned around and walked off.

Ralph raised an eyebrow. Was he acting in a particularly lecherous manner, he wondered? He thought of all the times he'd heard Church leaders say comforting words to older, unmarried women. If they lived righteously, they'd find eternal companions in the hereafter. Those words were never directed toward men.

Men had to find someone in this life or they were out of luck. He wasn't sure if this was fair or not. Men had so many other benefits, though, and women had so few. It only seemed fitting women were given at least *one* break. And yet the double standard still irritated him. If the Church were true, why were there double standards at all, for anyone?

Ralph went back to his cabin and read a couple of chapters of *The Hunger Games* before getting ready for dinner. He put on some nice dress slacks but no tie, and he headed for the dining room, where he found the tables set apart for the LDS group.

He'd hoped for name cards but there were none. This meant he'd have to time his seating just right, wait for at least a few people to sit so that the remaining options were limited, and then sit near someone who looked interesting, while there was no time or space left for those he'd ambushed to find other seating.

He chose a table where two young men and a young woman were sitting, but also a woman in her thirties and another in her forties. That meant the two older women would have no choice but to talk to him. Ralph smiled as he sat down and was relieved to see both women smiling back. The girl ignored him, but that was to be expected.

"Do you like being on the water?" Ralph pointed the question in the general direction of both older women, figuring he'd let whoever felt prompted answer first.

"I love water," said the woman in her early thirties. "I'm a firefighter."

Ralph raised his eyebrows. "Where?" he asked.

"In Washington State. I fight forest fires in the summer. The rest of the year I'm a pilot."

"A pilot and a firefighter?" asked the woman in her forties. Ralph was irritated that she was horning in on the conversation, but maybe that would make it easier to transition to her if the need arose.

"Well, I fly small, corporate flights. Just a handful of people on board. Once, there was a crack in the door seal and we had decompression in mid-flight and I had to make an emergency descent."

"You must be very good at your job to have avoided disaster," Ralph said.

"Most of the time it's routine. That's why I need some adventure in the summer. Last summer, we had to cut down several trees, and one of them almost fell on me." She smiled brightly, and Ralph looked at her appraisingly. She had shoulder length brown hair, almost straight, with a "sturdy" look to her, just slightly overweight, but most of it probably muscle.

"Are you a lesbian?" he asked.

The other woman gasped, and the thirty-something just looked at him coldly. "Real women can do any job they want," she said icily. "There's nothing about flaps on a plane's wings that are particularly masculine."

She looked as if she was about to stand and walk off, but the food arrived just then. She glowered a bit but then picked up her fork.

"No offense intended," said Ralph. "My ex-wife is a lesbian." He wondered if he'd driven Heidi to other women because his own body was so repulsive. He seemed to be pushing this woman away, too. "I'm Ralph," he tried again.

"Wonderful," the thirty-something said coolly.

"And your name?" he pressed.

"I'm Claudia," she finally said after a long pause.

"I'm Sheree," said the forty-something.

"And what do you do, Sheree?" asked Ralph.

"I'm an elementary school teacher."

"Is that feminine enough for you?" asked Claudia, putting a biteful of Romaine lettuce into her mouth as she stared directly at Ralph.

"You're eating that salad awfully daintily," he said in return.

Claudia put her fork down and glared at him. This wasn't working well. Ralph wondered what he was doing wrong. He'd just been making conversation, but he seemed to keep putting his foot in his mouth. For the rest of the meal, the two young men and the young woman talked to each other, and the two older women turned to one another and shut Ralph out of their conversation.

He had four more days. Maybe things would go better in the morning. Ralph took a stroll around deck and then headed back for the cabin to read. When he stepped in the bathroom, he saw two great big flakes of dandruff on his head. He knocked them off, brushed his teeth, and then read three more chapters before turning out the light at 9:30.

Ben and Andrew came in sometime later and turned on the bathroom light. Ralph glanced at his watch. 10:13. It never failed. But just what was the temptation he was supposed to overcome? He listened to his roommates whisper for a while and then finally climb into bed.

Sunday morning, Ralph woke before his roommates and decided to take a long stroll before having a quiet breakfast by himself. Then he took yet another stroll. He was leaning against the railing, looking out at the tiny waves, when he heard someone coming up beside him. “How’d your first night with the Mormon girls go?” It was Terri.

“Not so great.” Ralph looked briefly at her and then back out at the water. He didn’t know why he was even bothering to talk to her. Obviously, nothing could come of it.

“Bombed?” Terri asked.

Ralph wondered where her notebook was. “Afraid so. I called one woman a lesbian.”

Terri guffawed. “Charming.”

“I was just saying.”

Terri laughed again. “Look, why don’t you have coffee with me this morning? It’ll loosen you up.”

“Oh, I couldn’t drink coffee. It’s…it’s…”

“A sin? What’s the worst that could happen? The lesbian won’t talk to you again?” She had the most annoying smile.

Ralph debated what to do. On the one hand, he wanted to get married in the temple, his last chance at salvation, and he certainly couldn't do that if he didn't obey the Word of Wisdom. On the other, he might end up jumping overboard before the end of the cruise in any event, so it hardly mattered if he added a couple of minor sins to his scorecard.

"Sure. Thanks." Terri strode off, Ralph following just a step or two behind.

They sat at a table and had lattes. It wasn't as if Ralph had never drunk coffee before. He'd tried it twice, in fact. How could one go to the Café du Monde in the French Quarter and not even be tempted? He was afraid it was a slippery slope, though. Once you let go of the iron rod, it would be easy to get lost in the darkness. He'd never reach the Tree of Life if he wasn't careful.

He looked around to make sure no one from the Singles group was watching. Most wouldn't recognize him anyway. It was too early in the cruise for them all to be familiar with each other.

"How was *your* evening?" asked Ralph.

"Oh, I had a great time. Cornered one of the ship's officers and interviewed him. Then we snuck back to my cabin and…" She took another sip of her coffee.

Ralph was appalled by her nonchalance. He stared at her, his mouth open. Maybe a cruise with non-members wasn't the kind of thing LDS Singles should do. He felt the slightest stirring in his crotch and took another sip of coffee. "Is *that* going in your article?"

Terri laughed. "I'm nothing if not discreet." Ralph felt her foot accidentally bump against his under the table, and he moved away uncomfortably. "So tell me your deepest secret," she pressed.

"You've got to be kidding."

Terri smiled but said nothing.

Something about her made him want to keep talking. His deepest shame was probably the dandruff, but since that was so public, it could hardly be called a secret. Would it hurt to tell this woman one small thing to satisfy her? He wondered what he might safely divulge. He thought of a dream he'd had the night before.

"Well," he began, noticing Terri's expression of apparent relaxation betrayed by her steel eyes. "I have a recurring nightmare. I suppose it isn't exactly a nightmare. I don't wake up drenched in sweat with my adrenalin flowing. It's really just a recurring uncomfortable dream."

"Yes?"

"It's been twenty-five years or whatever since I graduated high school, but I find myself back there, and I need to get into my locker, but I can't remember the combination. Are you enough of a Freudian to figure it out?"

Terri shrugged. "Is that your only recurring dream?"

Ralph figured he had nothing to lose at this point. "There's another uncomfortable one," he admitted. "I'm in college, it's finals week, and I realize I haven't gone to my math class in a month and a half. I'm hopelessly behind, it's too late to drop the class, and I don't even know exactly what day or time the final is, or where the professor's office is to talk to her."

"Interesting."

"And I have to talk to her *before* the exam or there's no hope."

"Hope for what?"

Ralph shrugged. "Do you know what the dreams mean?" He really had no idea. All he knew was that he felt very unhappy when he woke up, not sure exactly what was making him feel that way, the dreams or what they represented.

"Do you have any *good* dreams that are recurring?"

Ralph shook his head. He wondered if he was too filled with dark emotions to have good dreams. Perhaps it was his negativity that drove people away. Could a thing like that drive Heavenly Father away, too? Wasn't God supposed to be above human weakness?

"You have something in your hair." Terri reached over and batted at his scalp. Ralph was mortified. "So what's on the agenda today?" she went on.

She hadn't been repulsed. Maybe she didn't realize it was dandruff. Ralph tried to focus. "We have a two-hour seminar today on the Book of Mormon."

"Sounds sexy." Terri smiled. "You can't help but hook up at something like that."

"Well," Ralph said a little defensively, "we're trying to connect on a deeper level, something that will last for eternity."

Terri nodded, and Ralph expected some crack about his divorce. "If I see you around later, is it okay if I talk to you again?"

Ralph shrugged. "Sure." Terri stood up, waved goodbye, and strolled away, looking this way and that as if surveying for something. Ralph looked down at the coffee mug and set it down quickly. He looked at his watch and headed for the seminar room. It was 10:13. He was late.

Steve was their teacher today. The printed program explained that he had an MBA and taught ballroom dancing in his own studio. In addition, he was a Gospel Doctrine teacher and a board member of the Book of Mormon Archeological Forum.

Ralph sat in the back of the room. That was always the safest place. Otherwise, he'd be thinking about the people behind him noticing the flakes on his shoulders throughout the entire session. Even with light-colored shirts, he could never really relax.

There were just over a hundred people in the room, about the number that showed up at his regular ward meetings in New Orleans. It had been difficult to assess the group the night before, but he could clearly see now that about 70% of those in attendance were in their twenties.

Still, that left a sizable portion old enough for Ralph to explore, and most of those were women. The problem was that the older women all sat near the front of the room, so it would be impossible to make asides to anyone. As it was, the only comments he overheard were from two young men sitting near him talking about politics, some comment about a Mormon neo-Nazi in Arizona who'd just killed four people.

"He hated Mexicans," said one of the young men. "Even wanted to put land mines along the border. Doesn't he realize they're mostly Lamanites? We should be *nice* to them."

"But Lamanites are sinners," the other young man replied. "That's why their civilization collapsed. That's why we're going to visit their ruins."

Ralph couldn't help but think of the DNA studies he'd heard about. Mormons claimed that Native Americans, at least those in Central America where the Book of Mormon always set so many of its stories near the "narrow neck of land," were from Israel.

But DNA analysis showed that Native Americans seemed to have more genetic links to Asia than to the Middle East. Some LDS leader had said at one point that in the Last Days, evidence would become so abundant that people simply wouldn't be able to deny the truthfulness of the Book of Mormon any longer. But that day hadn't come yet.

The teacher went on at length about how the ruins they'd be visiting could very well be the remains of cities spoken of in the scriptures. It was all very interesting, and Ralph hoped it was true. Perhaps his lack of faith was why he couldn't find a good wife. Hadn't he just demonstrated that faithlessness by drinking coffee?

What if Heavenly Father was going to punish him throughout the rest of the cruise, making him unable to meet any good women? He sent up a prayer of repentance and vowed to be better from then on.

There was a little mingling after the seminar, and Ralph approached a woman in her early forties. "I liked the comment you made during class," Ralph told her. She'd said good Mormons didn't need evidence, that faith alone would get them to heaven.

She smiled. "It's just that it's too much like all those studies that come out in the newspaper. Tomatoes are good for your health. No, they cause cancer. Wait, they reduce the risk of stroke. No, they cause kidney stones. Whatever. There are inevitably going to be contrary points of view on a subject. If we rely on those kinds of things, we'll always be disappointed."

"My name's Ralph." He offered his hand.

"I'm Nila." She smiled again.

"Would you like to have lunch together?"

"Sure."

They walked down to the dining room, and Ralph felt happy for the first time in ages. They ordered cheeseburgers and fries, a comfortable meal, and made small talk until their food arrived. Nila was from Memphis, a convert at the age of nineteen. She was forty-three now. She'd never married but had come close a couple of times. Nila had artificially blond hair with highlights or frosting the color of champagne.

It was an odd look, Ralph thought. She was a hair stylist with a mostly older clientele. "The hard part about that is the constant recruitment." She laughed. "You know, five percent of my clients die off each year." She looked at his hair for a moment then, her smile fading as she looked away.

"Excuse me," said Ralph. "I'll be right back." He headed to the bathroom, and sure enough, there was one medium-sized flake on the side of his head, only apparent if he turned his head a certain way, but Nila had clearly seen it. He took a few minutes patting out several flakes. Then he returned to the table. Their food had arrived.

Ralph was surprised to see Nila cutting her burger with a knife and eating bite-size pieces with her fork. As he sat down, he saw her cut a French fry in half and eat that with a fork, too. "You're very neat," he observed.

Nila smiled again. "You should see me at home eating Cheetos in front of the TV."

"Yes?"

"I use chop sticks. I don't like my fingers to get all cheesy." She picked up her napkin and wiped the corners of her mouth.

"I wouldn't mind licking the cheese off your fingers." Ralph smiled to show he was joking, but Nila put her napkin down, looking horrified. It wasn't as if Ralph had said something about sex. He frowned. What was the big deal?

They ate most of the rest of their meal in silence, and then Nila excused herself and headed off. There were activities scheduled for the afternoon, fun on the water slide and in the pool. Ralph figured there was hardly any point showing up in a bathing suit.

If he couldn't interest someone with his clothes on, he certainly didn't have much chance after taking most of them off. He strolled around deck by himself, hoping perhaps he'd run into Terri, and finally ended up going back to his cabin and reading a few more chapters before taking a nap.

Meeting with the Singles was becoming painful, but Ralph put on a fresh shirt for dinner and spent an extra few minutes on his hair to try to eradicate the flakes that might ambush him after he left his cabin. He chose a new table tonight, this one with one other man around his age but three women in their thirties and forties, plus one woman in her fifties. He vowed not to say anything stupid.

The meal was eggplant lasagna, one Ralph enjoyed after having served a mission to Italy many years earlier. He told a couple of stories about proselytizing near the Coliseum but mostly tried to fly under the radar. Perhaps if he didn't make a bad impression on these women, he could slowly build up to making a good one sometime later on the trip.

"And what do you do?" Ralph finally asked the woman in her fifties. The others at the table had pretty much ignored her throughout the meal, and though Ralph wasn't interested, he wanted to behave decently toward her.

"I'm a librarian," she said proudly. "My first husband left me plenty of money when he died, but I decided I wanted to go out and be a contributing member of society. I pay my own way."

"That's very admirable," said Ryan, the other man in his forties who was at the table. The librarian smiled.

"But isn't that a little selfish?" Ralph asked, the words coming out without warning. "With the unemployment rate over 9%, shouldn't you make yourself useful doing volunteer work and leave the paying job to someone who needs it?"

The rest of the meal went poorly. Fortunately, by this point, they were already on dessert. When Ralph made it back to his cabin and looked in the mirror, there wasn't a single flake in his hair. People had disliked him simply for who he was.

He tried to read another chapter but felt so low he couldn't concentrate. He wondered if he should jump over the railing tonight after most of the others aboard were asleep. Perhaps no one would even notice. But then, he really did want to see the Mayan ruins. Maybe he'd wait to kill himself the following evening. He lay on his bed for the longest time, but when he checked his watch and saw it was 10:13, he turned off the light and went to sleep.

They docked at Progresso on the Yucatan peninsula sometime during the night. Ralph woke up early and strolled around, hoping to see Terri, and he did see her, having coffee with a man about forty. He nodded to her with a forced smile and kept walking.

The excursion to Chichen Itza took most of the day. The LDS group, led by Steve, the ballroom dancer/Gospel Doctrine teacher, left at 7:00. The hundred or so people in their party formed several smaller clusters, and Ralph drifted from group to group throughout the day.

He started out among some twenty-five-year-olds, hoping that would make him feel young. Steve pointed to the scenery around them and explained, "This is an arid region, and most of the rivers here run underground, but nearby are a few large sinkholes called cenotes that provide drinking water year-round. That's probably why the city developed in this area, though an extended drought may be why the city eventually fell into ruin."

Ralph wondered about Church leaders deliberately choosing to relocate to the Salt Lake desert. It was land no one else wanted—aside from the Utes and Paiutes and Shoshone, of course—which gave them some peace from persecution for a while, but ultimately, he wondered that with a continually growing population, if Salt Lake might not collapse from lack of water as well. Would archeologists a thousand years from now be giving tours of the granite temple in downtown Salt Lake?

It was 10:13 in the morning. Ralph frowned. Shouldn't he be thinking about how they'd be in the midst of the Millennium a thousand years from now? He'd thought they'd be in the Millennium already. He'd read somewhere that Christ was born in 4 B.C., so he'd been hoping for the Second Coming since 1996.

Here it was 2012, sixteen years later, and nothing. Part of the reason he'd wanted to come on this cruise was because the Mayan calendar suggested the end of the world would take place later this year.

But if Mayans were corrupt Lamanites who'd killed off the prophets, why should he believe anything they had to say in the first place?

Ralph wanted the world to end. If he somehow passed muster and gained entrance into the Millennium, everything would be wonderful. And if he didn't, at least the misery of this life would be over. He wanted *someone* to be happy, and the sooner the Millennium came, the sooner those few good people would have that opportunity. Even if it wasn't him, it would be someone, and just knowing that was comforting.

Steve pointed to a cenote and explained that the Mayans had thrown in gold, jade, pottery, and other objects, but they also sacrificed humans here, hoping to appease the rain god Chaac. People always spoke of these ancient empires with reverence, Ralph mused, but just because a culture could build a beautiful pyramid didn't mean they were very nice people.

He thought briefly about how Heidi had been kicked out of the Church after falling in love with another woman. At the time, he'd been grateful for the validation her excommunication gave him, but now he wondered just for a moment if that wasn't a kind of human sacrifice, too.

Ralph went along with a group of Singles in their forties to the Temple of the Warriors, strolled through the columns of a thousand warriors, and explored the great ball court and the observatory. He'd had no idea the complex was this large, but it was a city, after all, not a solitary building. "It takes a village to raise a good Mayan," he joked to a woman about his age, thinking of Hillary Clinton's book.

"That's probably why this civilization fell," she returned coolly. "That horrible woman will do the same thing to us if we don't squelch her." Ralph's first reaction was irritation. There was nothing about his joke that implied he actually agreed with Clinton, so why the disdain? As he walked on, though, he wondered if the woman weren't simply projecting.

Didn't Mormons more or less believe the same thing? Yes, the family was the essential structural unit, but there were also Primary teachers, Sunday School teachers, Seminary teachers, Beehive instructors, Deacons Quorum instructors, and so forth. It took the entire community of the Church to properly raise a good Mormon. Some Mormons might believe in home schooling, but the Church certainly didn't permit home churching. Mormons had to go to church for full gospel growth.

And yet Ralph was growing tired of boring church meetings. If he didn't find a wife, he was afraid he'd stop going altogether and his soul would dry up and wither away.

Ralph wondered if there was some lingering influence of apostate Lamanites hanging over the area, infecting him with traitorous thoughts. He was here to be strengthened, and all he seemed to be doing was falling further from the Church. Why did God curse him with a grumpy personality and a repulsive body, and then order him to have a successful marriage? Even if Heidi hadn't been lesbian, she'd probably have left by now.

As he approached the great pyramid, El Castillo, tagging along with an age-mixed group this time, Ralph listened while Steve explained that Chichen Itza had been a major center from around 600 A.D. to 1200 A.D. Six hundred years, thought Ralph. It was astonishing. Of course, the Roman Empire had lasted longer than that, but nothing modern had.

Even New York was only three hundred years old. He honestly couldn't even comprehend it still being there three hundred years from now. Despite his hope for the

Millennium, he'd seen *Mad Max* too often to really believe in a happy future.

"The Church has only been around just over 180 years," Ralph said to Ryan, his table mate of the previous evening, who didn't seem to dislike him as much as the women last night had. "We talk as if we're the continuation of the Jews, but *they've* been around for thousands of years, and they're still here. Even the Catholics have been here ages longer than we have."

"But we're the true Church," Ryan said.

"When the Mayans were at the height of their civilization, don't you think they thought pretty highly of themselves, too?"

"But we're *true*," Ryan insisted. "Don't you have a testimony?"

Ralph wasn't sure he did. So why did he care about marrying in the temple anyway? Or marrying again at all? Maybe he should finally let himself look at some pornography and simply masturbate once in a while. If he couldn't develop a meaningful relationship with anyone, perhaps he should just get used to living alone and accept that as his fate. The prophet Moroni lived alone his entire adult life, didn't he? It wasn't the end of the world.

Ralph wished again it was the end of the world. He was so tired of trying all the time. Trying and trying and always failing.

He followed along with the others and looked at the feathered serpent and the jaguar throne and all the other fascinating features of the ruined city. All it did was make him feel nostalgic for his time with Heidi, for his time in Italy when he still believed so fervently, for his childhood when his biggest problem was being teased on the school bus, the kids calling him "Snowman" because of his dandruff.

When would that snowman ever melt away and become a cenote full of life-giving water? Was he destined to always be nothing more than an ugly curmudgeon that sucked happiness from others? A cenote that claimed life rather than gave it?

They made it back to the ship around 7:00. Ralph took a quick shower and then napped while Ben and Andrew took their showers afterward. Then it was time for dinner. Ralph felt so old and so tired and so down that he thought seriously about skipping.

Then he decided it was all Satan's doing, trying to keep him from finding the woman who would make his life complete. He dressed carefully, went back in the bathroom to make sure his hair was free of particles, and forced a smile on his face as he headed for the dining room.

"I'm beat," said a woman named Trisha next to whom Ralph had positioned himself. She was in her late thirties and had dark, almost black hair. It was slightly wavy and came down just below her shoulders, about as long as someone her age could dare let it grow, yet it still looked good on her. Perhaps she really was the one. She was a few pounds overweight and might not mind Ralph's extra pounds.

"Me, too," said Ralph, cutting into his steak.

"We have another full day tomorrow at the Tulum ruins," she went on. "And it isn't till we start back for New Orleans that we get Naomi's seminar." She sounded unhappy about it.

Ralph vaguely remembered reading about Naomi in the tour's program guide. "She's 'Utah's Dating Coach,' isn't she?" he asked. He remembered that Naomi was also a licensed marriage and family therapist.

"Don't you think it would've been more useful to have that seminar at the beginning of the trip?" Trisha asked. "I mean, she's even written books about dating."

Ralph remembered from the program. "*The Secret of Dating Successfully* and *How to Marry the Right Man*." He chuckled. "I'm not sure I really need to read that last one."

"Sure you do," Trisha returned. "If you see that the description of the right man doesn't fit, you know you need to change."

"Then why doesn't Naomi write about how to become the right woman?" Ralph stared thoughtfully at his water glass. "Seems like there are a lot more unmarried women here than men. Maybe the women aren't getting asked for a reason."

Trisha looked at him. "I've heard about you. But I told myself I'd keep an open mind. Why don't you go back to your cabin? No one wants to talk to you." She cut a tiny bite of meat on her plate and then added, without looking up again, "And by the way, you have dandruff. At first, I thought you'd put salt in your hair as some kind of bizarre superstitious ritual." She looked up again now. "But you're really just decaying in front of everyone's eyes, aren't you?" She put the steak in her mouth and began chewing calmly, looking directly at him.

Ralph felt his face go hot, and he looked at the others sitting at the table. They were all looking back at him, and not one of them said anything in his favor. No one scolded Trisha. No one said, "You have a point about the book." No one offered even a kind glance.

Ralph stood up and walked away. Mormons were nice people, he told himself. That was one of their hallmarks. They were always nice. Unless you didn't belong.

He must not belong.

Maybe his soul wasn't outright evil, but it must at least be damaged, and that seemed enough to create a reaction. It was like blood-clotting factors sensing a wound, like T-cells finding an invader. The system had to sacrifice some cells to save the rest of the body.

He'd have to give Heidi a call when he got home and invite her to dinner with her partner.

Ralph was too keyed up to go back to his cabin. He walked around the deck over and over, not so much in a hope to burn calories as to stay busy. He thought briefly again about jumping overboard after most people were in bed, but instead of feeling depressed, he felt a little angry now. He wouldn't give them the satisfaction.

Finally, after a few hours of walking, he leaned up against the railing and sighed. It was no fun being socially awkward, but if he hadn't learned social etiquette by this point, he had to accept he never would. And if there was no cure for his dandruff, he had to stop pretending he wasn't disabled. Life might never be wonderful, but perhaps it could only be bearable if one lived honestly.

He frowned. Wasn't it always his honest comments that drove people crazy?

"Hey, tiger," said a woman coming up beside him. He wasn't sure if he was happy to see Terri or not. "No midnight romance yet?"

Ralph laughed, surprising himself. "Furthest thing from it. They kicked me out of the group."

"For having coffee?" Terri sounded genuinely shocked.

"For being me."

Terri gave him an appraising look. "I don't get it. You're no George Clooney, but…"

Ralph shrugged. "It's the dandruff. It makes me so self-conscious that I can't act like a normal person. And Mormons are unable to accept anything outside of the norm."

"So why don't you shave your head?" Terri asked.

Ralph looked at her.

"Your skull has a good shape. You'd look okay bald. And lots of people choose baldness deliberately. If you don't like it, you can always grow your hair back."

Ralph kept staring at her. Why had this never occurred to him before? He blinked. "I guess it's worth a try."

Terri put her hand on his arm. "Come on back to my cabin. I'll shave it for you."

Ralph couldn't understand why this woman seemed to like him. Was she only trying to get material for her article? Maybe it was simply easier to let someone in if you were only gauging their appropriateness for an evening, or a few months, or a couple of years, instead of for eternity.

He looked out over the Gulf. If even great civilizations only lasted a few hundred years, wasn't expecting a marriage that lasted really and truly *forever* a bit much?

Ralph looked at his watch. It was 10:13. He smiled and then chuckled as he took Terri's hand, and they walked slowly in the moonlight past the other tourists on deck before heading below to her tiny cabin. Terri unlocked the door, and Ralph walked calmly on inside.

Temple Man

"Hey, Scoop," Mr. Rutkin said, "get over to Parleys Way in Sugar House right now."

"What's up?" I asked, ignoring my boss's insult. I was new at the *Salt Lake Herald*, eager to make my mark, and Rutkin couldn't help making fun of me. He was heavy and bald, like Lou Grant, only taller.

"Some guy just tossed a brick through a car window to rescue a dog." He slapped down a slip of paper with the address. "Go get the story."

"You're kidding me, right?"

Rutkin raised an eyebrow in reply. I grabbed my iPad and took off, grumbling to myself most of the way over to this older part of the city. It was the middle of summer, and we'd been having a heat wave, with temps almost to a hundred every day the past week. It would be cruel to leave a dog inside a car in this weather for even five minutes, but it hardly seemed like front page news. I wanted a real scoop.

When I reached the address on East Parleys Way, it was obvious at a glance what had happened. A dark blue Toyota Camry was parked on the street, with a police officer talking to an older woman on the sidewalk beside it. The rear window on the passenger side was bashed in.

I pulled to the curb just ahead of them and climbed out. Hanging back a few feet, I listened to the officer and the woman, typing what they said as quickly as I could. I wasn't sure how long they'd been talking, but the officer seemed to be finishing up.

"You're sure you've never seen this guy before?" the officer asked, a well-built man around forty, perhaps a few pounds overweight. "He must be from the neighborhood."

"I told you, I couldn't identify him even if he was my next-door neighbor. He had on a mask."

"All right, ma'am. Thanks for your help." The man closed his notebook and walked back to his cruiser. Normally, I'd have wanted to interview him as well, but I was afraid the woman would leave if I didn't approach her first, so I sacrificed the officer. I could always call the station later.

"Good afternoon, ma'am." I stepped in quickly. "I'm Mark Sanderson with the *Herald.* Do you mind if I ask a few questions?" I smiled the friendly smile that had won over my wife. "Could you tell me what happened here today?"

The woman sighed. She was probably sixty, short, with gray hair, wearing a simple green house dress not much more elegant than a muumuu. "I was walking home from the grocery," she began, and I now noticed her personal handcart filled with bags a few feet away, "when I heard muffled barking coming from this car." She pointed. "There was a little terrier inside. I tried to open the doors, but they were all locked. I stood on the sidewalk and called for help, and just sixty seconds later, this man showed up."

"And you didn't see where he came from?" I asked, agreeing mentally with the officer. "He must be a neighbor."

"I tell you, I didn't."

I nodded, not wanting to irritate her further. "Okay. And next?"

"Well, as I told the policeman, I was shocked to see his outfit. He was wearing a white, pleated robe, white slippers, and a white hat. And he had on this odd green apron in the shape of fig leaves. Plus, he had on a black mask like the Lone Ranger. I didn't know what to think, so I backed off."

Whoa, I thought. Some guy wearing Mormon temple clothes in public? That was a major no-no in the Church. This woman clearly wasn't LDS or she'd have recognized the outfit. Of course, the mask was a new addition. I didn't know what to make of that myself.

"The man came over to the car, saw the dog inside, and went up to that house right there..." She pointed again. "...and then grabbed a brick from the front porch. He came over, told me to go in the street and call the dog over to that side of the car, and then he bashed the window in. The man didn't even have to unlock the door. That dog just jumped out right into his arms, and the man walked off down the street with him."

"He stole the dog?"

"He saved that dog's life!" The woman wagged a finger at me. "The criminal here is the owner of that car. I want him arrested for endangering that poor creature!" She looked off in the direction of the officer's car. He'd driven away while we were talking.

I stepped behind the Camry and wrote down the license plate. We could look up the owner in the newsroom as well. I thanked the woman, typed in her name and contact info, and snapped a photo of the damaged car. Then I climbed back into my own vehicle and thought for a moment.

Within seconds, sweat began forming on my forehead. The dog's owner really had been a bastard. It was worth covering the story just as a reminder to the community. But I wanted something more. I turned on the engine and switched the air conditioner to high.

On my way back to the office, I thought and thought about how to approach Rutkin. It was the mask that intrigued me more than the temple clothes. That guy had been up to something.

Back at my desk, I typed and retyped. I called the police station and spoke briefly with the officer who'd responded. I found the name of the car owner. When I finished my story, I handed it to Rutkin. He read the headline, then the first paragraph, and his mouth fell open.

"'Temple Man, Salt Lake's Newest Superhero, Saves Dog's Life'? Are you crazy?"

"I'm telling you, we're going to see this guy again. KSL or KUTV or KSTU or, God forbid, *Main Street News*, is going to catch on eventually. We want to be first with the story, don't we?"

"*Main Street* would never print something like this."

"So we distinguish ourselves from them once more. Even if this guy never shows up again, we've got a fun piece."

"We'll get letters." Rutkin frowned.

"It's always good to be noticed, sir."

"I'll think about it."

The article appeared the next day, and that was that. I kept my ears alert for any more cases of a guy wearing temple clothes, but nothing showed up. So much for my intuition. Still, it had been an entertaining story while it lasted.

Then exactly a week later, it happened.

"Hey, Scoop," Rutkin said, slapping an address on my desk. "Seems some guy wearing temple clothes is on his cell phone at a local market over in Sandy calling for a tow truck to take away a car without a placard from a handicapped parking space. Go see what you can come up with."

I smiled and jumped out of my chair. Of course, the man was gone by the time I arrived, and I could see the tow truck heading off down the street with a Chevy Equinox trailing behind. Temple Man had just made an enemy, I thought. A small group of spectators was still milling about, so I approached the entire group. "What happened?"

A teenage girl, maybe sixteen, with stringy blond hair, laughed. An older man around seventy, with a stern face and glowing white hair, pointed at a sign in the empty parking area.

"Some jerk was parked in the handicapped space. People don't realize we need those spaces ourselves. Not me personally, of course, but people like me. I was driving around, looking for parking, and I saw this guy in temple clothes and a mask calling on his cell phone, reading off the license plate. I thought, 'Good for him.'"

Well, *this* witness was a Mormon.

"Just how was the man dressed?" I asked. "You said he—"

"What the hell is going on?" said a thirty-something man coming out of the grocery with a cart full of food. "Where the fuck is my car?"

Hopefully not a Mormon.

The girl kept laughing. The older man said, "Got towed, you son of a bitch. You're not handicapped."

"Goddamn shit!" the man said. "I was only in there a few minutes. It's not my fault! Such a goddamn tiny parking lot!"

Two or three of the other onlookers started backing off.

"Stop laughing, you stupid bitch!"

The girl kept laughing but walked away. There was no more I was going to get here, but I drove back to the newsroom and called the towing company to get the car owner's name. Public humiliation sounded like a good idea. Then I tried to track down the mysterious caller, but it turned out the call had been placed on a burner. This guy planned to show up again.

I wrote my story.

Rutkin strode over to my desk, slapping it with his palm. "'Temple Man Tows Faker.' It's great work, Mark." Shelly, two cubicles over, stuck her head out and stared. Apparently, Temple Man was doing heroic work here in the newsroom, too, getting Rutkin to be more human. I smiled and called Cathy.

Over the next month, Temple Man made five more appearances. He showed up at a public park and stopped a bully from tormenting a kid. Two mothers reported on that, one of them catching a shot of the guy with her cell. That made page three. Another day, a man dressed in temple clothes and a mask handed out sandwiches and water bottles to the homeless. Page five. Late one evening, a guy dressed in temple clothes helped a young mother change a flat tire on the highway. Page six.

Yet another incident involved someone identifying himself as Temple Man calling the police and reporting a drunk driver. Sure enough, the police found a drunk driver, and just like before, the call had been placed from a burner. Page seven.

Then one afternoon, Temple Man showed up at Trolley Square to give a man who'd had an apparent heart attack CPR until the paramedics arrived. That finally made the front page, complete with a photo by an onlooker. I wondered then how Temple Man always seemed to be at the right place at the right time.

Was he inspired? Was he for real? Was it just a coincidence? Perhaps he kept his temple clothes in his car so he could jump into them at a moment's notice. The back seat of a car couldn't be any less comfortable as a changing room than a phone booth used to be.

Maybe he had a van.

Of course, I also realized we could have a copycat on our hands, someone who'd read the stories and was trying to emulate him. The paper published an Op-ed about the need for the common man to step up and do the right thing by his neighbors as Temple Man was doing. There was an Op-ed in *Main Street* bemoaning the sacrilegious nature of the "self-righteous, self-proclaimed superhero."

Letters to the editor in both papers were published asking whether this was for real or if the guy was poking fun at the Mormon Church. One letter writer said simply, "Finally, a Mormon who *does* good rather than just going around *saying* all the time that he does good."

I wondered if maybe the man had been secretly called by his bishop or stake president to be a hero. Perhaps it was some kind of pilot program to replace the retired Home Teaching fiasco.

At least Temple Man wasn't picketing coffee shops or snatching cigarettes out of the mouths of smokers. Something a Mormon superhero might very well do. This guy seemed to be focusing on real problems, even if most of them weren't especially noteworthy.

People weren't going to care about towed cars forever.

Still, more readers began noticing my byline and Cathy could see the gleam in my eye. One evening over dinner, she was unequivocal. "You better not ever publish this guy's name and ruin what he's doing."

"It would be a great scoop," I said.

"You'd ruin the mystery," she replied. "He's more powerful as a mystery."

While my wife had a point, the desire to have a *real* scoop burned inside me. A few attention-grabbing articles would be generated through interviewing the guy and finding out what motivated him, and maybe some additional good could come from those revelations. Still, I'd read enough comic books as a kid to know that Cathy was probably right.

But it wasn't only my personal ethics being thrown into disarray by Temple Man. As a faithful Latter-day Saint, I attended the Jordan River temple once a month. When I started an endowment session several weeks after I began covering the story, I simply couldn't see the temple ceremony the same way. Here was a room full of men and women in their temple clothes. Part of me had always felt silly wearing the goofy little apron and the baker's hat tied to the robe to keep it from slipping off my shoulder.

In some ways, Temple Man was making the outfit "sexy," yet at the same time, he was clearly no Spiderman. There'd never be a movie about him. His latest two appearances had been to fill in a notorious pothole by himself and to hang an Olde Brooklyn Lantern from a post where a streetlight had burned out, apparently weeks earlier.

I looked about me in the endowment room as we performed one of the secret handshakes. Was one of these guys *him*? Or were we all congratulating ourselves on our faithfulness, while the real hero was out there rescuing a cat from a tree?

I shook my head at the mental image.

The following day at work, Rutkin came running over to my desk. “Get out to Millcreek. There’s a fender bender. Apparently, Temple Man is on the scene trying to calm frayed nerves.”

I drove on over, but not as quickly as I might have. A fender bender, I thought? Why wasn’t Temple Man out there preventing murders and rapes? Why wasn’t he foiling bank robberies and muggings? Was stopping at the scene of a minor accident the most we could expect out of a real-life hero? His escapades suddenly seemed less endearing and began to feel rather pathetic.

Was the guy just someone off his meds?

By the time I arrived, the police were talking to the drivers, and there was no sign of Temple Man. I interviewed the witnesses, got permission to use another cell phone picture, and soon had my story ready for the *Herald*. I went home early, wondering if I’d chosen the wrong profession.

I’d always liked ornithology.

“You didn’t get fired, did you?” Cathy asked when I walked in the door at 3:00. We didn’t have any children yet, but as good Mormons, we still felt it best she didn’t work full time outside the home. Cathy worked fifteen hours a week as a real estate agent, which we figured was a good profession in case she ever did need to work after the kids came. Flexibility.

She'd also taken up designing stained glass windows to feel productive. And teaching ESL to immigrants downtown.

"I'm just not feeling well."

"You don't look so good, either. You better get to bed."

I heated a can of Campbell's chicken soup, ate a third of it, and climbed under the covers. I slept fitfully, dreaming about Arnold Schwarzenegger and Sylvester Stallone and even Halle Berry. I woke up at 2:00 in the morning, went to my computer, and thought about resigning. We could put off having kids a few more years while I went back to school and Cathy worked full-time. Maybe I could be a falconer.

I could write something like *The Zookeeper's Wife*.

I'd read about people with big dreams, and when they finally fulfilled those dreams, they thought, "Is this all there is?" Writing about Temple Man may not have been my dream, but writing about something exciting was, and Temple Man had churned up a great deal of excitement. If not in the community at large, at least among a few news writers.

The national press hadn't picked it up yet, probably out of a sense of delicacy, afraid to be perceived as mocking religion, but every reporter in town—print, radio, and television—was talking about it.

Several reporters were buying squares to guess the date "it would all come out."

I listened to my police scanner when I could, always hoping for that "big moment," and half-heartedly turned it on now while reading my emails. I had three messages from folks claiming their neighbor was Temple Man. Four or five of those tips made it to my inbox every day. I'd given up checking them out.

One email today was from my cousin in Denver saying she was jealous to hear how well I was doing. Another was from Rutkin, saying he hoped I felt better because he was going to assign me to a drug case soon.

Just what I needed, to get shot by a drug dealer.

I'd never be a Woodward or a Bernstein, I thought. I'd certainly never be a Richard Engel.

The scanner soon crackled to life. A man was holding his wife hostage over in Magna. I breathed a sigh of relief. Something real for a change.

I jumped into my clothes and ran out the door. Since I didn't live all that close to the copper mine, I was surprised to discover the police still hadn't shown up.

The front door was open. I could see a man in his boxers and T-shirt holding a gun to a woman's head. But someone else was at the door, too, just off to the side as if afraid to block the message on the welcome mat.

"Love at Home."

Oh my god. It was him. Temple Man. He must own a police scanner, too. That could explain a few of the other incidents, I supposed, like the fender bender, but the guy was clearly small-time. This was something new.

All of a sudden, I felt like a journalist again.

I needed to get closer without provoking the armed man or putting myself in danger. I took a picture in case one of our photographers didn't arrive in time, but before I could do anything else, two police cars pulled up and four men filed out.

One of the officers, a tall African American, spotted me and held up his arm in warning. "You keep back." He stayed on his walkie talkie while his partner and two other officers slowly approached the house.

"I got a gun here!" the man at the door shouted, shoving it up against his wife's head. She squealed in terror, her flimsy nightgown offering little protection against the cool night. Temple Man stood by calmly. He seemed to be talking, but I couldn't hear him.

The officers stopped advancing, their guns ready. "It's okay," one of them shouted. "We're just here to talk."

"Get the fuck off my property!"

"Sir, we need you to put the gun down so we can talk. We don't want anyone to get hurt."

"Get out of here or I'll blow her brains out!"

The woman whimpered again.

"Hey, you!" shouted one of the officers, pointing toward Temple Man. "Back off!"

Temple Man said something to the husband which I couldn't hear, and to everyone's amazement, the man threw the woman to the ground and grabbed Temple Man instead.

The woman jumped up, one knee bleeding, and ran toward the officers. I was close enough to hear her. "That man asked Jerry to take him hostage instead of me! Said he was famous and Jerry would get what he wanted!"

I focused on the woman, looking up again when I heard the front door slam. Two of the officers ran to the entrance, standing just to the side as if debating what to do next. A moment later, there was a shot. The two police officers still near their cars ducked behind them, one officer dragging the woman with him. The officers nearest the house kicked in the front door.

When it was all said and done, the husband lay dead in the living room. There was no sign of Temple Man. No one knew if the husband had killed himself, if the two men had fought over the gun and it had discharged accidentally, or what.

The woman said that a guy wearing strange clothes had shown up shortly after the shouting started inside, long before any neighbors could have called 9-1-1. He'd tried to calm her husband down. She'd never seen the man before.

The officers didn't seem compelled to find him, even to take a witness statement, and I wondered if their personal religious beliefs influenced that decision. Was the guy a police officer himself? In any event, the deceased seemed the obvious criminal. I wrote my longest story yet for Rutkin and he loved it. Another front page.

Three weeks later, Rutkin came by my cubicle and slapped my desk. "What happened?" he demanded.

"What are you talking about?" I asked.

"Where is he?"

"Who?"

"You know damn well who. There's been no sign of Temple Man for almost a month!"

I shrugged. "Maybe seeing real danger scared him off. Made him realize he was taking too many chances."

"I don't want to hear that. That's *Main Street* talk." He pulled a stick pin out of my cubicle wall, making one of my notes fall to the desk. He stuck the pin back in without the note.

"Maybe he was just some college kid looking for adventure and now he's had his fill."

"Hmmph."

"Perhaps he was some terminally ill guy out to fulfill a fantasy."

"Mark…"

I shrugged again. "Maybe he was one of the Three Nephites."

Rutkin slapped my desk. "Write it up," he ordered.

"What?"

"All of it. Everything you just said. There's still a chance we can get a Pulitzer out of this."

I did write it up, editorializing a bit on how there might be a hero inside each of us, if we dared to put ourselves on the line. Saving a cat from a tree might not change the whole world, but it changed the world for that cat. Saving a dog meant the world to that dog. Saving a bullied kid meant the world to that bullied kid.

Even saving an old man with a heart condition so he could live even six more months was something.

I probably overdid it. The piece was far too sappy to gain any critical recognition.

But it persuaded me. I began to see the potential for heroism everywhere again. In my wife, the neighbor on our left, my cousin in Denver. Even Mormon missionaries, I supposed. If some guy wearing Dearfoams slippers could make a difference, anyone could.

People often talked about the banality of evil, but perhaps the truth was that heroism could be just as banal.

That night, for the first time, Cathy and I chose not to use a condom.

After she was asleep, I took the mask I sometimes used on Date Night and stuffed it in my pocket. Then I pulled out the little suitcase in our closet with my temple clothes, put it in the trunk of my car, and went for a drive.

Books by Johnny Townsend

Thanks for reading! If you enjoyed this book, could you please take a few minutes to write a review online? Reviews are helpful both to me as an author and to other readers, so we'd all sincerely appreciate your writing one! And if you did enjoy the book, here are some others I've written you might want to look up:

Mormon Underwear

Zombies for Jesus

A Gay Mormon Missionary in Pompeii

The Golem of Rabbi Loew

Sexual Solidarity

Marginal Mormons

Gay Gaslighting

Going-Out-Of-Religion Sale

Gayrabian Nights

A Mormon Motive for Murder

Out of the Missionary's Closet

Invasion of the Spirit Snatchers

Escape from Zion

The Last Days Linger

The Mysterious Madness of Mormons

Sins of the Saints

Human Compassion for Beginners

Breaking the Promise of the Promised Land

I Will, Through the Veil

Am I My Planet's Keeper?

Have Your Cum and Eat It, Too

Strangers with Benefits

Constructing Equity

Wake Up and Smell the Missionaries

Racism by Proxy

Orgy at the STD Clinic

Please Evacuate

Recommended Daily Humanity

The Camper Killings

An Eternity of Mirrors: Best Short Stories of Johnny Townsend

Kinky Quilts: Patchwork Designs for Gay Men

Inferno in the French Quarter: The UpStairs Lounge Fire

Latter-Gay Saints: An Anthology of Gay Mormon Fiction (co-editor)

Available from your favorite online or neighborhood bookstore.

Wondering what some of those other books are about? Read on!

Invasion of the Spirit Snatchers

During the Apocalypse, a group of Mormon survivors in Hurricane, Utah gather in the home of the Relief Society president, telling stories to pass the time as they ration their food storage and await the Second Coming. But this is no ordinary group of Mormons—or perhaps it is. They are the faithful, feminist, gay, apostate, and repentant, all working together to help each other through the darkest days any of them have yet seen.

Gayrabian Nights

Gayrabian Nights is a twist on the well-known classic, *1001 Arabian Nights*, in which Scheherazade, under the threat of death if she ceases to captivate King Shahryar's attention, enchants him through a series of mysterious, adventurous, and romantic tales.

In this variation, a male escort, invited to the hotel room of a closeted, homophobic Mormon senator, learns that the man is poised to vote on a piece of anti-gay legislation the following morning. To prevent him from sleeping, so that the exhausted senator will miss casting his vote on the Senate floor, the escort entertains him with stories of homophobia, celibacy, mixed orientation marriages, reparative therapy, coming out, first love, gay marriage, and long-term successful gay relationships.

The escort crafts the stories to give the senator a crash course in gay culture and sensibilities, hoping to bring the man closer to accepting his own sexual orientation.

Inferno in the French Quarter: The UpStairs Lounge Fire

On Gay Pride Day in 1973, someone set the entrance to a French Quarter gay bar on fire. In the terrible inferno that followed, thirty-two people lost their lives, including a third of the local congregation of the Metropolitan Community Church, their pastor burning to death halfway out a second-story window as he tried to claw his way to freedom.

A mother who'd gone to the bar with her two gay sons died alongside them. A man who'd helped his friend escape first was found dead near the fire escape. Two children waited outside a movie theater across town for a father and "uncle" who would never pick them up. During this era of rampant homophobia, several families refused to claim the bodies, and many churches refused to bury the dead.

Author Johnny Townsend pored through old records and tracked down survivors of the fire as well as relatives and friends of those killed to compile this fascinating account of a forgotten moment in gay history.

A Gay Mormon Missionary in Pompeii

What is a gay Mormon missionary doing in Italy? He is trying to save his own soul as well as the souls of others. In these tales chronicling the two-year mission of Robert Anderson, we see a young man tormented by his inability to be the man the Church says he should be. In addition to his personal hell, Anderson faces a major earthquake, organized crime, a serious bus accident, and much more. He copes with horrendous mission leaders and his own suicidal tendencies. But one day, he meets another missionary who loves him, and his world changes forever.

The Golem of Rabbi Loew

Jacob and Esau Cohen are the closest of brothers. In fact, they're lovers. A doctor tries to combine canine genes with those of Jews, to improve their chances of surviving a hostile world. A Talmudic scholar dates an escort. A scientist tries to develop the "God spot" in the brains of his patients in order to create a messiah. The Golem of Prague is really Rabbi Loew's secret lover. While some of the Jews in Townsend's book are Orthodox, this collection of Jewish stories most certainly is not.

Am I My Planet's Keeper?

Global Warming. Climate Change. Climate Crisis. Climate Emergency. Whatever label we use, we are facing one of the greatest challenges to the survival of life as we know it.

But while addressing greenhouse gases is perhaps our most urgent need, it's not our only task. We must also address toxic waste, pollution, habitat destruction, and our other contributions to the world's sixth mass extinction event.

In order to do that, we must simultaneously address the unmet human needs that keep us distracted from deeper engagement in stabilizing our climate: moderating economic inequality, guaranteeing healthcare to all, and ensuring education for everyone.

And to accomplish *that*, we must unite to combat the monied forces that use fear, prejudice, and misinformation to manipulate us.

It's a daunting task. But success is our only option.

Wake Up and Smell the Missionaries

Two Mormon missionaries in Italy discover they share the same rare ability—both can emit pheromones on demand. At first, they playfully compete in the hills of Frascati to see who can tempt "investigators" most. But soon they're targeting each other non-stop.

Can two immature young men learn to control their "superpower" to live a normal life...and develop genuine love? Even as their relationship is threatened by the attentions of another man?

They seem just on the verge of success when a massive earthquake leaves them trapped under the rubble of their apartment in Castellammare.

With night falling and temperatures dropping, can they dig themselves out in time to save themselves? And will their injuries destroy the ability that brought them together in the first place?

Orgy at the STD Clinic

Todd Tillotson is struggling to move on after his husband is killed in a hit and run attack a year earlier during a Black Lives Matter protest in Seattle.

In this novel set entirely on public transportation, we watch as Todd, isolated throughout the pandemic, battles desperation in his attempt to safely reconnect with the world.

Will he find love again, even casual friendship, or will he simply end up another crazy old man on the bus?

Things don't look good until a man whose face he can't even see sits down beside him despite the raging variants.

And asks him a question that will change his life.

Please Evacuate

A gay, partygoing New Yorker unconcerned about the future or the unsustainability of capitalism is hit by a truck and thrust into a straight man's body half a continent away. As Hunter tries to figure out what's happening, he's caught up in another disaster, a wildfire sweeping through a Colorado community, the flames overtaking him and several schoolchildren as they flee.

When he awakens, Hunter finds himself in the body of yet another man, this time in northern Italy, a former missionary about to marry a young Mormon woman. Still piecing together this new reality, and beginning to embrace his latest identity, Hunter fights for his life in a devastating flash flood along with his wife *and* his new husband.

He's an aging worker in drought-stricken Texas, a nurse at an assisted living facility in the direct path of a hurricane, an advocate for the unhoused during a freak Seattle blizzard.

We watch as Hunter is plunged into life after life, finally recognizing the futility of only looking out for #1 and understanding the part he must play in addressing the global climate crisis…if he ever gets another chance.

Recommended Daily Humanity

A checklist of human rights must include basic housing, universal healthcare, equitable funding for public schools, and tuition-free college and vocational training.

In addition to the basics, though, we need much more to fully thrive. Subsidized childcare, universal pre-K, a universal basic income, subsidized high-speed internet, net neutrality, fare-free public transit (plus *more* public transit), and medically assisted death for the terminally ill who want it.

None of this will matter, though, if we neglect to address the rapidly worsening climate crisis.

Sound expensive? It is.

But not as expensive as refusing to implement these changes. The cost of climate disasters each year has grown to staggering figures. And the cost of social and political upheaval from not meeting the needs of suffering workers, families, and individuals may surpass even that.

It's best we understand that the vast sums required to enact meaningful change are an investment which will pay off not only in some indeterminate future but in fact almost immediately. And without these adjustments to our lifestyles and values, there may very well not be a future capable of sustaining freedom and democracy…or even civilization itself.

The Camper Killings

When a homeless man is found murdered a few blocks from Morgan Beylerian's house in south Seattle, everyone seems to consider the body just so much additional trash to be cleared from the neighborhood. But Morgan liked the guy. They used to chat when Morgan brought Nick groceries once a week.

And the brutal way the man was killed reminds Morgan of their shared Mormon heritage, back when the faithful agreed to have their throats slit if they ever revealed temple secrets.

Did Nick's former wife take action when her ex-husband refused to grant a temple divorce? Did his murder have something to do with the public accusations that brought an end to his promising career?

Morgan does his best to investigate when no one else seems to care, but it isn't easy as a man living paycheck to paycheck himself, only able to pursue his investigation via public transit.

As he continues his search for the killer, Morgan's friends withdraw and his husband threatens to leave. When another homeless man is killed and Morgan is accused of the crime, things look even bleaker.

But his troubles aren't over yet.

Will Morgan find the killer before the killer finds him?

Escape from Zion

In these short stories by ex-Mormon author Johnny Townsend, parents hire men to pose as the Three Nephites to teach their children the Book of Mormon is true. A shy single woman meets the man of her dreams at an endoscopy party.

An anti-Mormon mob threatens a church outing. A deceased sinner plots to break out of Spirit Prison. Aliens visiting the UN reveal that God really does live on the planet Kolob. Mormons survive the zombie apocalypse because of their two-year supply of food. A young couple desperately try to escape after America becomes a theocracy.

Another fun collection from the author of *Recommended Daily Humanity* and *Please Evacuate*.

The Mysterious Madness of Mormons

When religious indoctrination clashes with reality, the outcome can't always be predicted. In these stories by the author of *Please Evacuate* and *Inferno in the French Quarter*, a Seminary teacher threatens to kill his students. A schizophrenic woman in a hurricane evacuation shelter finds love. A Relief Society president's silicone breast implants develop into a new life form. A sister missionary suffocating under family pressure volunteers to be held hostage during a bank robbery. A teenage girl is haunted by the ghost of Emma Smith. A devout Mormon takes up sex work to raise money to help the poor.

Sometimes, behavior that seems perfectly reasonable in one culture can seem disturbing to those outside it. But whether reasonable or disturbing, their stories can also make compelling reading.

What Readers Have Said

Townsend's stories are "a gay *Portnoy's Complaint* of Mormonism. Salacious, sweet, sad, insightful, insulting, religiously ethnic, quirky-faithful, and funny."

D. Michael Quinn, author of *The Mormon Hierarchy: Origins of Power*

"Told from a believably conversational first-person perspective, [*A Gay Mormon Missionary in Pompeii*'s] novelistic focus on Anderson's journey to thoughtful self-acceptance allows for greater character development than often seen in short stories, which makes this well-paced work rich and satisfying, and one of Townsend's strongest. An extremely important contribution to the field of Mormon fiction." Named to Kirkus Reviews' Best of 2011.

Kirkus Reviews

"The thirteen stories in *Mormon Underwear* capture this struggle [between Mormonism and homosexuality] with humor, sadness, insight, and sometimes shocking details….*Mormon Underwear* provides compelling stories, literally from the inside-out."

Niki D'Andrea, *Phoenix New Times*

"Townsend's lively writing style and engaging characters [in *Zombies for Jesus*] make for stories which force us to wake up, smell the (prohibited) coffee, and review our attitudes with regard to reading dogma so doggedly. These are tales which revel in the individual tics and quirks which make us human, Mormon or not, gay or not…"

A.J. Kirby, *The Short Review*

"The Rift," from *A Gay Mormon Missionary in Pompeii*, is a "fascinating tale of an untenable situation…a *tour de force*."

David Lenson, editor, *The Massachusetts Review*

"Pronouncing the Apostrophe," from *The Golem of Rabbi Loew*, is "quiet and revealing, an intriguing tale…"

Sima Rabinowitz, Literary Magazine Review, *NewPages.com*

The Circumcision of God is "a collection of short stories that consider the imperfect, silenced majority of Mormons, who may in fact be [the Church's] best hope….[The book leaves] readers regretting the church's willingness to marginalize those who best exemplify its ideals: those who love fiercely despite all obstacles, who brave challenges at great personal risk and who always choose the hard, higher road."

Kirkus Reviews

In *Mormon Fairy Tales*, Johnny Townsend displays "both a wicked sense of irony and a deep well of compassion."

Kel Munger, *Sacramento News and Review*

Zombies for Jesus is "eerie, erotic, and magical."

Publishers Weekly

"While [Townsend's] many touching vignettes draw deeply from Mormon mythology, history, spirituality and culture, [*Mormon Fairy Tales*] is neither a gaudy act of proselytism nor angry protest literature from an ex-believer. Like all good fiction, his stories are simply about the joys, the hopes and the sorrows of people."

Kirkus Reviews

"In *Inferno in the French Quarter* author Johnny Townsend restores this tragic event [the UpStairs Lounge fire] to its proper place in LGBT history and reminds us that the victims of the blaze were not just 'statistics,' but real people with real lives, families, and friends."

Jesse Monteagudo, *The Bilerico Project*

In *Inferno in the French Quarter*, "Townsend's heart-rending descriptions of the victims…seem to [make them] come alive once more."

Kit Van Cleave, *OutSmart Magazine*

Marginal Mormons is "an irreverent, honest look at life outside the mainstream Mormon Church….Throughout his musings on sin and forgiveness, Townsend beautifully demonstrates his characters' internal, perhaps irreconcilable struggles….Rather than anger and disdain, he offers an honest portrayal of people searching for meaning and community in their lives, regardless of their life choices or secrets." Named to Kirkus Reviews' Best of 2012.

Kirkus Reviews

The stories in *The Mormon Victorian Society* "register the new openness and confidence of gay life in the age of same-sex marriage….What hasn't changed is Townsend's wry, conversational prose, his subtle evocations of character and social dynamics, and his deadpan humor. His warm empathy still glows in this intimate yet clear-eyed engagement with Mormon theology and folkways. Funny, shrewd and finely wrought dissections of the awkward contradictions—and surprising harmonies—between conscience and desire." Named to Kirkus Reviews' Best of 2013.

Kirkus Reviews

"This collection of short stories [*The Mormon Victorian Society*] featuring gay Mormon characters slammed [me] in the face from the first page, wrestled my heart and mind to the floor, and left me panting and wanting more by the end. Johnny Townsend has created so many memorable characters in such few pages. I went weeks thinking about this book. It truly touched me."

Tom Webb, *A Bear on Books*

Dragons of the Book of Mormon is an "entertaining collection....Townsend's prose is sharp, clear, and easy to read, and his characters are well rendered..."

Publishers Weekly

"The pre-eminent documenter of alternative Mormon lifestyles...Townsend has a deep understanding of his characters, and his limpid prose, dry humor and well-grounded (occasionally magical) realism make their spiritual conundrums both compelling and entertaining. [*Dragons of the Book of Mormon* is] [a]nother of Townsend's critical but affectionate and absorbing tours of Mormon discontent." Named to Kirkus Reviews' Best of 2014.

Kirkus Reviews

In *Gayrabian Nights*, "Townsend's prose is always limpid and evocative, and…he finds real drama and emotional depth in the most ordinary of lives."

Kirkus Reviews

Gayrabian Nights is a "complex revelation of how seriously soul damaging the denial of the true self can be."

Ryan Rhodes, author of *Free Electricity*

Gayrabian Nights "was easily the most original book I've read all year. Funny, touching, topical, and thoroughly enjoyable."

Rainbow Awards

Lying for the Lord is "one of the most gripping books that I've picked up for quite a while. I love the author's writing style, alternately cynical, humorous, biting, scathing, poignant, and touching…. This is the third book of his that I've read, and all are equally engaging. These are stories that need to be told, and the author does it in just the right way."

Heidi Alsop, *Ex-Mormon Foundation Board Member*

In *Lying for the Lord*, Townsend "gets under the skin of his characters to reveal their complexity and conflicts....shrewd, evocative [and] wryly humorous."

Kirkus Reviews

In *Missionaries Make the Best Companions*, "the author treats the clash between religious dogma and liberal humanism with vivid realism, sly humor, and subtle feeling as his characters try to figure out their true missions in life. Another of Townsend's rich dissections of Mormon failures and uncertainties..." Named to Kirkus Reviews' Best of 2015.

Kirkus Reviews

In *Invasion of the Spirit Snatchers*, "Townsend, a confident and practiced storyteller, skewers the hypocrisies and eccentricities of his characters with precision and affection. The outlandish framing narrative is the most consistent source of shock and humor, but the stories do much to ground the reader in the world—or former world—of the characters....A funny, charming tale about a group of Mormons facing the end of the world."

Kirkus Reviews

"Townsend's collection [*The Washing of Brains*] once again displays his limpid, naturalistic prose, skillful narrative chops, and his subtle insights into psychology...Well-crafted dispatches on the clash between religion and self-fulfillment..."

Kirkus Reviews

"While the author is generally at his best when working as a satirist, there are some fine, understated touches in these tales [*The Last Days Linger*] that will likely affect readers in subtle ways....readers should come away impressed by the deep empathy he shows for all his characters—even the homophobic ones."

Kirkus Reviews

"Written in a conversational style that often uses stories and personal anecdotes to reveal larger truths, this immensely approachable book [*Racism by Proxy*] skillfully serves its intended audience of White readers grappling with complex questions regarding race, history, and identity. The author's frequent references to the Church of Jesus Christ of Latter-day Saints may be too niche for readers unfamiliar with its idiosyncrasies, but Townsend generally strikes a perfect balance of humor, introspection, and reasoned arguments that will engage even skeptical readers."

Kirkus Reviews

Orgy at the STD Clinic portrays "an all-too real scenario that Townsend skewers to wincingly accurate proportions...[with]

instant classic moments courtesy of his punchy, sassy, sexy lead character…"

Jim Piechota, *Bay Area Reporter*

Orgy at the STD Clinic is "…a triumph of humane sensibility. A richly textured saga that brilliantly captures the fraying social fabric of contemporary life." Named to Kirkus Reviews' Best Indie Books of 2022.

Kirkus Reviews

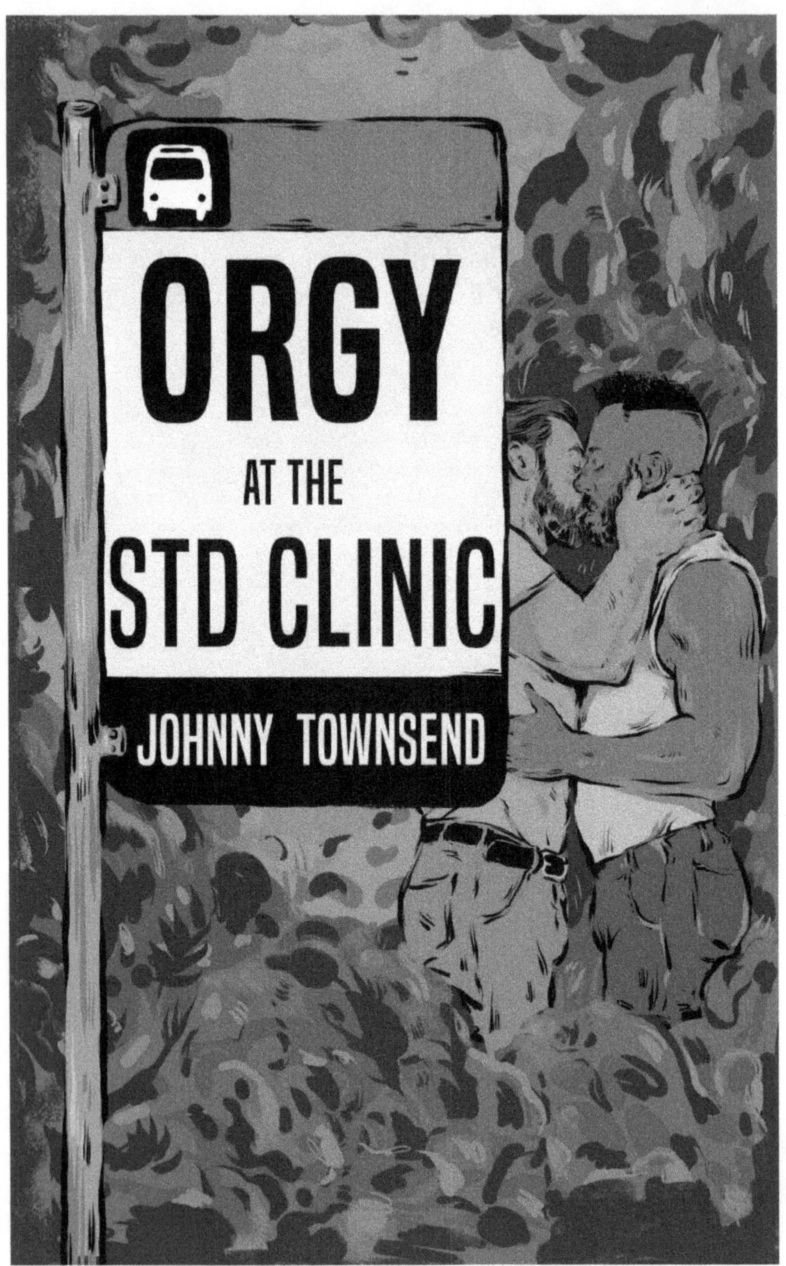
ORGY
AT THE
STD CLINIC
JOHNNY TOWNSEND

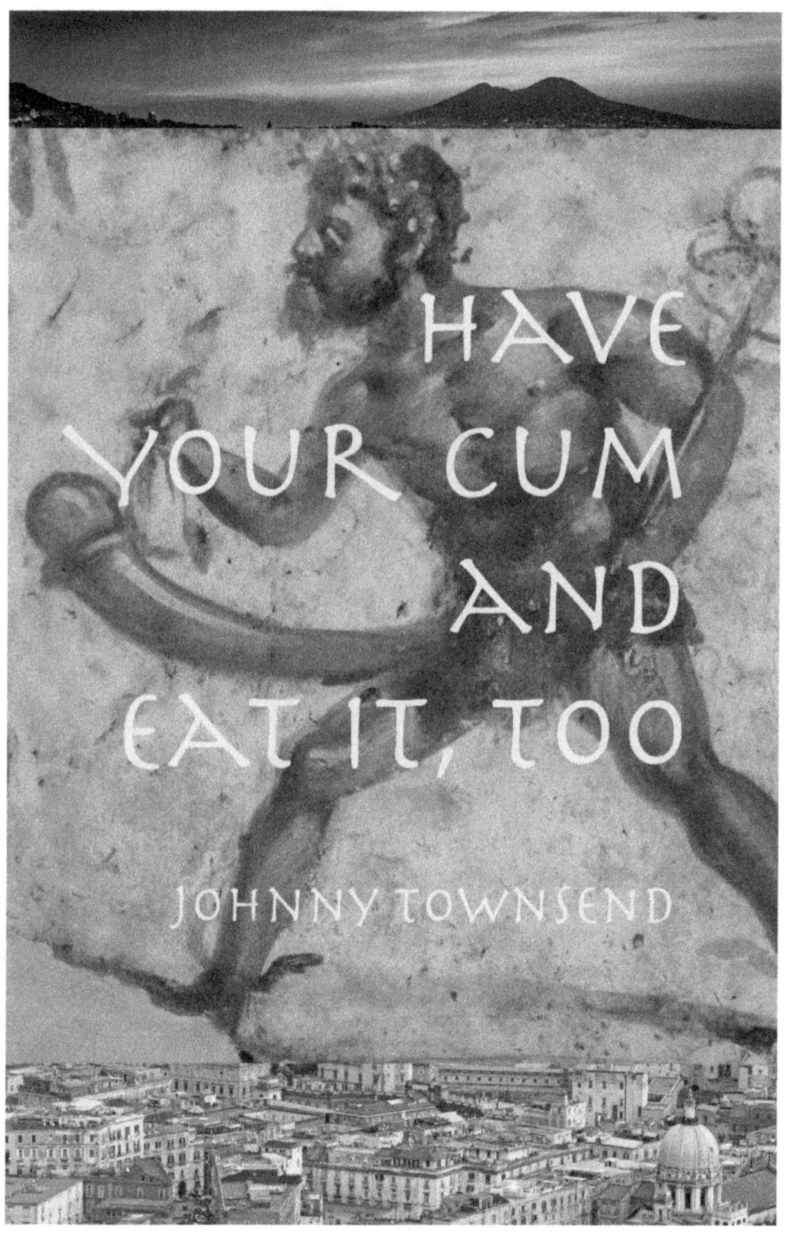
HAVE
YOUR CUM
AND
EAT IT, TOO
JOHNNY TOWNSEND

JOHNNY TOWNSEND
ESCAPE FROM ZION

Printed in the USA
CPSIA information can be obtained
at www.ICGtesting.com
JSHW020541270224
57928JS00003B/90

9 781961 525054